Hypocritic Days

Hypocritic Days

David Fiore

SEROTONIN | WAYSIDE

INSOMNIAC PRESS

Edited by Marisa Grizenko and Jon Paul Fiorentino

Library and Archives Canada Cataloguing in Publication

Fiore, David, 1974-, author
Hypocritic days / David Fiore.

ISBN 978-1-55483-138-8 (pbk.)

I. Title.

PS8611.I665H97 2014   C813'.6   C2014-907351-8

The publisher gratefully acknowledges the support of the Canada
Council, the Ontario Arts Council, and the Department of
Canadian Heritage through the Canada Book Fund.

Printed and bound in Canada

Insomniac Press
520 Princess Avenue, London, Ontario, Canada, N6B 2B8
www.insomniacpress.com

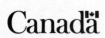

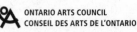

Daughters of Time, the hypocritic Days,
Muffled and dumb like barefoot dervishes,
And marching single in an endless file,
Bring diadems and fagots in their hands.
To each they offer gifts after his will,
Bread, kingdoms, stars, and sky that holds them all.
I, in my pleachèd garden, watched the pomp,
Forgot my morning wishes, hastily
Took a few herbs and apples, and the Day
Turned and departed silent. I, too late,
Under her solemn fillet saw the scorn.

—Ralph Waldo Emerson, "Days"

Book One

Chapter One

I had programmed the Duke Ellington Orchestra's "Jump for Joy" as my incoming ringtone.

Wishful thinking, I know, but today it sort of fit. I had just put the finishing touches on a tough article, and I felt like sharing the news with some captive telemarketer.

I slid my fingertip across the green phone icon. "Hello?"

"Universal Pictures. What's the story with that place?"

I'm sure a lot of people would've dropped the call right there, but I've got to tell you, this is exactly the kind of talk I like. I liked the voice doing the talking, too. It belonged to a woman who had obviously had a lot of experience being listened to. An attractive woman, if the little hairs on the back of my neck were any judges. Still, some caution seemed warranted, before I allowed my excitement to bubble over.

"This isn't leading into some kind of product survey, is it?" I crashed face first into the couch.

"Oh, don't be ridiculous, Douglass."

"Do I know you?" I asked for no good reason. I

knew a grand total of five women, only two of whom were speaking to me—and she wasn't either of them.

"Nope," she said playfully. "But you're Douglass Infantino, right? You write the *Nitrate Nuggets* column, on the Turner Classic Movies website?"

"Uh...yes...." I tried my best to keep the foolish smile out of my voice. "Do you read it?"

"Just found it this evening," she said matter-of-factly. "I like it."

"You like it enough to call me in the middle of the night?"

"Why not? One of your articles got me thinking about something—and your number's in the book. I figured if you were sleeping, you wouldn't answer."

"You're talking about my piece on the early 1930s at Universal? On Carl Laemmle, Jr.?"

"That's the one."

Of all the things I'd written for my column, that was indeed the one, as far as I was concerned. I hoped it really captured the excitement and frustration of a remarkable period in Hollywood history. Carl Laemmle, Sr. gave Universal to his son as a birthday present in 1929—and the kid actually used the studio to make a personal statement about life and art during the Great Depression. Even Laemmle, Jr.'s downfall spoke volumes about the era: A consortium of bankers snaked Universal out from under him just before his absurdly (and daringly) faithful version of *Show Boat* took the box office by storm in 1936.

I'd loved a lot of people and things during my thirty-five years, but my relationship with 1930s Hollywood had stood the test of time far better than the rest of them. That probably sounds even sadder than I think it does, but it's the truth. I've never considered myself a kinky guy, but the idea of a threesome with this woman and those movies brought my blood to a temperature that would have exploded the negatives.

"Do you realize this is the only reason I've been letting Verizon bleed me dry all these years—to get a phone call like this?"

If I was coming on a little too strong—and I think it's pretty clear that I was—she gave no indication of it.

"That's great, Douglass," she said. "But let's have the rest of the conversation in person, hunh?"

"You mean now?"

"I mean as soon as you can get here."

If I ever get that cellphone back, I'm sticking with Duke Ellington.

Chapter Two

Her name was Dorothea Cullen. She was a physicist. She lived in Greenwich Village. I could've walked there in about forty-five minutes, but this was no time to be saving on cab fare.

It was the night of November 2nd (or the morning of the 3rd, if you want to be absolutely strict about it), 2010, and Tea Partiers were dancing in the streets over the results of the midterm congressional elections. If I had seen any of them outside my window, I might have instructed the taxi driver to splash some mud on their parade. But the drive was uneventful.

I got out at the corner of Bleecker and Bank, paid the man, and buzzed at my physicist's door.

The woman who answered it did not disappoint.

Her brown-gold eyes popped with buttoned-down enthusiasm. The lightly latticed skin beneath them told me everything I needed to know about a life spent squinting at books, screens, and theories, and the carefully maintained brows above them showed a little earthly vanity. She had dark, curly hair and pale, freckled curves every place I looked. I guessed she was in her mid-forties.

"Hello, Douglass."

She seemed kind of glad to see me, too.

"Hello," I replied.

She led me down a hardwooded hallway with my trench coat in her arms.

"You want a snack, Douglass? I've got English muffins."

"Sounds great." I nodded, taking careful note of the lush movie posters that covered nearly every square inch of the walls: *Portrait of Jennie*, *Vertigo*, *Berkeley Square*, *Peter Ibbetson*, *Spellbound*, *Yolanda and the Thief....*

"You're more of a romantic than most of the scientists I meet up with in the middle of the night."

"Ha-ha." She turned to face me, throwing my coat on a chair and gesturing toward its neighbour. "I suppose I am, although I didn't choose those posters."

I took a seat. "You didn't?"

"Well, I guess I did, in a way. Let's just say I happened to be a different iteration of myself at the time."

"That's not the kind of thing people usually say after the words *let's just say*."

"You didn't come here for the usual, did you?" She smiled, touching my shoulder.

I liked the way her hand felt.

"Jam, Douglass?" she asked. "I've got strawberry and blackberry."

I watched her stroll toward the fridge. "I'd rather you came back and put your hand on my shoulder...."

"Stay on target, Douglass." She wagged a knife. "We've got a lot to discuss!"

"Okay," I sighed. "A little of both, please."

Dorothea applied herself to the muffins, toasting one for herself as well. She also put on a large pot of coffee, either guessing that I never say no to caffeine or knowing that its effects would be needed to sustain us through the coming marathon. I couldn't have asked for more pleasant surroundings in which to undergo the ordeal, if that's what it proved to be. The room featured a fascinating blend of high-tech gadgetry and art deco furnishings—almost entirely in white, black, and red, with a little gleaming silver here and there. I felt as if I had wandered onto the set of a "kitchen of the future" two-reeler.

"What does that do?" I asked, pointing at a black witch-hat-shaped thing on a circular pedestal.

"Good eye, my friend!" she beamed. "That's a prototype, the only one of its kind. A wine accelerator. It'd make wine cellars obsolete. 'Tomorrow's Tannins Today!' I designed it myself."

"Impressive...."

"I know." She nodded, a little shyly, before setting our snacks on the table. "Only problem is I hate wine.... Cream? Sugar?"

"Neither, thanks."

"Ah, good."

She pushed a steaming mug into my waiting hands. It smelled wonderful.

"Have you been messing with the Bean, too?"

"Never!" she exclaimed in mock horror. "That's a

sacred process. I'm kind of a traditionalist, you know."

"I believe it."

I took a sip of the coffee. It was wonderful.

"You're also quite a tease," I said. "I'm on tenter-hooks here!"

"Okay." She wiped a bit of jam from her lip. "I'm ready. Are you?"

"Of course." I leaned forward, wanting to go the whole way, almost tasting those berries.

She took a deep breath. "I want you to remember that I didn't have to handle things this way, Douglass. I do really need your input right now, but I think I could probably have secured it in any number of other ways."

"Undoubtedly." I nodded.

"All right then. Well. I'm a physicist—you know that. I teach at Columbia, and I've got research assistants there, but I keep the really important projects to myself."

"It's nice to have free time."

"Oh, I've got that in spades." She grinned. "In fact, my discovery makes the whole idea of a life lived in time obsolete."

"Just like the wine cellars."

"That's right." She nodded toward the accelerator. "I've been working on time machines since I was a teenager."

"Ah, *time machines*. I had a feeling they'd rear their ugly gears before too long. Ever since you brought up other iterations of yourself...."

"Yes"—she smiled pityingly—"and I had a feeling you'd react this way, so...."

She removed her watch (a stylish gold number with five ornate interlocking dials on its face), adjusted its settings, pressed a button on the left, clamped it onto my wrist, and pressed a button on the right.

In the blink of an eye, she was gone. I was alone in the room with a scorching August sun. I stumbled down the hallway to the front room, which opened onto a balcony. I pulled the sliding door open and found Dorothea out there, tanning in a green bikini. She had aged ten years. Her hair had gone almost completely gray.

"Hi, Douglass." She smiled, without any trace of bashfulness.

I raised a hand weakly.

"I've been waiting a long time for this." She stood up, grazed my left hip with her palm, and sort of waltzed into my chest. Halfway through our spin, her mouth was deep in mine, and I had my fingers in her hair. We stumbled into the wall. She kissed the side of my neck, where a brick had scuffed the skin. Then she drew back a step, with my hands in hers, and exhaled: "Now I can finally get out of this lease."

Suddenly, the summer glare faded and a cool November breeze tickled the wet spot on my neck. It was nighttime again. There were leaves on the patio furniture, which hadn't changed one bit. I slumped into the glass door, trying to get my bearings. I couldn't open it. Soon, Dorothea (the 2010 version) appeared on the other side of the barrier and flipped the lock.

She handed me a fresh mug of coffee and flashed a shy, wry grin. "Convinced?"

"I guess I have to be, don't I?"

"Good. I promised myself that we'd waste as little time as possible on that part of the story."

"Mission accomplished."

"And I'm not going to explain how it works either. Would there be any point?"

"None."

"That's what I figured…. Come on back to the kitchen. I'll reheat your muffin for you."

"Why not just send me back a few minutes?"

"Don't be silly."

I unclasped the watch and handed it back to her. "I'll try not to be."

Things were different between us when we settled back down. Was it due to the kiss (which couldn't possibly have been planned), or simply because she had disburdened herself of an immense secret? Whatever the reason, we sat much closer to each other now, made more eye contact, fewer jokes.

She told me the story of her life:

"I was a lonely kid, Douglass. Of course, I didn't notice half the time, because I was usually busy solving problems and making up new ones to puzzle over. But cheering parents and teachers don't make very good friends.

"So I watched movies for companionship.... The old black and whites on the PBS channel. Every night at eleven, I'd cozy up with hot chocolate and a snack for another visit with Barbara Stanwyck, Jean Arthur, Jimmy Cagney, Cary Grant.... When they played two in a row, I stuck with them. I never needed much sleep anyway.

"Westerns and war films usually bored me, but I was always game for just about anything else. The musicals were my favourites. Busby Berkeley, Fred and Ginger, the Freed Unit, Eleanor Powell, Bing Crosby.... Alice Faye's movies at Fox didn't make a whole lot of sense, but I loved them just the same. They topped my list until I saw Cynthia Ward in *Chorines in Arms*."

"Don't know that one," I interrupted her.

"Ah." She frowned slightly. "No, I'm afraid you wouldn't. But it's a classic 'backstager' just the same. Three downtrodden showgirls in a breadline spend the whole movie discussing (and dreaming about) their plans for ending the Depression.... One of the best fantasies involves some tongue-in-cheek revolutionary activity kicked off by the pro*leg*tariat."

"You're telling me this was some kind of a Marxist musical?"

"Is there any other way to describe it?" She smiled. "Still, the tone was light enough to keep the censors from howling. But the movie sticks to its guns where it counts: No one gets anything they want in the end. Except for soup and a bread roll, I guess."

"Wow. When the hell was this made?"

"It came out in 1931."

"Okay." I nodded. "It does sound like something that might just barely have made it under the radar in Pre-Code Hollywood. They would have pulped that script immediately after 1934. Where'd it come from? Some Poverty Row studio ten layers deeper in the muck than Monogram?"

"No, Douglass. Universal made it."

The whole evening was beginning to make an eerie kind of sense.

"Not anymore they didn't. I would know about it if they had."

"No kidding. They didn't make *any* of her movies."

"What are you saying? You popped back in time and killed your favourite actress?"

"She was everyone's favourite." Dorothea ignored my insinuation. "And a genuine *auteur*, too—even though she never directed a film. The best people bent over backwards to work with her, and her box office pull made strange things possible. Like, René Clair came over from France in 1934 to adapt Irving Berlin's *As Thousands Cheer*, which gave Ethel Waters her breakout role in Hollywood...."

"Come on! They let Ethel Waters sing 'Supper Time' in a 1934 movie? An anti-lynching song from a black woman's perspective?"

"I've seen it, Douglass." She nodded. "Waters is

completely magnificent. I'm sure Southern state censors cut that scene to pieces, but the movie did get made."

"All right." I bowed to her transdimensional wisdom. "So where is it, then?"

She shook her head. "We'll get to that shortly, I'm afraid. There's not much left to say about Cynthia Ward in Hollywood. She died in 1936, at the age of twenty-nine. No one ever called it a suicide, but she pretty much killed herself with booze."

"Hazard of the profession," I said, shaking my head.

"Yeah...well...biographers have spent decades trying to come up with something a little more analytical than that...."

"And you tried using one of them as a how-to guide to fixing the past?"

"Right." She shrugged.

I touched her hand. "That's pretty cool."

She got up and started pacing. "Thanks. But you'd never know it from the results...."

"So what did you do, exactly?"

"I saved a man's life."

"What man?"

"Cynthia Ward's husband. He was mugged and killed in November 1929. On Thanksgiving Day, actually. The 28th. Right outside of this building, on Bleecker Street, at 5:46 p.m. I went back there and stopped it from happening...."

She sat down, but the words kept on coming: "According to everything I've read, she never recovered from his death. Started drinking the minute it happened and didn't stop until her liver exploded…. But now it looks as if the guy's death also made her, as an artist. Until November 28, 1929, Eileen McWade (that's what she called herself, before Hollywood beckoned) was just a pretty ingénue with a knack for jazz singing. Two months pregnant and ready to give it all up for her man, Village restaurateur Pat Corelli"—those names rang gong-sized bells in my skull, but I did my best to muffle them—"after that date, she became the classic shooting superstar, rising from the abortionist's table to dazzle Paul Whiteman and Carl Laemmle, Jr. at a New Year's Eve party, securing herself a specialty number in 1930's *King of Jazz*, parlaying that into a contract with Universal…."

"Jesus," I choked, hoping that Dorothea would ascribe my distress to the general cultural dissonance she had generated.

"Yes…and from there, everything was simple, except for getting through the off-hours. She found the ideal collaborator in James Whale, who let her write her own dialogue, knew how to film it to best effect, and was quite willing to roll with any notions that entered her head, after *Chorines in Arms* did so well.

"Laemmle, your favourite studio head, protected her reputation in the press and kept her as busy as he could. She still found a way to raise hell with people like Helen Chandler and Lillian Roth, but the movies just got better and better, and so did Universal's gate receipts."

"Dorothea, do you realize that in this...what? Timeline? Is that what we're calling these?"

"Sure. We can if you want to."

"Okay, well, in *this* timeline, Universal went completely bankrupt in 1936...."

"I know," she said. "From your article. That's why I called you, remember?"

"I remember. You said it got you thinking about something."

She walked over to the stove and added fresh grounds to the coffeemaker.

"That's right," she said. "It did."

"Are you going to tell me what you thought?"

"Not just yet. I'm developing a theory, and I don't want to prejudice you in its favour."

"A theory about what? The best way to keep a film history nerd in suspense?"

"No. About how Universal going bankrupt could have wrecked American politics this badly."

"Wrecked American politics? Could they possibly get worse?"

She lit the burner and turned around. "Not by much they couldn't. That's what I'm saying, Douglass. Two days ago, in my timeline, they were a whole lot better."

"Really?"

"Really." She nodded. "It's like the New Deal never happened here!"

"Oh, it happened all right, but it's got a lot of Republican teeth marks in it at this point."

"Right." She rubbed her chin. "See, that's the part I don't understand. I mean, it's not as if we didn't have Republicans. I guess they'll always be with us. But in the country I grew up in, conservatives were always on the defensive. Now, all of a sudden, I find we can't even push through nationalized health care without the threat of mass revolt. I can only imagine how these people would have dealt with the Free Access to University Act, the Equal Rights Amendment, and the massive wealth redistribution tax measures passed under McGovern during the mid-1960s."

"*President* McGovern?" I laughed. "Really?"

"Sure." She smiled. "He beat out Lyndon Johnson for the Democratic nomination in 1964, running against the escalation of Kennedy's Vietnam crisis, which never made much sense to anyone anyway. And his administration pushed the Great Society reforms through Congress."

"Amazing."

"It just seems like history to me."

She poured out more coffee.

I took a big gulp from my mug.

"I wonder if it has something to do with the Blacklist?" I said. "I've got theories of my own."

"Do you now?"

"I've been nursing this one since college, actually. I majored in U.S. history."

"So let's hear it."

"Okay. You know the Blacklist, right? The Red Scare?"

"I've been reading about them, yes."

"But only since you showed up here?" I gripped a silver-bullet-shaped pepper shaker as if it were unique to this timeline.

"That's right. Oh, we had a House Un-American Activities Committee, too, but it was such an obscure little chapter that I'd almost forgotten about it until now."

"Well, it wasn't obscure around these parts," I grumbled, with a kind of masochistic pride. "Before they got through tampering with the media, both formally and informally, the average U.S. voter couldn't tell the difference between social justice and totalitarianism. And they still can't."

"I guess that's it, then," she said thoughtfully.

"It is?"

"Douglass"—her voice was electric—"just try to imagine postwar Hollywood with Carl Laemmle, Jr.'s Universal in the mix."

I should have been thinking about this the whole time, obviously. But it just seemed too good and too strange to be true. "I guess it might have changed a lot. Before 1936, Universal was the only really large studio that wasn't owned by a faceless collection of shareholders. It really was a family business. So I guess they'd have had the freedom to buck the Blacklist, if they'd wanted to."

"In which case," Dorothea leaped ahead of me, "there wouldn't have been a Blacklist at all, right? These things depend upon total collusion."

"In principle, yes," I agreed. "But, family business or no, there were still a lot of reasons to go along quietly."

"Of course." She moved closer to me. "But, Douglass, it was your article—and your portrait of Carl Laemmle, Jr.—that put this idea in my head. He was utterly reckless during your early '30s. Why not during my late '40s, too?"

"My column impressed you that much?" I couldn't help asking.

"I told you I liked it. In fact, I was kind of surprised I'd never seen it before. It's exactly my kind of thing."

I knew why she'd never seen it before. "Well, thanks again." I think I blushed a little.

Then I took her idea and ran my mouth: "And, yes, I think Laemmle, Jr. might very well have done something like this. Most of the other Hollywood moguls were older men who had either been born in pogrom-ridden Europe or in miserable circumstances here in the States. These were some of the only people who had actually managed to live out the American Dream, from rags to incredible riches, and they took their patriotism quite seriously, for all sorts of reasons—the most important one being self-defense. No one is more likely to come under fire than an 'ungrateful' immigrant. But Carl, Jr. was born here, and raised in luxury by the founder of Universal, his dad. He never worried about being labelled 'un-American.' He knew damned well how American he was."

"And there you have it." She grinned. "That's why we never had a Blacklist. The whole thing was scuttled behind the scenes. Of course, HUAC did keep the pressure on for a while, and a few diehards did go to jail for contempt of court."

"The 'Unfriendly Ten.'" I nodded.

"Right. But when those people were released, they went right back to work in Hollywood."

"Amazing. The studios had so much power, and they let themselves be railroaded into working against their own best interests by a bunch of rednecks."

"I guess so," she said. "You don't appreciate the drama until you start creating divergent realities."

"God." I winced. "And I had to be born in this one."

"You were born in all of them, Douglass. We're not stuck here. It just feels that way because we have to let Pat Corelli die in order to put things right. But this timeline is the aberration, not mine."

I added a silent footnote to the statement—and it made me want to throw up.

"This coffee is taking its toll," I said. "Which way is the bathroom?"

"First door to the right. Are you okay?"

Was I okay?

I splashed water in my face, stared in the mirror, and made my decision. Then I took a long piss. The coffee actually had been taking its toll, but the pain in my gut stayed right where it was. I tried another blast of water and towelled off.

"I'm fine," I confirmed, upon re-entering the kitchen. "So, I gather you're planning to take care of things right away?"

She rubbed the back of her neck. "Yes. I don't want this on my conscience another minute." Her sharp-cornered smile returned with a tremor. "I'm glad you'll never have to know anything about this."

"You like me that much?"

"The next time I see you, you won't know me." The naked affection in the last syllable nearly killed me. "There's no harm in telling you."

"This seems like the worst possible time for you to leave."

"Ah." She grinned. "But I'll be back in a second. Literally. And I'll find you."

No, she wouldn't.

I appealed to her technical side: "And you can actually set the controls to take you to a specific day and time?"

"Sure." She took the watch off and stretched it out on the table in front of me. Then she draped herself over my shoulder. "See, the dials are for minutes, hours, days, months, and years. They're not actually dials at all, as you can see. They're digital readouts. But I did my best to camouflage them beneath the gold filigree. I'm still not sure what I'll do if I ever shoot past the mechanical era entirely. Maybe people'll think it's a bracelet?"

"I'd be more worried about overshooting the bifocal era." I squinted at the tiny numbers on the watch face.

She smiled and then worked the buttons on the right to plot a journey to 4:30 p.m., on November 28, 1929. "This toggle on the left has settings for backward, forward, or return journeys." She adjusted it to go back. "I sent you about ten and three-quarters years into the future, on a five-minute return setting."

"So I gathered."

"How did I look?"

"Good." I kissed her, ran my fingers up and down her back, under her shirt.

"Do you have any more of these machines?" I asked.

She let out a heartbreakingly trusting snort. "Are you kidding? It would take me another twenty-three years to win enough grant money to replicate this thing. You wouldn't believe the crazy rare materials I had to use!"

I stepped back and took firm possession of the watch. "Good."

"Douglass!"

"I'm sorry. I'll be nicer in another timeline. I promise."

I pressed the "go" button on the right.

I suppose I should have told her that Pat Corelli is my grandfather.

Chapter Three

Dorothea had undoubtedly intended to set forth on her journey from a discreet corner of the back alley. In my haste, I plunged out of the frying pan of our dismal parting into the potential flames of an alien kitchen more than eighty years in the past. My one hope, as I pressed the button, was that Dorothea's long-ago predecessor in the apartment would be out having Thanksgiving dinner at some rich relative's house. Of course, given the economic maelstrom I had leapt into, it was quite conceivable that this modest flat's occupant had suddenly become the rich relative. In which case I would have a lot of explaining to do.

As before, the trip took no time. Dorothea's hurt visage gave way, in my sightline, to an imitation Renoir, possibly painted by the tenant, hanging on the wall. The room was dark. I did not smell turkey. I wanted to look around, touch things, memorize every detail of the evaporated scene. But it was 1929 outside the window, too, and that's where I went. Down the fire escape.

Fear of detection spurred me forward, along with the knowledge that I would have to find some way to foil a violent crime within the next hour or so. Would I spot signs of the assault in time to prevent the worst from happening? Would I even recognize my grandfather, who had died long before I was born? I had seen a few pictures, of course, but, for the life of me, I couldn't call them to mind. And my life did depend upon success in this endeavour, almost as completely as his did.

But I needn't have worried, at least about finding my mark on the stage. As I waited to cross Bethune Street, brushing rust and paint chips off my clothing, I spotted Dorothea in the park across the street. It was a place I knew fairly well: Abingdon Square, a cozy little garden, watched over by the commemorative bronze statue of a World War I "Doughboy."

The incognito physicist grabbed a seat on a bench near the statue and started pretending to read. I couldn't quite make out what the book was, but I'm sure it was as period appropriate as her clothes. She looked fantastic and tolerably well insulated in a lime-green wool coat with matching felt hat and giant scarf—but she still can't have been too comfortable in the damp 40°F air.

She was certainly on her game, though. She spotted me right away. For a moment, I wondered if she had been lying about the time machine's uniqueness. The very idea made my blood run cold, and it must have showed on my face, because she responded with the warmest-eyed smile I have ever seen.

This only made me feel like more of a jerk for having treated so remarkable a person so shabbily. Luckily, the woman I was admiring through the afternoon's exhaust had no inkling of what I had done to her future self, and if my plan succeeded in every respect, she never would. For of course this was no desperate Dorothea pursuing a silver-tongued shadowman of her own creation through the funhouse of time but rather the noble scientist taking her invention for its first spin, on a mission of mercy.

A mission that my intense gaze (or, more likely, my luridly white sneakers) had distracted her from. I realized I would have to do something about *them*, but that would have to come later. The first order of business was to put my unwitting competitor off her guard before the moment of crisis arrived. I strolled a few blocks northward on Hudson and then quickly doubled back in search of the perfect observation post.

In the end, I chose a bench on the other side of the square that was pretty well shielded (by trees) from Dorothea's scrutiny, as long as she didn't get up and turn around. A bush would have been preferable, certainly, but getting arrested for lurking in the park in a pair of crazy shoes wouldn't have helped the cause at all. I settled into a cross-legged position, which extinguished my foot glare, and waited for something to happen.

Here was my first real opportunity to survey history in its daily course. November. Twenty-eighth. Nineteen twenty-nine. Thanksgiving. Earlier that afternoon, a gargantuan parade, still in its infancy as a tradition, had thrilled New Yorkers who had no reason to associate the event with Edmund Gwenn and Natalie Wood.

I would never be one of them. I had viewed my life through the prism of classic films for so long that the prospect of seeing this body of work come into being, year by year, in piecemeal fashion, filled me with the terror and awe that a *normal* person might experience if he or she were presented with season tickets to the creation of the universe. I could adjust to the *real* 1929. Indeed, I would have to if I hoped to secure both Dorothea's American pastoral and my own place at the picnic table. But the *psychic* 1929 was off limits. Hindsight may be 20/20, but I had wandered into its blind spot.

So I squinted at the details.

I watched a procession of 1929 model cars motor down Hudson and 8ᵗʰ, marvelling at their baroque chrome peninsulas. I kept an eye on the moon, taking shape in the dusk. It seemed much farther away than it ever had before. I wooed a crowd of pigeons, with the same lack of success that I always had with their descendants whenever I forgot to come provisioned with bread. I sniffed the crisp air and thought I detected more burning wood on its currents than I would have on a comparable night in 2010. But there was no change at all in the gooseflesh it raised on the backs of my hands, and the wind flashed a red, orange, and yellow semaphore that had meant "November" since before calendars were born.

A strong gust rummaged through the trash bin to my left, pulling out yesterday's sports section and a flamboyant crimson leaf. I flailed at the latter as it flew past my face, losing the prize to a huge German shepherd that had snuck up on my right.

"Whoa!" I exclaimed, as quietly as I could manage.

The dog tried to toss the leaf back to me, but it dribbled to the pavement. I rubbed her chin instead.

"Sorry, girl."

"She'll be sorry all right," agreed a striking woman, picking up her end of the muck-encrusted leash. "Don't you ever do that again!" She wagged her finger at the dog, who deflected the criticism with an endearing shrug of ear and tail.

"You're an inconsiderate beast, aren't you?" I added sternly, moving up to stroke the dog's whiskers. "It's not easy to run in heels."

The beast's owner looked herself up and down, lingering with a smile on the black shoes in question. "I think I managed rather gracefully."

"Of course you did." I nodded. "That stage training has many applications."

She fiddled with a pearl necklace. "You recognize me?"

I did. Even forty years out of focus and swathed in alien finery, the autumn-green eyes were unmistakable. My grandmother, aged twenty-two. She looked like a movie star. She wasn't one though. Not yet.

"Uh-huh."

"From what?"

"Oh." I stood up to meet her inquisitive gaze at eye level. "I'm not sure, actually. *The Follies? The Scandals?*

The Vanities?"

"You're an addict!" she laughed. "It's *The Scandals*. And before *that*, vaudeville—ever since I was ten...."

"It must have been vaudeville." I grinned. "I'm too poor for the big time.... But I'm glad you weren't."

"Gee...thanks." She sat down, shedding every vestige of self-consciousness. "Things are comin' along nicely...."

"They must be." I patted the dog's stalwart shoulder. "You both seem quite prosperous."

"Lulu is my husband's dog, actually. He keeps her in kibble...."

"And you in pearls?"

"Welll..."—she reached instinctively for her throat—"just these ones."

"Aw, I was just fooling around. Why shouldn't he get you pearls? Is he in the show business too?"

"Oh, no!" She shook her head, relaxing for good this time. "He hates it. Wants me to give it up.... He owns that fine establishment over there." She indicated an Italian flag-striped awning near the corner of Hudson and Bethune. I could just barely make out the restaurant's name, scrawled in elegant black cursive across the canvas.

"Risotto Voce?"

"Cute, hunh? I named it. Pat says I can sing for the customers whenever I get a yen to...."

"Sounds a little patronizing."

"Oh, it is." She smiled. "But he's a great guy....

He'll be along any minute now.... We always meet in the square."

"It's a good spot for it."

"It's home." She extended her arms behind her head, ending the stretch in a gesture that encompassed the entire park and everyone in it.

We were seven, at that moment, if you counted Lulu. In addition to Eileen and myself, there was Dorothea, of course, still peering over the edge of her book like that drawing of Kilroy; there was a cabbie who had parked his car near the gates of the square and begun pacing the inside of its perimeter, rehearsing his side of some imminent argument with his wife; and there were two youngish black men playing chess at the next bench down the path.

I could feel the moment closing in.

But Eileen couldn't.

She regained my attention with a wave of her hand. "You from New York?"

"Uh...." I pondered the merits of a truthful response. Did I know enough about the minutiae of my native city's past to convincingly portray a man who had lived there since 1894? I decided that I didn't. "No...I'm from Montreal, actually."

"Montreal?"

"Oui." I smiled. "I'm Douglass Infantino."

We shook hands.

"Eileen McWade."

"A real pleasure."

"Not *enchantée?*"

"When in Rome...."

"Were you ever in Rome?"

"What do you think?"

"I think you should go. Everyone should. Although I suppose it might be a good idea to wait until they get rid of Mussolini."

"A very good idea. It'll happen someday. I'm sure of that, at least."

While Eileen pondered that ambiguous statement, I watched Dorothea stand up, toss her book aside, and draw a revolver from beneath her green coat.

That's how she stopped the mugging? Dirty Harry–style?

I kept an eye on her eyes and got ready to sprint.

My plan wouldn't work unless I did the saving.

"You all right, Douglass? You're acting kinda weird all of a sudden," Eileen interrupted.

Torrents of sweat came gushing from my temples; I massaged the dog's left ear obsessively; my foot tapped frenetically. I was acting very weird....

Two guys in top hats and ill-fitting coats entered from stage left, heading south on 8th Avenue, jostling and joking as they went. They seemed pretty unimportant until Dorothea aimed the gun at their heads.

I turned to Eileen. "The really weird part begins now."

I plotted an intercept course that would also obstruct Dorothea's shot, praying that she wouldn't just fire through me. As I approached her targets, at a full gallop, I read the histories of violence off their dead-pans, spelled out in cold eyes, broken noses, and badly healed scars. I noticed that the shorter of the two men (both were quite a bit taller than my 5'7") had a knife at the ready.

Across the street, a car pulled up near the intersection of 8th, Bleecker, and Bank. My grandfather (I did recognize him) stepped onto the curb, as oblivious of the men with hard faces as they were of me. That is, they saw me running but had no reason to suspect me of planning an open-field tackle at 1:2 odds.

I crashed into them five steps from their quarry. We all fell down. The knife clattered into the street. Its owner beat me to his feet—and kicked me in the head. The rest is pretty confused in my mind. A woman screamed from a window. The two assailants made tracks for the park. Pat Corelli leaned over me, asking if I was all right. Eileen McWade repeated the question a little while later. The dog licked my face. Police sirens wailed.

I passed out.

Chapter Four

I woke up in the most comfortable bed I had ever lain in. Flannel sheets. Down comforter. Something wonderful in the pillows. Dog at my feet.

The room was small and crammed full of coziness. There was a roaring fireplace; a mantelpiece stocked with first editions of Dreiser, Ferber, Hemingway, Millay, Benét; a curvy old radio and an old-fashioned globe on a big cedar chest; a lamp at the bedside.

I sat up and switched on the light. My head *hurt*. My face was definitely swollen. I tasted blood in my cheeks and noted the absence of two cherished back teeth. The dog wagged her tail pityingly as I flopped out of bed, directly onto the parquet floor. I spotted the moon through a green stained-glass transom. Was it still Thanksgiving night? Twenty-four hours later? Christmas? Nineteen fifty-eight? I couldn't guess any better than I could stand. So I crawled to the fireplace and shoved my marshmallowed face into its glow.

"Be careful, Douglass!" Eileen appeared at the doorway, with a glass of water in one hand and two pills in the other.

"Don't worry." I curled up on the hearth rug. "This

is not the world's clumsiest suicide attempt. That warmth is good for what ails...."

"So're aspirin," she soothed, helping me back to the bed, "and they don't give off sparks."

"I'm bringing out the mother in you."

"She was already on order. This room'll be a nursery in about seven months."

"Oh really?" I tried to smile. "Congratulations."

"Thanks."

She straightened out the blankets and sat down near my knees. "Can I read you a story, young man?"

"You can tell me the one about what the hell happened after I passed out."

"Ah...well"—she blinked the irony out of her eyes and focused directly on mine—"you saved Pat's life."

"Good, good. So everyone's okay...."

"Yes."

"How long was I out?"

"More than a day."

"Wow...what about the lady with the gun?"

"Gun? What are you talking about?"

"The woman in green, she was sitting near the statue."

"Oh! Right. I remember now. You stopped listening to me and stared at her back for about three solid minutes. I started thinking I had lost my touch.... I saw her pull something out of her coat, but I never dreamed it was a gun."

"Believe me. It was."

"Well, she didn't use it. In fact, I completely lost track of her as soon as you dashed off."

"The police didn't question her?"

"No. She must have run out before they got there. Can't say that I blame her. Those questions were endless.... You're lucky you slept through it. Although I suppose they'll catch up with you, now that you're awake. They're pretty curious to know how you anticipated the robbery. So am I, frankly."

I aimed my face at pure guilelessness. "Well, I guess you'd call it a premonition"—I paused for effect, savouring the chance to rehearse my act before the professional critics got a look at it—"something...told me... that...if I paid attention to the woman in green, she'd... I don't know...show me what needed to be done...."

She squinted at me. "And then you saw her pull a gun?"

I nodded. "Right. Maybe the gun wasn't even there." I backtracked as far as I could. "Maybe that's why you didn't see it.... But I read it as a symbol of violence, and transposed that meaning onto the men she seemed to be pointing at."

"Maybe." She seemed dubious. "So you decided to tackle them both?"

I shrugged. "It was the only thing I could think of to do."

A hand appeared on Eileen's shoulder. "That certainly jibes with your account, honey."

The confident voice belonged to Pat Corelli, who

would die of a heart attack in 1958. Here, in 1929, he looked invincible, towering over his wife in a black smoking jacket, thoughtfully rubbing his square, scarred jaw, peering down at me with one-way window eyes, tinted blue. It was hard to believe that he would have been killed without the intercession of his scrawny grandson. Seeing him and observing his effect upon Eileen, who hadn't spoken a word since he had entered the room, I wasn't so sure I was glad that I had saved him. She obviously adored him, but the adoration was laced with the seeds of an abjection that I remembered from the eyes that had watched over me in my childhood.

Was Eileen really condemned to either superstardom and implosion within seven years or a lifetime on dim? My mission was to hack a third way through this underbrush of possibility and to keep my mind on the situation at hand.

"Of course it tallies," I said. "That's what happened."

His face opened up a little. "Hey, I believe you, buddy. I'm just trying to see it from their perspective."

"*Their?*" I sat up. "The police, you mean?"

"Right. They're not handing out any free passes on this one."

Eileen stood up and walked to the window. "They...they dragged those two coloured men off to jail, Douglass...."

"What?"

Her voice cracked. "As possible accomplices! They were only trying to help! One of them even got cut defending me."

Pat clamped a hand around her waist. "But they didn't stop 'em, hon."

Tears edged into her voice. "How could they have? They didn't have any weapons. They were playing chess!"

The hand climbed up her spine. "The police must have some reason for suspecting them, Eileen...."

"We both know what their 'reason' is!"

"Okay." He turned to me. "Eileen is going to bed."

"No, I'm not. Douglass needs to hear about this! He can corroborate my statement."

"And I *will*," I said, rather more dramatically than I would have believed myself capable of sounding.

"Great." Pat smiled mirthlessly. "You just make sure you don't get yourself into any trouble while you're doing it...."

"Some trouble you don't mind getting into." I smiled back.

"Do what you have to do, buddy."

He pulled Eileen toward the door. "Come on."

"Get some rest, Douglass." She waved.

I waved back. "Good night."

Chapter Five

The bed did its work.

The morning sun found me bright-eyed and considerably less bushwhacked. My jaw still ached, and my teeth couldn't be regenerated, but I felt certain that history could be.

There was no clock in the room, but it seemed to be quite early, just a few minutes past dawn. I grabbed *An American Tragedy* off the shelf and read the first page to Lulu.

A knock at the door interrupted our session.

"Yes?" I chirped.

Corelli walked in, carrying a breakfast-in-bed tray. The coffee smelled wonderful. "Hey, you look great, buddy!"

"Thanks. I feel like great's second cousin. Which isn't so bad, all things considered."

I reached for the steaming cup and took a quick sip. "Now this is great." I smiled. "Hey, I really appreciate the effort here, Pat, but I think it might do me some good to move around a bit...."

"Whatever you say." He bowed and then beckoned. "The kitchen's this way."

We chugged down a railroad passage decorated with Dutch master knockoffs and modernist efforts by the neighbours, some of them quite interesting. At the end of the line, we emerged into a multiwindowed, yellow-green kitchen sizzling with greased skillets and percolating with coffee.

"Have a seat, Doug." He pulled out a chair for me.

"Thanks." I sat in it.

He refilled my coffee as I took my first bite of French toast.

"I'm sorry about last night." He flopped his palms onto the table, face up. "I was still pretty rattled, I guess. But that's no excuse for bein' a jerk. You and Eileen were right. We gotta make sure those guys are turned loose....

"She and I don't really agree...politically.... I'm a businessman...been trying to make something of myself since I started bussing tables, when I was twelve, and you've got to learn a little selfishness if you want to get anywhere in that racket....

"Eileen wants to help *everybody*, which is nice. I wish we could. But not by taking food out of my kids' mouths, y'know? That's the world we live in. I've got a restaurant to run. I don't want any trouble. But those guys, I figure we can help them without overthrowing the government, right?"

"I hope so." I nodded.

"You like the food?" His eyes widened.

"It's fantastic."

He blinked contentedly. "That's good. There's more of everything. And Eileen should be up soon. You two really hit it off, hunh?"

The question sounded innocent but had the potential to take on accusatory connotations in a hurry.

"Well, I've seen her on the stage. She's amazing. I had to tell or so. It was pretty great of her not to high-hat me. And then I got my psychic newsflash...."

"Yeah, she told me you were *meditating*, or somethin', when she ran into you...."

I considered correcting him on this point, but the detail seemed to fit (in Pat's mind) with the "harmless, helpful friend of the family" characterization that I needed to establish, so I let it stand.

I nodded spiritually. "I was communing with the autumn."

"Sounds nice," Eileen interjected, yawning her way to the table.

"Good morning, hon." Pat lavished her with kisses and a plate laden with delicacies.

"Isn't he amazing, Douglass?"

I accepted another round of French toast. "I'm overwhelmed."

Pat beamed. "My first place was a breakfast joint. It's still my favourite meal of the day. But there's a lot more money in a night spot."

"All he thinks about is money." Eileen tsked him lovingly.

"Someone's got to, no? You taking another day off

– 46 –

from the show?"

She shrugged blue-kimonoed shoulders. "Hey, Benny suggested that I take a few days to regroup. They don't want me up there ruining the fun by flashing back to hopheads with knives. Besides, I think they want to see how Jessie handles the material."

She turned to me. "Jessie's in the chorus, but I've been working with her on her delivery. She's getting pretty good."

Pat shook his head. "Helping out the competition.... Where did I go wrong?"

Eileen scrunched her face at him. "You didn't raise me, Pat. I was like this when you met me."

He refilled our cups. "And I loved you from the start. It's no skin off my nose if you want to sabotage your career.... You *know* how I feel about that anyway."

I jumped in: "Oh, but you're not going to *quit*, are you?"

She leaned back in her chair. "Well, I haven't really decided that yet. I feel like I'm *this* close to crashing through. Bu-u-ut"—she patted her tummy—"there are other factors to consider now...."

"But lots of stars have babies. Why not you?"

A look of queasy pride came over her face. She eyed Pat nervously. He picked up some dishes and stalked off.

"Well," she said, "in the first place, I'm not a star.... And I'm not likely to become one if I take a year off. And in the second place, well, believe me, I used to feel as strongly about this as you do"—she said this under her breath—"but, like I said, there are other factors to consider...."

I followed her gaze to the sullen man at the sink. "Yeah." I nodded.

She snapped her fingers. "But what about *you*, Douglass? Things have been so crazy.... All I really know is that you've seen me perform and you're from Montreal. Presumably you came here to accomplish something. Where've you been living? And what've you been doing?"

Pat cocked an intent ear in our direction.

"Actually, to answer your questions as simply as possible: Nowhere. And nothing."

"What?"

I knew I was taking a chance here, but, I figured, what the hell, it's the dawn of the Great Depression; the cities are full of displaced losers.

"I did have a room of my own, at a boarding house in the Bowery, but they kicked me out of there a few days ago. I came here to write for the pulps. Science fiction stories are my thing. But I haven't made any real headway there, and now I've lost all of my manuscripts, along with my typewriter and my clothes.... They warned me they'd get rid of my stuff if I didn't pay up, but I didn't believe they'd be that petty!"

"Never underestimate a landlord's pettiness, Douglass."

Pat rejoined us, stroking his wife's plaid-kerchiefed curls. "That's my little radical...."

"You know I'm right, Pat." She shrugged him off.

"You are," he conceded, then turned to me and added: "That's the world we live in, buddy."

I nodded. "I guess it is."

"You're welcome to stay with us for a while, Doug. We've got a nice typewriter that no one"—he grinned at Eileen—"ever uses. And I can always use some help around the restaurant while you're waiting for your break."

"Wow," I exhaled, "really?"

Eileen's eyes bulged. "Douglass! Of course! It's the least we can do for you. We know a few publishers, too. I'll see if I can get you an interview or something."

"That'd be fantastic." I jumped up, quite sincerely thrilled. "And, I mean, I do have editorial experience. It's not like this is some pipe dream. I can write."

"No kidding!" Pat slapped me on the back. "You write when you talk. It'll do Eileen some good to have another intellectual around the house for a while. But no Red meetings in the kitchen, you hear?"

"Don't worry, honey," she replied, "the stink of bourgeois aspiration in this place will keep all progressive thought at bay."

"You mean the olive oil?" He smirked.

"I mean *you*." She kissed his nose.

He kissed her back. On the mouth. "I'd better take my shower now. Gotta get down to the Voce. Thanksgiving weekend is huge for us. Have some more coffee, Doug."

He bustled off down the hallway.

She watched after him, quite lustfully.

"You two really have something, don't you?" I asked.

She smiled. "We do."

"A shame he's got to be such a gender Nazi."

Her brow bunched up. "A what *what*?"

Neither term, of course, had any meaning to an American in 1929.

"Oh, uh, Montreal term," I explained. "I mean he's a traditionalist."

"Ah, yes. It's always going to be a problem between us. But I don't know that I'd want him to change...."

"That's social conditioning."

"Sure, Douglass. I guess it is. But what can I do? I'm conditioned. No changing it now. You want to go back in time?"

"No. I want you to forge ahead with your career and drag him kicking and screaming behind you. He's *not* going to leave you over this. He just wants you to think that he might."

"You're probably right," she yawned. "But what do *I* really want? That's the question. I've got a competitive streak, for sure, and right now I'm battling for the spotlight, like everyone else, but I'm not sure how much winning that game would do for me, on a personal level."

"Hard to argue with that."

"So why argue?" she laughed. "You trying to distract me from prying into this vagabond life you've been leading? I might want to write something about you. That's where my real ambitions lie, you know."

"But what about your singing?"

"Oh, I've worked hard on it. But now I've just about got it licked. I'm as good as I'm going to get. Acting still excites me. But I don't have enough control over my material to explore the problems that really interest me.... Take you, for instance. What were you planning to do with yourself, that day in the square?"

I shrugged. "I guess I was just hoping I'd catch a break before I starved."

"Come *on*! You're not that stoic. You had to be making some kind of a plan! Were you gonna sell that crazy watch?"

I grinned and glanced at my left wrist.

The watch wasn't there!

"Where is it?!" I almost screamed.

"Take it *easy*, Douglass," she soothed. "I put it away for safekeeping, just before the doctor and the dentist went to work on you, Thursday evening."

She darted out of the room.

She was gone just long enough for me to contemplate the spot I'd be in if I ever lost that machine. It was probably good for me, in a way. Got me right into character as a man on the edge of oblivion. But I would have preferred to go on hamming my way through the act. The lesson was clear: "No more getting kicked in the head."

"Good idea," Eileen giggled, and I realized I'd spoken those last words aloud.

She spread the watch on the table with exaggerated ceremony.

I looked up at her gratefully.

She mussed my hair. "Don't look so *haunted*, Douglass. You're breaking my heart."

"I'm okay." I forced a smile.

Her eyes reddened in sympathy. "It's pretty valuable, hunh?"

"Yeah." I nodded. "It's pretty valuable."

Chapter Six

We played cribbage most of the day, as we would often do again during the early '80s. (She improved with age, as did I, which put her at a very peculiar disadvantage in our current situation.) Pat went down to the restaurant at 9:00 a.m., after taking our dinner orders (veal scaloppini for Eileen, gnocchi primavera for me).

"He'll be down there all day." She rolled her eyes. "But he always eats with me before I head off to the Apollo."

We decided to face the inquisition as soon as possible. Eileen called them right after breakfast. She argued that I ought to delete the months of New York flaneurism from my resume and pose as a newly arrived literary hopeful instead. I embraced this idea with alacrity. Nothing suited me better than backing out of a backstory that I couldn't possibly have corroborated.

"But how'd I lose all of my stuff?" I wanted to know.

"You got robbed at the bus depot. They'll believe that. Actually, I can't believe you weren't."

"Sounds good." I nodded, claiming the victory slot.

"Christ!" She replaced the pegs at the start line and

began shuffling with a will.

"You weren't kidding about that competitive streak, were you?" I jabbed.

"Of course not. And I'm not kidding around with you anymore either!"

"Better get serious about your pegging then," I advised her.

A couple of rain-drenched detectives appeared at the door, putting a damper on the fun. They introduced themselves as Fredericks and O'Meara. Both were tall, dark, and solidly built, without an iota of geniality between them, although I wouldn't have called them *mean*-looking either. Human watchdogs, that's what they were. Quick on the scent and never lost for a snarl, in the appropriate context, but robbed by nature and self-imposed reserve of the prick-eared joy that real watchdogs bring to their nasty work. They didn't even seem to notice the beautiful dark-haired woman who admitted them to the kitchen and made coffee for us all. They only had eyes for swollen-faced me.

"What's this about you not having any identification?" barked Fredericks, whose graying hair marked him as the senior partner.

"A citizen's welcoming committee processed me at the gates of your fair city. Didn't Ms. McWade tell you?"

"Yeah," O'Meara grunted, "*Mrs. Corelli* told us. Bad luck for you, friend. You're from Canada, right?"

"That's right. I came here looking for magazine

work, not trouble."

"Well," Fredericks began, in what seemed like his friendliest tone, "you won't get any more than you deserve. Not from us, at any rate. So take it easy."

"All right."

O'Meara joined the love-in. "You helped people in trouble. That sits well with us. As long as you didn't stage the whole thing yourself."

Eileen punched the table. "Another criminal mastermind in your custody?" she yelled.

"Don't worry about your chess players, lady," O'Meara grunted. "They both work in better homes than we'll ever have. We released 'em yesterday."

"Perfect!" she exploded. "Some rich white people might be inconvenienced, and suddenly you're all heart."

"That's the world we live in." I dropped my chin onto my knuckles.

"You said it, friend," O'Meara agreed, in an almost aggressively ambivalent tone. Orders were orders for him. But his partner wasn't so incorruptibly corrupt. I could see that Eileen's bravura performance had found an audience.

"Well." She pressed her advantage, crowding her target. "I'm a fairly well-known Broadway personality.... And my husband is an up-and-coming entrepreneur in this neighbourhood. Doesn't it mean anything that we vouch for Douglass?" She practically whispered the last sentence. Her mouth was barely two inches from Fredericks', and those last esses in my name just enveloped him.

"Yeah, it does," O'Meara groaned, a little louder than was necessary, "as long as you aren't being hood-winked."

Fredericks stood up. "She isn't."

O'Meara took one last hasty sip and picked up his hat. "So does this mean we aren't gonna trouble Mr. Infantino for a *statement?*"

Fredericks stared dazedly at his partner. Doubtless, he was nearing the same conclusion that I had reached. He had been *movie-starred.* "Oh, uh, of course." He peeked apologetically at Eileen. "We will need to get his statement...."

O'Meara shook his head. "Yeah, *sorry*...." He pulled out a notepad, and I dictated the blandest possible account of my adventure.

Did I know the perpetrators?

Of course not.

How had I known what they were up to?

I had played a hunch.

What did they look like?

Big Caucasians with stubble and very dirty suits. One brown and one gray.

"That's not very helpful," the officer sighed, flipping his book closed.

"I never thought it would be."

Fredericks patted my shoulder. "Okay.... Get some rest, kid...."

O'Meara slipped into a disingenuously obliging

tone of voice: "I wish you a speedy recovery, sir...but please don't stray.... We might require your assistance at a later date."

"I'm not going anywhere."

Fredericks gave Eileen a brief salute.

O'Meara bowed, with a sneer.

They wandered off into uncertain weather.

Eileen reshuffled and dealt.

"Now you're gonna see some pegging." She smiled.

Chapter Seven

Love had skipped a generation in my family.

I didn't blame my mother for this. She had had me at the age of forty-five, in a desperate attempt to save a marriage that had gone on failing despite her best efforts, bottoming out in a divorce when I was two. Children had never really figured in June Corelli's plans, and she made few attempts to hide that fact.

My father (that's "Mr. Infantino" to you) had even less interest in parenting, at least until he started on his "do-over" family in the mid-'80s. By then, we were used to not being used to each other. He sent me money every Christmas.

If I sound bitter, it's only because I've discovered that people expect me to be. In fact, I have no complaints about my childhood. No one was ever actually mean to me (which is more important than you might think), and my grandmother was fantastic. We never had any financial worries either, thanks to Mom's editorial prowess at a popular women's magazine. She wasn't home much, and didn't know what to do with me when she *was*, but she always made it clear that the responsibility for that was hers, not mine. Maybe too clear. Like clockwork, every night, after her third drink, she would tell me what a "great kid" I was, in a tone which implied that I deserved better than her.

Eileen, too, had tippled throughout my childhood, albeit in a far more elegant fashion. She always drank sherry, which I had assumed to be "harmless," until I actually *tried* it. It had never interfered with her card playing. But it was alcoholism all the same. Growing up, I had often wondered about the cause of this ailment that, unlike my mother's more verbal strain, had no symptoms except for a phantom sheen in her eyes that replaced the real tears I imagined would collect there if she ever sobered up.

The fact that she had sung on Broadway was never a secret, and I positively lived for her yearly renditions of "Have Yourself a Merry Little Christmas" and "The Christmas Waltz," but no one had ever so much as hinted at the potential for stardom that her career had held. Later on, after the disease had helped to kill her, fifty years past her expiration date in the timeline that Dorothea hailed from, I had filed her lifelong sadness under the heading of "just not quite good enough." Now I knew better.

On December 1st, I attended my first performance of *George White's Scandals of 1929* at the Apollo Theatre (no, not the really famous one in Harlem; this less-storied neoclassical venue was on 42nd Street, near Times Square—and was destined to become a burlesque house before the Depression was through with it). It was Eileen's first night back on the job, and, by all accounts, she put a little something extra into her number, just for the occasion. The song was a DeSylva, Brown, and Henderson comedy ballad called "18 Days Ago."

It suited Eileen to a T. *This* Eileen, I mean. Not the caroler I had grown up with. She could rankle without rancor, suggest and keep you guessing, slip her heart out onto her sleeve when you weren't expecting it. And she knew just how long to leave it there, too.

I made two more trips to the Apollo, on complimentary passes, later in the week. I really wasn't used to live entertainment, and I actually needed those replays of Eileen's five minutes before I could think about them. One thing I did grasp right away, though, is that "revues" annoy me. This might seem odd, given my obsession with '30s and '40s "backstagers" (which are always about putting on a variety show), but, in fact, those movies are held together by stories—insipid stories, to be sure, but that's part of their charm. *The Scandals* could have used some of that charm.

All of which was beside the point, because, as a supporting character in Eileen's real-life backstager, my job was to accentuate the positive, as Johnny Mercer would someday say. Aided by a few thousand years of patriarchal tradition and Eileen's own history of indoctrination, Pat was absolutely killing in the role of philistine obstacle, and I would have to parry his every macho thrust if I meant to keep him from puncturing the fragile bubble of Eileen's ambition.

And yet, I *liked* Pat. Bussing tables at Risotto Voce on my nights between *Scandals*, I couldn't help falling in love with the place, which offered great food, good music (sung by voice school trainees, for the most part), and an intangible aura of artistic aspiration. Perfect Village atmosphere. No checkered tablecloths (those went with lower prices), but no one other than me seemed disappointed by that. Pat never made a wrong move in public, and the clientele adored him.

He got a lot of mileage out of the mugging. Every time he described it, the implied threat grew more serious, and my intervention more preternatural. He still never came close to guessing that I had travelled back from 2010 to snatch him from the jaws of certain death.

By Friday, he had the story down. The emphasis, by necessity, fell mainly on the debaucherous prelude to the incident, from the perspective of the villains and putative drug users of the piece.

"...so they blew out their credit at whatever lowlife den they were usin' and got tossed on the street," I heard him tell one willingly captive audience. "But they weren't done for the day."

"'Course not," agreed a graying man in a tailored brown suit. "That kind just keeps going until they pass out or get arrested...."

"Exactly." Pat nodded. "But you don't pull stuff in your neighbourhood, if you can help it. So they stumbled north. It musta felt like a week in the desert to them, and I had the water. Or anyway, the stuff that buys the water. I've never seen such desperate looks in my life. And then I saw the knives."

A couple of the younger men at the table whistled. The lone woman, who appeared to be with the man in brown, muttered, "I know that feeling."

"Oh, jeez, Helen," Pat yelped, genuinely concerned. "I'm so sorry! Is this bringing back the wrong kinda memories?"

Helen, a lovely blonde in green with a hermetic smile, shook her head and lit a cigarette. "You know me better than that."

"Yeah." Pat smiled. "You're tough.... Anyway, you wouldn't believe how many thoughts crowded into my head during those few seconds. Could I take them? They were tall but kinda skinny, y'know? Wrecks. Still, they looked capable of anything. And they had those knives.... I wanted to *run*, but I didn't like to turn my back on them...."

"I thought about Eileen, of course. And the baby. We're having a *baby*. Did you all know that?"

Celebratory noise filled the room.

"Thanks, thanks," he beamed.

I wheeled my cargo of sauce-encrusted plates into the kitchen, missing the next few minutes of the performance, but I knew from experience that he always spent quite a while praising his wife for planning to give up "the life" in favour of living for her family.

I didn't want to hear that stuff.

But I reappeared on cue for Pat to introduce me as "the struggling writer who saved my life."

Earlier in the week, I had been simply a "benefactor" or, more extravagantly, a "clairvoyant Good Samaritan." The new occupational detail, I soon learned, had been added for the benefit of the man in brown.

"Oh? What do you write?" this stalwart asked me.

I set down my last fork. "Well"—I thought for a moment—"magazine work, mostly. A lot of mystery stories. Some fantasy."

"Really?" The man's gaze swivelled toward Pat. "Did you plan this?"

"I guess I did," the proprietor said, "but Douglass wasn't in on it."

I was genuinely puzzled. "Plan what?"

Pat rubbed my shoulder. "Douglass Infantino, meet Tom Katz. He publishes things."

We shook hands.

"I publish a lotta garbage." Katz shrugged. "But we get it out there every month. And we're gettin' better."

I stepped up to the plate. "I can help you."

He nodded. "As a close friend'a Pat's, you'll get a chance to try."

And I knew I'd succeed. Devouring a few thousand old movies will give you storytelling moxie, and I had a pretty good idea of where pulp fiction was headed in the '30s. Plus I could write. Maybe too well. But I could tone it down if I had to.

The following Monday, I got my start on assistant

edits at *Corking Tales*, a thick grab bag of genres with an increasing bent toward science fiction, published out of a crusty office in Chelsea. I made fifteen dollars a week, supplemented by one penny for every word of stories that I wrote myself (dealing with subjects such as bordellos on Venus, dogs trained to smell the future, and a scheme to stop werewolves by exploding the moon).

I enjoyed doing that kind of writing, could tolerate the editing, and loved the fan letters. The first reactions to my own work came in May. They were positive, on the whole, despite my fatal (in the eyes of some aficionados) indifference to "hard science."

By then, I was comfortably ensconced in a boarding house near the corner of Greenwich Avenue and 10th Street (having moved out just after New Year's), seeing three "talkies" a week with a variety of casual dates, and failing disastrously in my mission. *The Scandals* had closed in late February, and Eileen had quietly bowed out of the running for the 1930 production. There had been no parties with Hollywood producers. No talks with them at all. *King of Jazz* had opened in April in the form I recognized from my own unacceptable timeline.

My friendship with the Corellis deepened over the course of the winter and spring. I saw them a couple of times a week, without fail. And I did my best to argue Eileen out of this disastrously premature retirement. But even I could see that she was relieved to be out of the spotlight and that she and Pat were absurdly happy together, in their even more absurdly gendered way. Meanwhile, my erstwhile adversary had given up sulking. In fact, he had even begun to encourage the discussion of career versus family once he realized that his wife had drifted closer to his position.

❖

The bridge fad was just revving up to high gear, and we got into the habit of playing on Wednesday evenings. My partners rotated. One hot night in early June, I drew an old voice-school chum of Eileen's who was in town for a couple of days. Nora Kelly had been engaged to a big-time Midwestern investor until the crash had wiped out his fortune, not to mention their relationship.

"It wasn't the *money*," she insisted, while sorting through her cards, "it was his loss of confidence that sank us. I tell ya, some men's backbones are in their bank accounts.... One diamond."

Eileen nodded. "Sure, but let's face it, Nora, he was hopeless when you met him. Maybe he didn't know it, but you did."

Nora fussed with her blonde bangs. "As long as he didn't know it, there was a chance that he'd improve. And I certainly hadn't received any better offers.... Are you going to *bid*?"

Eileen flailed at the air. "Pass."

"Nora's right," I jumped in. "Self-knowledge isn't nearly as attractive as the philosophers would have us believe."

"No. It isn't." Nora's blue-green eyes sparked. "Alcibiades might have wanted to fuck Socrates, but I'll bet the rest of their friends wanted to fuck Alcibiades, the vain bastard."

Eileen covered her vastly expanded stomach. "Nora!"

"Jesus Christ, Eileen! You're on the wicked stage!"

"Not anymore." She shook her head beatifically.

"Well, no, of course not. Not until you lance that boil." She poked the engorged area, then shot me a wink. "Or is it a *goil*?"

Eileen shrugged her off. "I'm not going back, Nora. I'm bored of it."

Nora slumped back into her chair. "That's the hormones talking."

"Maybe so, but they sound a lot better to me than my singing ever did."

I could tell that she had nudged Pat under the table. A tripwire smile passed between them. I had seventeen points in my hand, with honours in spades.

"One spade," I sighed.

◆

Nora and I cleaned up that night, winning three rubbers by a combined total of twelve hundred points, but the six dollars (we played penny-a-point) I earned hardly made up for the decades of reactionary politics that Eileen's withdrawal from public life would ensure.

Nora was disgusted on general principle. She asked me to go for a drink with her as the evening wound down.

Pat jabbed my arm at the door. "We won't wait up for her, buddy." He winked.

Chapter Eight

We strolled a few blocks to a speakeasy that Nora knew from, as she called them, "the good old days"—before she had moved to Chicago in order to please her ex-fiancé.

"I'll be back here before long," she told me confidently, over gins and tonics. "Just have to arrange another transfer."

Nora worked as a buyer for Sears, Roebuck & Co. She carried herself like a society deb, but she wasn't one. Like Eileen, she had grown up in Flatbush, Brooklyn. The child of a tobacconist, she had made it to Radcliffe on an academic scholarship and had studied philosophy there—

"—but it didn't curb my instinct for the main chance. I worked on my brain because I thought it would impress the fraternity boys! That was the acme of my idealism." She signalled for another drink and focused her dark green eyes on my throat. "Good thing my body kept pace with my grades."

Her grades must have been very good. Her Chanel-style "little black dress" enveloped her curves with obvious pleasure.

I changed the subject. "So you speak Greek?"

"Like a native, Old Soc." She raised her glass to me. "Of *Periclean* Greece, I mean."

I gave in and changed it back. "Would you be my Aspasia?"

"For tonight?" She smiled. "For sure."

And she wasn't kidding.

The offer expired around 4:00 a.m. Some internal alarm went off, and she made a beeline for her clothes.

I followed suit and accompanied her back to the Corellis', kissing her hand at the door.

That seemed to amuse her.

My place was about five blocks away. The walk home was fairly dismal, although the feeling was somewhat mitigated by exhaustion and the sure knowledge, from past experience, that this feeble encounter would someday sprout melancholy flowers in my memory.

And it has.

Part of the explanation for my seamless plunge into the life of a time traveller is that, in a sense, I had always been one. I have never been very adept at living (or feeling things) "in the moment." I tried doing it on my doorstep, staking my existential claim in the Greenwich Avenue pavement, at precisely 5:03 a.m., June 10, 1930. But it didn't even come close to penetrating the layers of associative memories evoked by the spot. I was just a block away, for instance, from the café where I'd asked my first important girlfriend to move in with me. That was (or would be) in 1996. I was only a little farther away from the apartment that she'd left me in sole possession of, in 1998. My mother had bought me my first root beer float in this neighbourhood, in 1978. And when I noticed a milk truck rumbling my way through the early morning mist, it conjured thoughts of a movie (*The Clock*), made in 1945, that I had fallen in love with when PBS aired it on a blustery afternoon in the fall of 1989.

I needed a strong person to anchor me in the present. *Any* present.

I fumbled for my keys at the door.

"Nice *watch*," an insinuating voice startled me.

There was no doubt in my mind that it was Dorothea. But *which version?*

I spun around, shielding my left wrist.

"Oh." I tried to look calm. "It's you."

"What do mean 'it's you'?" Her forehead crinkled. "Who do you think I am?"

"Dorothea Cullen. Genius inventor. Temporal tamperer."

She blushed a little. "That sounds about right. And you?"

"I'm just a guy following orders. Yours."

"We're about to get paradoxical here, aren't we?"

"I'd say there's a pretty good chance, yeah."

"Can we do it over coffee?"

More than anything, I wanted my bed. However, under the circumstances, coffee would have to do.

I nodded emphatically.

We made haste to an all-night diner, ordered cheese omelets, and got started.

"I've been keeping tabs on you since Thanksgiving," she explained, "when you spoiled my turkey shoot."

"Were you really going to kill those thugs?"

She smiled enigmatically. "Don't you *know?* If I sent you here, I must have done it after that little stunt."

"You never said anything about a gun."

"I guess I didn't hire you for muscle." She grinned.

"No, indeed. You're primitive enough for both of us. And you handled the mugging perfectly, whatever you did. It's the aftermath that got fubared."

"Fubared? Are you being deliberately anachronistic, or do you actually speak this way?"

"No, but I've always wanted to say *fubared*. And the *mot juste*, in this case, *is fubared*. Fucked up beyond all recognition...."

I proceeded to describe the world I had grown up in. I gave Dorothea a near-verbatim account of our first deductive dialogue, emphasizing my expertise as a cultural historian. I also invented a career for myself in film production, reasoning that the credentials would help to convince her that I was the right person for the job she had supposedly assigned to me.

It worked.

"Except you've completely *failed*, Douglass," she concluded.

"Well...it's going slowly, I'll grant you that, but I'm not done yet."

"I'm afraid you are." She stood up. "Don't feel bad. I like what you tried to do. But it doesn't sound like you ever had a chance. Eileen clearly isn't the woman I thought she was. And I've seen enough of *Pat* to know that the world isn't going to miss him."

My lip quivered. Totally involuntary. But it did the trick.

She sighed and put a hand on my shoulder. "You think I'm a monster, don't you?"

The look of thwarted logic on her face was transfixing. I kept staring.

"There's something going on between us, isn't there?" she whispered.

I shrugged.

"All right, let's discuss this some more. At my place."

Dorothea's apartment was on Thompson Street, near Washington Square. That suited me fine, considering that my bed was still messed up from Nora's visit. It was a palace compared to my garret.

"Well, of course I brought a lot of '20s money with me," she said matter-of-factly, locking the door and slipping her hand under my shirt. "Didn't I make the same arrangements for you?"

"No." I jerked into her. "We figured I'd be more likely to elicit sympathy if I showed up broke. It's the method school of time travel."

"Gosh," she beamed, "we're sm—"

The "—art" came off on our lips.

Chapter Nine

Ten hours later, she fell asleep.

The interim had been wonderful. And wonderfully nerve-wracking. It had finally dawned on me that Dorothea was, for all intents and purposes, my creator. Not an easy thing to face. And yet, there was an incredible thrill in knowing more, about this one aspect of the multiverse, than my maker.

Not very romantic sentiments, I grant you, but then how much room for tenderness can there be in a heart ravished by the grand existential passion for survival? Not merely on the physical plane. I was fighting to preserve my place in the continuity: my birth certificate; my funeral, whenever that was destined to be; my third-grade crush on Ms. Von Blerk.

Dorothea was brilliant, stunning, and genuinely loveable when she wasn't talking about erasing me from the space-time continuum. But the odds were against anything very good happening between us in the long run. So I kept my guard up and probed her mind for loopholes during the sweat-soaked intervals.

"Can we talk about this timeline thing some more?" I whispered into her neck.

"What for, Douglass?" Her chin jerked upward. "So you can beg for the life of this miserable alternate reality? Just because we presume that our old one is still alive and kicking somewhere?"

"Well, I don't think I would have put it that way...."

"Obviously not," she laughed. "But isn't that what's going to happen anyway? If the multiple timeline thesis applies, nothing I do in the past can hurt *these* people. Their world'll go on. I"—she corrected herself—"we...just won't be here to share it with them. We'll create a *third* timeline that's pretty much identical to the first one."

That sounded all right, if I could only believe it.

But I didn't.

"Are you sure about that?" I slumped back onto the pillow. "What if there's only one infinitely malleable timeline...."

"Of course I'm not sure.... About any of this stuff." She burrowed into my chest. "*But* if there is just one timeline, then it's even more crucial that we allow Pat Corelli to die. Isn't it?"

"Yeah." I could've kicked myself even harder than Pat's once-and-future murderer had. "I guess that's true...."

She slid on top of me, and I stopped caring for a while.

"But can't you give me just a little more time?" I asked her when I regained the power of speech.

"Time to do *what*, Douglass? You're up against cultural attitudes that were millennia in the making. That's worse than fighting windmills."

"But if we set things back the way they *were*, she'll be *dead in six years*." I could feel my eyes silting over.

The sad act didn't work nearly as well this time. She touched my cheek and pressed onward to the logical conclusion. "No kidding. I'm the source of that information, remember? Cynthia Ward never even got a chance to *exist* in your timeline."

"True." I tried to steer her back toward the multiple timeline idea. "But doesn't the fact that you remember two distinct versions of the world prove that each of them really does exist?"

"First of all, I'll bet you remember some dreams you've had, don't you? Do they exist?"

"Maybe?" I grinned.

She kissed my nose. "And maybe *not*. Also, just in case you forgot, I *don't* remember the alternate history you're talking about. That was a version of me that you met in 2010. I haven't gone back there yet. And I *don't intend to* until we've got this thing straightened out."

"Oh, that's right!" I yelped. I actually had forgotten that detail. Or perhaps *suppressed* is the more accurate term, considering my role in that unfortunate sequence of events. But it all came back to me now. Especially my exit line, something about a promise to be nicer the second time around.

A promise I wouldn't be keeping.

"Well"—I moderated my tone—"believe me, you

were keenly aware of the discrepancy. You made it live. Made me feel that I could get from one place to the other."

"And so we *can*, Douglass." Her cheeks flushed with the thrill of conjecture. "But not through the usual channels. We like to say 'the mind is its own place' and that people 'contain multitudes,' and this is part of what we mean by that.... There's no concrete travel involved. You get from a messy bed to a *made* one by smoothing out the sheets."

If I hadn't been lying on my back, I would have swooned.

"Let's keep it messy a while longer." I pulled her toward me.

But once she dozed off, I unfastened the watch from her wrist, added it to mine, and slipped away.

Book Two

Chapter Ten

It was 1929 again. Everything was back in its place, like a diligent child's nursery at dusk, and all for my benefit.

I had set the controls for a 5:00 p.m. touchdown on the crucial Thanksgiving. A few minutes later, I was back in Abingdon Square. The stage was set: chess men on their squares, the cabbie on his rounds, and Dorothea on her bench, more oblivious than ever to the mounting catalogue of wrongs I had done her.

I strolled over and sat down.

"You screwed it up," I whispered. "I'm here to fix things."

She turned with the intention of gasping incredulously, but I stopped her with my watch (the original—I had pocketed the second one. Which was also an original, I guess).

"I came at your request, of course."

She smiled.

As usual, our rapport developed quickly. We excelled at first meetings, no matter what the circumstances. I considered it something of a tragedy that I always found myself lying to her in the midst of those pheromone fests.

On the other hand, what choice had I ever had? She wanted to abort my familial line. Not much scope for compromise there, or honesty.

I felt even more under the gun than usual during this particular encounter. Primarily because I knew she was packing one, but also because I kept expecting my old white-sneakered self to stumble onto the scene. I was kind of hoping that the old sci-fi saw about two identical bodies not being capable of coexisting on the same material plane would cut through my potential dilemma, but I didn't want to be counting on it.

I took her hand. "Why don't we discuss this someplace warm?"

"You mean like my bedroom?" Her eyes widened bemusedly.

"Uh"—suddenly she had my hand—"sure." I nodded. "Why not?"

She laughed and let go. "Because I don't have a bedroom, remember? I'm just here to intimidate some thugs and then it's back to the 21st century for me. You *too*, no?" Her eyebrows had risen to their zeniths.

"Of course I'm going back. But I can't go right away."

She curled her knees into her chest and settled into the far corner of the bench. "Why not?"

"I told you. I'm on damage control here."

"Damage that I did?" she whispered innocently.

I nodded gravely. "You turned American politics inside out, simply by giving our friend Eileen a reason to quit the stage before Hollywood beckoned."

"I did?"

"Yes. So we're gonna try something different."

I reached for her arm. "Can we please go somewhere else? I...don't want to be here when it happens. Do you?"

She jumped up. "You mean we're going to let him die?"

"We *have* to. If he lives, he'll pull her down. Actually," I reconsidered, "she'll pull herself down."

"This is horrible." She kicked the ground.

"Yes," I agreed, "it is. And it's your freakish brain's fault."

I started walking toward Hudson Street.

Curiosity forced her into step with me.

Out of the corner of my eye, I thought I spotted my anachronistically dressed twin watching us from his bench in the distance. I hoped he'd have the good sense to leave well enough alone. But Dorothea didn't give me any time to worry about it.

"So you're telling me those movies are worth Pat's *life?*" her voice quavered. "I mean, I love them, but still...."

"I've never seen the movies, Dorothea, so I can't rightly say. But I have seen footage of the Vietnam War...."

"Don't you mean the Vietnam *Crisis?*"

"No." I picked up the pace. "I definitely mean the Vietnam *War.*"

We ducked into a diner, ordered coffees, and commandeered a booth.

"How can Hollywood musicals prevent wars?" she demanded to know. "Especially wars in *Vietnam*? What the hell were we fighting for in Vietnam anyway?"

Her ignorance was blissful to behold. Unfortunately, it also reduced her chance of understanding the "domino theory" to nil, despite her 200 IQ. The Cold War was a chill that you felt in your bones, not an idea you could grasp.

"Nothing." I shook my head. "We weren't fighting for anything."

"Okay." She paused, eying me cautiously. "What's your name?"

"Douglass."

"Douglass." She smiled. "So...Pat dies. Eileen goes west. Becomes Cynthia Ward. Makes a bunch of great movies. Rots out her innards by twenty-nine. And the rest of us, including the people of Southeast Asia, live happily ever after?"

"That's one scenario, certainly." I shrugged, dreading the return to deception after such a nice long detour through the truth. "But we don't have to give up on everything."

"Meaning?"

"Well, I got to know Eileen pretty well last time...."

"*Last* time?" She leaned across the table.

"Yeah." I nodded. "I made a trial run. I had to learn more about the Corelli codependency, didn't I?

And I wasn't going to get any of it from books. No one writes books about the kind of people they turned into.... Anyway, I think I can get her to Hollywood *and* keep her sober once we're there...but not with Pat in the picture...."

I expected Dorothea to react in horror to that last clause, but it's amazing how quickly those calluses develop once you begin tinkering with history.

She moved toward me on her elbows, arching her back into the air. When her nose got to within a centimetre of mine, she took a deep breath. So did the counterman, who watched the whole scene play out in the mirror near the cash.

"Did you *fall in love with her*, Douglass?"

I cupped her cheeks in my hands and kissed her. We fell back together onto my side of the table. I massaged the bare skin above her shoulder blades.

Our host stormed over. "Awright! What the hell is this?"

I kissed her again. "If I've fallen in love with anyone during the course of this insanity, it's you, Dorothea."

She put her forehead on my chin. "It's funny. I had a feeling there was something between us the minute you sat down on the bench. The way you looked at me. So direct. But not invasive. Not like seduction. More like afterglow."

I smiled. "Well, I suppose that's because, just a few hours ago (by my messed-up body clock), we were in bed together...."

"Amazing!" She kissed my nose. "I wonder if all 'love at first sight' is a trick of time displacement?"

The counterman tugged at my shoe.

"Get *outta* here, ya *freaks!*"

◆

We got out. And it was just as well. On the sidewalk, I convinced Dorothea that I ought to go ahead with my plan to recombine the known elements of Eileen's separate fates. Immediately. For my companion, of course, our reunion in the present would be pretty nearly instantaneous, but I would have to sacrifice several years to the cause. She applauded the selflessness of my resolve, and I let her do it, despite the egocentric aspects of the plan. After all, I did want only the best for Eileen and the world, and I was willing to endure anything short of self-annihilation in the pursuit of their well-being.

If I had my way, only Pat Corelli would suffer by my actions. Not because he deserved it, but because there really wasn't any other choice. "Besides," I added, as we walked, "he's already dead."

"You mean before we began interfering?" she sighed philosophically.

"No." I gestured to my watch. "I mean right *now*. It's past six o'clock."

"Oh, God." She stepped backward off the curb, nearly falling into a puddle in the process.

"That's us." I pulled her toward me.

"Maybe." She smiled weakly. "But we're pretty limited deities. Don't forget that."

"I'm not likely to. I don't even understand how you managed to adjust your machine for daylight saving time."

We kissed on Bleecker, a few blocks from Abingdon. Then she slipped three thousand dollars' worth of greenbacks into my pocket and set her watch for the new, improved 2010 we'd envisioned. I hoped that's where I'd see her next.

In any other scenario, we'd be enemies.

Chapter Eleven

Even, or perhaps *especially*, on Thanksgiving, misfortune draws a crowd. Of course, the New York air had been thick with calamity since October, but now that mood closed in on a precinct of the city far removed from the haunts of the financial classes, leaving Eileen McWade gasping for breath on the running board of a police car. Fredericks and O'Meara stood over her, contorting their stolid faces into masks of concern. Behind them, a group of professionals busied themselves with cameras and notebooks. Just a few feet from the body, someone had tethered Lulu to a black rail fence, diligently wrapping the leash around a pole just enough times to crop her moist eyes and snout from the crime stills. The dog's mournful barking provided the soundtrack for my long skulk onto the scene.

My grandfather was dead, and I had a clean slate, if not a clear conscience. I took a deep breath, squared my shoulders, and barrelled through the police scrum toward Eileen.

"Are you all right?" I blurted.

She didn't look up.

O'Meara bit into my bicep with jawlike fingers.

"This lady's husband just got killed, friend. You know anything about it?"

I pulled back but couldn't get free. "Killed?" I choked, with genuine empathy. "I'm so sorry, Ms. McWade."

"Her name is Mrs. Corelli," Fredericks interrupted, stepping toward me from the other side. He tapped Eileen's shoulder with more tenderness than I would have believed he could muster. "You know this clown, Mrs. Corelli?"

She tilted her chin slightly, then shook her head. But the quizzical look in her eyes confirmed my suspicion that our friendship was just as eerily inevitable as my rather different rapport with Dorothea.

The policemen closed in on me.

"What's the big idea, friend?" O'Meara demanded to know.

"Big idea?" I squirmed. "There's not even a small one. I was just strolling along, pondering a plot problem (I'm a writer), when I spotted my favourite Broadway ingénue (McWade *is* her stage name, isn't it?) in some kind of distress. I just wanted to see if I could help."

O'Meara let go of my arm. I rubbed the affected area, and this actually coaxed a smile from him. "Oh, did you now?" The smile widened. "That's nice. Maybe you wanted to help out so badly that you created a little opening for yourself?"

"That wouldn't be very nice, would it?" I smiled back, just as mirthlessly. "Murder?"

"Naw, we know it wasn't you. We've got descriptions of the hoodlums. But you certainly might have paid them to do it. A husband can be a hell of a plot problem."

"What's with you guys?" I kicked at the curb. "I told you I just wanted to help. But you're always inventing complicated backstories! I hope you live to see Kennedy in Dallas. That mess will sustain you through your golden years."

Neither man saw fit to respond.

I turned my back on them and walked away. It was a risky play. They could easily have cuffed and frisked me. And who knows what they would have made of the giant wad of bills in my pocket? They followed me into the street but didn't restrain me. Upon reaching a respectful distance from the bereaved party, I stopped and growled quietly, "I didn't arrange any killings this week! And I'm not going to talk about this in front of that poor woman!"

Fredericks actually looked humbled; O'Meara just looked outmaneuvered. He did the talking.

"Yeah, sometimes we think out loud a little too noisily for comfort. This job ain't easy, friend. Try and remember that...."

Of course, they had no intention of letting me entirely off the hook. Nor would I have wanted them to. I had to remain involved somehow. I gave them my name and address (I intended to move into the boarding house on Greenwich a couple of months ahead of schedule), pledging to remain available for questioning. But my concerned citizen gambit had so completely turned the tide that they allowed me a minute alone with the object of my "chivalrous" outburst, after she requested it.

This time she half stood to greet me, keeping one unsteady hand glued to her almost imperceptibly swollen belly. "Who *are* you?"

I repeated the information I had given to the police. In her distraught condition, Eileen looked, unfortunately, more than ever like the woman who had raised me. Some of that shock of recognition must have fed back to her, because she simply didn't treat me like a stranger.

"I know what you're thinking about." I touched her hand lightly. "Don't do it."

She looked down at her stomach. "Don't do *what*?"

I deflected her deflection. "At least talk to someone before you decide anything. Talk to me. I'll be at home the entire weekend. Any time. Please?"

She took a deep breath and said, "Okay."

"Twenty-two Greenwich Ave."

Chapter Twelve

Twenty minutes later, Mrs. Duncan showed me to my old room. Number 12, on the third floor. It was too good to be true. I had expected that I would be forced to settle for an identical cubby somewhere else in the building. Duncan herself was an even more welcome sight. We had gotten to be pretty good friends, during my last incarnation, and I looked forward to renewing her acquaintance.

In many ways, she was your stereotypical landlady. In fact, given the number of theatre people she had probably sheltered throughout the '20s, it was reasonable to assume that she had helped to establish the character in the collective mind of that influential contingent. Gray hair (often up in curlers, despite the fact that she never seemed to leave the building), thin neck, body always wrapped in onion-layered housecoats. You couldn't hide a thing from Mrs. Duncan (except perhaps the fact that you had been born forty-five years in the future), but, then, you didn't have to. She was the kind of busybody that every neighbourhood needs. Pragmatic but never judgmental. A little too interested in your sex life, perhaps, but she never put the really damaging bits of gossip that she learned into circulation. Moreover, she paid her way into your private affairs with good advice, a lenient policy concerning tardy rent, and chicken soup on demand.

Her husband (Sam) had kicked off during the Big Flu of '18, leaving her all alone in the world, with eighteen rooms to let. She missed him, but they'd had twenty good years together, and he'd been so devastated by their (only) son Jimmy's death in the Argonne that she half suspected him of surrendering to the virus. Esther Duncan (nee Ashberg) had no use for that kind of self-pity. "Sammy was a beautiful man," she had told me one evening, "but he was weak.... I knew he was a goner the minute he looked up from that telegram. And sur'e-nough, four months later, he was dead."

Since then, she had dedicated herself to "making the best of things." It was the only moral commandment she recognized. And the times had obliged her by supplying no end of amusements for unescorted ladies of the old school. Chief among these, in Mrs. Duncan's domestic pantheon, were the *New York World* crossword puzzle, *Black Mask* magazine, Paul Whiteman's radio program, and the inevitable *Amos 'n' Andy*.

That last item had been the biggest thing in American entertainment during the spring of 1930, a fact that I, in my selective nostalgia for the period, had never fully dealt with. My friendship with Esther had put an end to that conceit, rubbing my ears in the duo's fifteen minutes of fame nearly every night, at dinnertime. It goes without saying that the program was incredibly offensive, but it took its protagonists' lives seriously, within the artificial limits imposed by white supremacist doctrine, and the narrative was genuinely propulsive. It was easy to understand how fifty percent of the radio audience got sucked into its serialized vortex. Quite an education. Although not one that I would have consented to endure twice.

This time around, I vowed to scrounge my meals elsewhere and drop in on my landlady during the more palatable phases of her mass cultural regimen. I was particularly looking forward to rekindling our uncanny crossword chemistry. We had made an unbeatable team, mercilessly filling those squares over coffee and pulp mag palaver (my inadvertent mention, some weeks into my residency, that I gained my livelihood at the typewriter had secured her undying devotion).

When she wondered aloud about the location of my personal effects, while unveiling the Murphy bed I had last shared with Nora on a hot summer night that lay more than six months in the future, I was grateful to be in possession of the map to Mrs. Duncan's heart. I took the short cut.

"Oh." I stretched beatifically. "I didn't bring much with me. Just one bag of clothes that I managed to lose along the way. Got money, though. I sold everything I owned when I decided to crash the magazine racket down here."

"Ah!" She let the bed drop with a thud. "You mean

you write stories? Or *highbrow stuff?*" Her intonation left no doubt as to her preference.

"Well, I—"

The tenant below smashed the ceiling with a broom handle or something.

"Justaminute." She gesticulated, diving toward the hardwood floor. "You better relax down there, Tommy!" she bellowed. "If there's any damage to the plaster, it's goin' on next week's rent! Not that you've *paid* any lately!"

A faint, chastened voice wafted up to us: "I'm saw-ry, Mizziz Duncan."

She straightened triumphantly, brushing dust from the "knees" of her outermost housecoat, smiling. "We got a nice buncha people in this building. You'll see."

"I believe it." I smiled back.

She sat down on the mattress. "So go on about your *writing*, young man. You're gonna take the *place*, right? It's ten bucks a week. A bargain, no?"

"Very good." I nodded.

"*Okay*, so let's get acquainted.... You write *murder* stories, Douglass?"

"A few." I paid obeisance to her pet genre. "I did a bit of *everything*, up in Montreal, where I'm from...but I think my forte is in science fiction."

"Ah," she beamed, "that's good, too! You gonna work for *Amazing Stories?*"

"It'd be great to start at the top, but I'm not picky."

"That's the spirit! Haven't had many writers here,

for some reason. Actors? Musicians? 'Models'? *Please.* We've been lousy with 'em! But writers? Scarce. Very scarce...."

She got up. "I'll let you get settled.... You want blankets? Pyjamas? I got tons downstairs...."

She led me to a massive linen chest in the nether reaches of the building. She piled flannel bedclothes into my arms, and I rushed back to the room, determined to use them.

No clock in the world could have told how long it had been since I'd slept.

Chapter Thirteen

Insistent knuckles broke into the soundest slumber I'd enjoyed since my beating, two Thanksgiving 1929s ago. After waking, I lay in bed for at least a full minute, wallowing in the percussive waves, wondering how long I'd been out, tonguing nostalgically at molar craters that had oozed blood the last time I'd lived through this date on the calendar.

November 29, 1929: sometime before noon, if the shadows on the floor could be trusted.

"Come in," I yawned.

Seconds later, a German shepherd hit the creaking Murphy bed. An apologetic Eileen entered the room in the wake of the dog's beachhead assault. My grandmother looked more dishevelled than I'd ever seen her during any phase of her life.

I saluted her with floppy plaid sleeves (Sammy Duncan had left some mighty big PJs to fill), then freed a hand from the flannel, for ear-rubbing purposes.

"And who is this?" I thought I'd better ask, before I called the dog by name.

"That's Lulu." She brightened a little.

"Hey, Lulu! You been taking care of Mom?"

"*Everyone's* 'taking care' of me," Eileen sighed. "Or thinks they are. Pat's parents. His sister. My agent. The producer. The restaurant people.... I don't need it!"

She jerked a dowdy, brown armchair (the only one in the room) toward the bed.

"What do you need?"

She sank into faded felt, a little uneasily. "To decide what to do next, I guess...."

"Makes sense."

She leaned forward, squinting. "What was that about yesterday, Douglass? What makes you think I'm pregnant? Were you a friend of Pat's or something? Did he tell you anything about me?"

I considered answering in the affirmative. It certainly would have helped to demystify my occult insight into Corelli family affairs. But if I *were* a friend of Pat's, wouldn't I have said so yesterday, at the scene of his murder? I decided that to change my story now would arouse even more suspicion than sticking to the original (and, admittedly, quite fatuous) course I had planned to pursue.

"I'm sorry, Eileen." I shook my head. "I never got a chance to meet Pat. I'm just a fan with a very keen eye for body language."

"Body language?" She looked baffled.

"You were cradling your belly in a very particular way." I tried to sound matter-of-fact. "Not like you were sick to your stomach—"

"Or reeling from the death of my husband?"

"No," I pressed on. "Not like that either. All of the pain was in your eyes. The anxiety was radiating toward your belly, not coming from it."

She looked away from me. "That's...ridiculous... Douglass." Her voice was a little muffled. "But...you're not wrong."

"I'm sorry. I wish I was."

"So do I." She faced me again. There were no tears in evidence. "You've got to understand, Douglass. I really want to be a mother. But there were some things I wanted to accomplish before I took that step."

"Sure." I nodded. "But you don't have to—"

"*Please*," she hushed me. "I need to get this off my chest. I'm not interested in advice. Can't you just sit there and hear me out?"

"I can."

"*Good*." She smiled weakly. "Because no one else seems to be up to the challenge.... All I'm getting is a lot of pious talk about how the sacred task of raising Pat's son will see me through the decades of my bereavement.

"I wanted to wait a few years, Douglass. See how far I could make it. On the stage—and maybe even in Hollywood.... But Pat wasn't having any of it. 'We're supposed to be a *family*, honey,' he'd say. 'Two people aren't a family.' Finally, I gave in. Because I *love* him"—she emphasized the tense—"But I'll be damned if I'm going to start a two-person family without him!"

I weighed my words carefully before starting.

"You've got me convinced. But I'm not the important one here. Please understand me, Eileen. I think a woman's right to choose is absolutely fundamental, no matter what the law books say. So you're talking to the right person here. I'm not here to give you advice. This has to be your decision. But make sure you're clear on what the options are. This isn't a choice between family and career. You can have your career either way. And you can have a family either way, too. This is a choice between having and not having *this* baby."

Her eyes watered. "I want to have this baby. But I don't want to stop performing."

"So don't." I touched her forearm. "Just decide right now not to do *anything* that you don't want to do."

"Easier said than done," she groaned. "You don't know Pat's parents...."

I had, in fact, met the pair in question at Risotto Voce during my previous sojourn through the upcoming months. The evening had been placid enough on the surface, but the elder Corellis' geniality did not quite conceal their predatory watchfulness for faults or unwanted brilliancies in their glamorous daughter-in-law's makeup. I had no hard evidence, had never had a chance to draw Dorothea out about the causes of Cynthia Ward's precipitous mid-'30s decline; however, from what I had seen of them, Francesco and Laura Corelli seemed very capable of driving a vulnerable Eileen to drink, and I had resolved to do my best to keep them away from her in this timeline.

"Maybe not," I said, "but you've already said enough to convince me that they aren't worth knowing. That should make it easy to cut them out of your life, if you have to."

"Cut...them...*out?*" She seemed genuinely startled. "Don't be ridiculous, Douglass. A child needs grandparents, and my parents are already gone."

"No." I shook my head. "Grandparents need their grandchildren, not the other way around. I'm sorry to be so cold-blooded about this, but it's the truth. I'm sure they had power over you in the past, but you'll be dealing with them from a position of strength from now on, if you keep that in mind."

She shifted on the bed, putting more of the dog's comforting body between us. "Douglass, I can see that you're trying to help me, but you're scaring me a little." She reconsidered. "More than a little, frankly. It's not just the Machiavellian tone. It's that you *can't* have learned this much about my troubles with the Corellis from my 'body language,' or from the couple of words I said about them...."

"Oh, no? I think you'd be surprised." I smiled. "But let's say, for the moment, that you're right, that there is more to me. What could it possibly be?"

"You could be a G-Man." She savoured the neologism.

"Right!" I saluted her. "A member of the crack in-law trouble squad."

"I'm being serious, Douglass," she said ruefully.

"Was Pat involved with the rackets somehow? If he was, I want to know it." Her face and voice toughened up. "Right now."

I had to hand it to her. She had reasoned her way to the most plausible explanation for our current situation (in a world that did not allow for the possibility of time travel).

"Eileen, I don't have a clue. I'm sure the police would have questioned you about it if he was. But I'm not any kind of an agent, believe me."

"Then how the hell do you know these things?"

"I...well...I get these flashes of...of insight," I sputtered.

"You're telling me you're a medium of some sort?" She laughed in spite of herself.

"No." I did my best to contain the damage. "No séances. No spirits. I just get these...hunches...about people sometimes. And sometimes, certainly not always, they're right."

"And what are these hunches telling you about me?"

I told her what I had never quite had the chance to tell my grandmother: "That there's something within you that's too big for your body. Too big for *any* body to contain. Something (we'll call it a 'voice,' but that doesn't even begin to describe it) that has to be shared, and will poison you from within if it isn't. At the same time, you're feeling a terrible pressure from without that comes from being a woman in a world and a culture that is crushingly unfair to women. Both of these forces will require your constant attention, if you're going to channel and resist them in good measure. And no one could accomplish this alone. You're going to need good friends around you to get where you're going, and you're going to leave even better people in your wake if you succeed."

She ran her fingers across Lulu's magnificent head and touched my hand. "Thank you, Douglass. I...think you're seriously overestimating my importance, but... well...I guess I can use a little of that right now. I definitely seem to have come to a crossroads all of a sudden, and it feels like there are trains bearing down on me from all directions...."

Her grip tightened. "You really think I can dodge them?"

"I do," I whispered.

"And I'll get to make movies?" Her tone became exultant. "The kinds of movies I've been dreaming about making?"

I shrugged. "*Well*, my hunches aren't very reliable about specifics. And they confiscated my crystal ball at the border."

Eileen laughed. Tentatively at first, and not for long. "What's the matter with me, Douglass? I should feel terrible, shouldn't I? And I did. But I've drifted away from it."

"It'll come back to you, I'm sure. But you can't force these things. So why not take advantage of the reprieve?"

"That sounds suspiciously like advice."

"Can't be. You're not accepting advice."

"That's right." She grinned. "I'm not."

Chapter Fourteen

Eileen and Lulu returned often during the following weeks. As I had hoped, my little room became the perfect place of refuge from the punishing round of obligations that can encircle and overwhelm a newly widowed spouse. She took a leave of absence from *The Scandals*, arranged a traditional Catholic funeral for Pat, and initiated proceedings for transferring ownership of Risotto Voce to its kitchen and wait staff. The Corellis nearly lost their minds over that one.

Eileen burst through my door one mid-December evening. "I'm *giving* them the insurance money. Where do they get off telling me what to do with the restaurant?"

I put my book on the bedside table and loaded coffee grounds into the silvery electric percolator I had just bought.

"They want to run it?" I asked.

"Oh, no." She shook her head. "They'd never leave Queens. They want me to sell it. Frank says that anything else would be disrespectful to Pat's memory."

"Ridiculous," I snorted.

"Well, the thing is"—she sat down in her accustomed spot on the brown armchair—"it's not. Pat wouldn't like this at all. More of my 'Red' nonsense, he'd say. And I guess it *is*—"

"Except that it's not nonsense," I jumped in.

"No, of course it isn't. I mean, they're saying now that the crash isn't going to be nearly as disastrous as we thought, but I think it's pretty clear that things aren't going to get any easier for working people for the next decade. And things were tough enough already."

"No argument here." I nodded. I didn't see any need to mention the Great Depression on the horizon.

"I can't do anything about Wall Street, or medieval anti-labour laws, but when they give me a chance to create a workers' cooperative just by signing a piece of paper, I'm going to take it."

Coffee steam filled the air. I pulled a pair of cups out from under the bed.

"I'll drink to that." I handed her a cup. "I hope you like it black. There's no icebox in this place. And I used to have some sugar, but the mice got it...."

"That's fine, Douglass, thanks."

I tried to read the look on her face. "Do you...feel like you're betraying him by doing this?"

"No...it's not that. It's just.... I feel like I'm cheating somehow.... Like I won the argument by outliving him.... But I guess the funeral was even worse, pretending he was right about everything, out of pity.... I just... really didn't want that fight to end."

"I know."

"I'll be all right." She took a quick sip and smiled. "Did you see that friend of Pat's about the job?"

She was referring, of course, to Tom Katz, of *Corking Tales* fame. I had only had to mention my pulp editor aspirations about a hundred times before the idea of introducing us had occurred to her.

"I did. And he hired me."

"Really? Douglass, that's great!"

It was. Although if anyone in the room should have felt like they were cheating in some way, it was me. No job applicant ever navigated the interview process with more panache than I had displayed during my second first meeting with Katz. The knowledge I had gained through implementing the man's no-nonsense publishing strategies for more than half a year made me an unbeatable candidate for the position in this fresh timeline. I had asked for (and gotten) twice as much money as I had received from him the first time around.

"I start next Monday. The 23rd. I'll probably even have to work on Christmas."

"Not too late, I hope." She sounded a bit disappointed. "I thought we could reheat some turkey on your hotplate and listen to carols on the radio. I don't want to be anywhere near my apartment that night."

"I'll be here. Six o'clock at the latest."

"Good. I won't have too many free nights myself, once I go back to *The Scandals*."

"New Year's Eve, right? You must be excited."

"I guess I am." She nodded. "I mean, I definitely needed the break. But now that I've regained some control over where and when I start bawling, I'm pretty eager to get back out there, before my belly eclipses the sets."

"Eileen, you haven't even started showing yet."

I thought about making another round of coffee, but then I remembered that someone, someday, was destined to discover that caffeine and pregnancy don't mix very well.

She sighed and stood up to go. "You're sweet, Douglass, but that'd probably sound a lot more convincing if it were coming from a guy who hadn't spotted my 'delicate condition' through a block-wide police cordon."

Chapter Fifteen

Knowing Tom Katz's mania for punctuality, I showed up half an hour early for my first day on the job at *Corking Tales*. Located on the sixth floor of a less-than-prepossessing building on West 29th Street near 8th Avenue, the office fairly twitched with the seedy dynamism of a growing pulp magazine on the make. The three-room suite consisted of a cramped reception area (always occupied by one of Katz's three interchangeable teenaged nieces, whose job was to smile at and pacify the throngs of bordering-on-hysterical freelance writers and artists who flooded the chamber whenever their uncle allowed them to unlock the door), an increasingly overstuffed archive that would never have passed muster with an unbribed fire inspector, and an editorial room with enough space to accommodate two people comfortably (it never had less than three bodies in it during the course of my tenure on the magazine, since Katz always stationed a nephew or two on the floor near the seldom-used drafting table, where they helped to screen out the least coherent story submissions and the most obscene letters to the editor).

A bright high school dropout without any family

connections to speak of, Katz had built his pulpish fortune on half-kept promises, sleeplessness, and a killer instinct for identifying the kinds of stories that his expanding audience of lower-middle-class introverts and autodidacts craved. Launched in 1915 as a globetrotting adventure magazine, *Corking Tales* had shifted its focus toward the stars during the past year or so, following the lead of Hugo Gernsback's trendsetting *Amazing Stories*. The publisher never concealed the primacy of his mercenary goals, but he did cherish a genuine fondness for the overwrought, idea-rich stews that had been thickening his circulation figures of late.

"I believe in scientifiction, kid," he announced on *both* of my first mornings in his employ. "There are a lotta changes comin' down the pike in this world, and the kids who read our stories are gonna be a big part of the machine that does the changin'. We ain't scientists"—he jabbed a thumb into his chest and then bounced it back at me—"but we can have our say about the world-a-tomorra by gettin' inside the heads of the children of today. They can make our dreams come true. It's important work."

I nodded (in this timeline—I forget how I responded to the first speech). "That makes perfect sense, Mr. Katz. But," I added mischievously, "does this mean you don't want any of our nightmares mixed in there to spoil the Century of Progress?"

He shot me a look of squinting admiration. "You don't wanna take me too literally now, Douglass. We've got books to sell. That's job number one. We ain't gonna influence *anyone* if we go outta business—and I ain't in business for my health. But I don't haveta tell you any of this, do I?"

"No, but it's fun to hear."

"We're gonna get along fine, kid."

And we did. I slid right back into the nine-to-five (or more like eight-to-six) routine I'd left behind in June 1930. Most of the work involved copy editing huge chunks of indifferently spelled and punctuated text, but I also had the honour of composing the pithy responses that enlivened our letters-to-the-editor column, and soon, I knew, Tom would delegate to me the pleasure of selecting about a third of the material we printed. I'm not being the least bit facetious when I describe that last task as pleasurable. I had always appreciated the unleashed *id*istry of the old pulps, and it was a real treat to read some of the pieces that were too lurid to make it under even Tom Katz's ultra-permissive radar.

Less than two days' worth of expertly feigned attentiveness brought me fully into the publisher's confidence, and he released me for the holidays upon my own recognizance at about 3:00 p.m. on Christmas Eve (with the proviso that I would make up the hours over the weekend if necessary, of course). I seized the opportunity to make a run over to Macy's on 34th Street, just a ten-minute walk away. The place was in the grip of a Boschian commercial frenzy the likes of which it would probably not see again for more than a decade, if ever. As I plunged into the evergreen scrum, I couldn't help thinking that many of my jostling throngmates would be out of a job by next Christmas. That melancholy insight helped me to keep a tolerant tongue in my head as I battled for access to the merchandise.

Knowing that my grandmother was destined, at some point, to fall in love with buckwheat blueberry waffles, I had decided to surprise her by recreating her future favourite dish (one she had often made during the festive seasons of my youth). Naturally, I'd need a waffle iron to turn the trick. The plan was to purchase a nice one from the department store, use it once, and then serve it up to Eileen as a Christmas gift.

I settled on a beautiful art deco model from the Samson Cutlery Company, which sold for nine dollars and fifty cents (a third of my weekly salary). Chrome plated, adorned with an oddly appealing parrot print on its ceramic lid insert, and heavy as hell, this cast iron monstrosity made the trip home on the jam-packed 6th Avenue streetcar even more of a trial than it usually was, but it gave every indication of being worth the effort.

I burst through the doors (muttering holiday greetings with every laboured step) at the corner of 6th Avenue and 10th Street. From there, it was just a short, but somewhat disturbing, jaunt around the haughtily Victorian grounds of the Jefferson Market Courthouse and its recently demolished Women's Prison (the city was in the process of building a brand new, and incongruously *art deco*, distaff detention centre on the site). The early winter mist mingled clammily with my transit sweats, and I rushed up the stairs to my wash basin. I deposited the hefty waffle iron on my two-seater "dining table" and eyed that thoroughly inadequate piece of furniture's spindly legs warily as I performed my ablutions.

They held up.

I recognized Mrs. Duncan's knock from the hallway. "Are you home, Douglass?"

"Am I home?" I chuckled, tossing aside my washcloth and throwing on a white undershirt. "Would you be knocking if I wasn't?" I opened the door and beckoned her inside. "You'd just be letting yourself in like you always do."

"Oh, *you!*" she laughed in her appealingly rubicund way. (But you'll notice that she didn't deny my allegations.) "I was just wonderin' if you wanted to come down and listen to *Amos 'n' Andy* this evenin'?"

"Sorry, lady." I shook my head. "I won't be able to make it. I'm glad you dropped up, though. I need to borrow your phone—and a few ingredients for buckwheat blueberry waffles."

"Of *course*, Douglass! No problem!" She took my arm. "Whaddya need?"

"Um...everything except for blueberries and buckwheat?"

"Ah! Such a *character!*" She bustled out of the apartment, pulling me along for the ride.

"*I'm* a character?" I nearly fell down the stairs.

But her mind was glued to the idea of that phone call. "You tryin' ta get in touch with your girl?"

"My *girl?*" I asked with genuine surprise.

"Yeah." She unlocked her door with a wink. "The beautiful young lady who brings her dog as a chaperone."

What was I supposed to say? *That was no lady—that was my grandmother?*

"You mean Eileen? Esther, her husband was killed less than a month ago."

"Uh-hunh." She went into the kitchen. "A real tragedy. I hear his resta'rant was good. But thaddont mean she don't need comfortin'."

"That's what I've been doing. But not in the way that you're implying."

"Who's implying?" She handed me a tray containing a jug of milk, a brick of butter, a carton of twelve eggs, a bag of flour, and some baking soda. "You're a wonderful man. Make her happy."

I accepted the ingredients with unspoken gratitude. Esther Duncan was not a woman who liked to dwell on the numerous favours she did for anyone and everyone who came within range of her kindness. "What are you talking about? Did you rush out to find a replacement after Sammy died?"

"Ah, but that was different, Douglass." She tapped my shoulder affectionately. "This girl is just gettin' started. I was nearly forty-five. *And* I'd had a baby...."

– 112 –

"Well," I announced, with perhaps a tad more pride than was warranted, on the surface, "Eileen is three months pregnant."

"Oh?!" Esther put her hand to her heart. "Is she really? Well, that makes a difference."

The feminist within me had no desire to let the matter drop there, but it seemed like the pragmatic thing to do.

She walked me over to the telephone (in her radio-dominated living room) and unhooked the receiver. I put the tray down on a marble coffee table and dialled Eileen's number.

"Still, Douglass," Esther whispered confidentially, "I'm sure that baby would like a little brother or sister someday...."

Eileen picked up just as Esther disappeared into her bedroom. "Hello?" She didn't sound very happy.

"Hey, there."

"Douglass?"

"Want to come over on Christmas Eve instead? I've always liked it better."

Her tone brightened. "I'd love to, but I haven't made the turkey yet...."

"No problem. Amazing things are happening here."

"When do I get to eat them?"

"Seven o'clock. Bring Lulu."

"Of course."

We hung up.

The landlady peeked out from her bedroom. "This dog thing is getting out of hand...."

I waved as I moved toward the door. "*Goodnight*, Esther. Come by for waffles later?"

"No thank you, Douglass. You'll be crowded enough up there as it is. Have a wonderful time!"

I ran up to my room and started working on the batter, using my large all-purpose pot as a mixing bowl. I needed no recipe book or measuring cup to complete the operation. My hands and eyes judged the proportions with an inevitable sureness that testified (as nothing else in my current existence did) to the reality of long-ago Christmas Eves at my grandmother's house that might or might not happen fifty years down the road, on this timeline.

At 7:00 p.m., I plugged Eileen's gift into the wall outlet and poured a cascade of thick berry-studded batter into the large waffle iron. My guests arrived a minute later.

Eileen sank into her customary armchair. "I can't believe how good that smells."

Lulu seemed to concur, making a beeline for my cramped cooking area. I let her lick the wooden stirring spoon.

"It's going to taste even better," I promised.

"You can't imagine how much I needed this, Douglass. The Corellis showed up for lunch. And they wouldn't leave. They're still camped out in my living room, waiting to continue our 'discussion' about my career and how it's going to destroy my child's life."

"So don't go back." I watched the new contraption do its work. "I can sleep on the floor. Or I could take the bed and let you have the floor, if you'd prefer to be comfortable."

"Oh, Douglass," she giggled nervously, "I...I couldn't...."

"Why not?" I opened the iron, showing off the brilliantly coloured parrot on its lid, and breathed in the golden-buckwheat-tinged steam. "You think I want to eat Christmas breakfast alone?"

For the first time since our Thanksgiving Day meeting, she looked really ill at ease with me. "No...but...we...we can't be together, Douglass."

"Be together?" I chuckled. "Have you been talking to Mrs. Duncan? Who says I want us to *be together*? We're having far too much fun for that."

I pulled the giant round waffle from the griddle with a spatula, cut it in two, and smothered the halves in Green Mountain maple syrup.

"Are you telling me the truth, Douglass?" She accepted her plate with tentative hands.

Since the waffle iron had hijacked nearly the entire surface of my table, I figured we'd just eat at our usual stations.

"Believe me." I sat down on the bed. "This isn't part of some complex courtship scheme. Obviously, you're an attractive woman, in every sense of the word, and I imagine you've had to put up with a lot in your life, but I genuinely don't want anything more from you than your acknowledgement that these are the finest waffles ever made."

Her entire posture relaxed as she joined me in that first satisfying bite. "It's official." She raised her fork to me. "They really are."

"Good." I switched on the radio I'd installed on a shelf next to the bed. "Now let's see what's playing."

It didn't take me long to find a dramatization of Dickens' *Christmas Carol* on WEAF.

"What a great idea!" Eileen was entranced.

The actor playing Scrooge wasn't up to Lionel Barrymore's soon-to-be-established standard, but the program was pretty enjoyable. I left the dial right where it was as we polished off every last bit of batter. The station proceeded to enrich our lives with a "Christmas Carol Sing" live from Madison Square Garden that featured the NYPD Glee Club, the Edna White Brass Quartet, and a special holiday message from graft guru Jimmy Walker.

"Do you find this as fascinating as I do?" I asked her.

"I'm pretty sure I don't," she yawned.

"Okay." I stood up. "Let's take Lulu for a nice long Christmas stroll." The dog's ears leaped to full mast. "But then you're coming back here, right?"

"Right." She smiled.

Chapter Sixteen

I had done rather a poor job of truly witnessing the late '20s during my first lap through the past, and I was determined to pay closer attention to the world beyond my little circle of friends and potential ancestors this time around. Case in point, on the *last* Friday, December 27, 1929, not long after sunrise, the NYPD had rounded up and arrested a peaceful group of "Red demonstrators" outside of a factory just a couple of blocks from the *Corking Tales* office, and I had had to read about it in the Saturday *Times*. And so I made a point of meandering forth into the sub-freezing 7:00 a.m. murk when that morning dawned anew.

The Palter Shoe Company was located at 151 West 26th Street, but I didn't need a map to find it that day. I just followed the sounds of irate car horns and enthusiastic proletarians serenading the state with the unmistakable lyrics of "The Internationale." As I rounded the corner at 7th Avenue, I merged with the mass of onlookers who'd staunched the traffic flow on 26th. Halfway down the block, I saw men and women swirling red banners at the crowd's core, but it was impossible to tell whether the majority of this alternately cheering and jeering group was with them or against them.

"What's the rumpus?" I couldn't help asking a tall, frosty-nosed man who looked like he'd been observing for a while.

"Aw, you know." He shrugged. "These guys think the world bein' unfair is front page news."

"Would it be such a bad thing if it *was?*" an even taller man in a postal carrier's outfit interjected.

"Mebbe not," the first man replied. "It ain't like I don't sympathize. It's just"—he spread his arms—"the world don't work that way."

"Well, how *duzzit* woik?" A young woman spun on worn-to-the-sole heels and joined the conversation. "Tell us, Big Boy."

The honking got louder, and the singers raised their voices accordingly.

"Not the way you wannit to, lady." The man shrugged. "Not the way I wannit to either."

"That's pretty defeatist talk, buddy." The postman shook his head.

"No kiddin'? And here I thought I was some kinda yu'man inspiration machine. But mebbe I oughtta let you have the job. You're workin' for the government, ain't ya? You got no kick."

Ignoring the last comment, the uniformed man turned to me and said, "To answer your question, friend: Those people came out this morning because ten of their fellow picketers got arrested for 'disturbing the peace' last week. I deliver mail on this block, and I can tell you they weren't disturbing *anything* but Dan Palter's greedy little dreams...."

"Dat's right," the woman with the Brooklynese accent chimed in. "Dey say dey're on strike. And de Dan Palter comp'ny says dey've been fi-yuhed. Which I guess dey have. Dere's a whole new crew woikin' up dere now...."

"All they want is a chance to tell their side of the story," the postman summed up.

"Oh." The woman shook her head. "I tink dey want more dan dat. But dey'll take what dey can get."

A few feet away, a sour-faced, sandy-haired man who had been yelling "dirty Reds" over and over again ever since I had arrived reached down and picked up a small rock. He smiled as he took aim at a woman carrying a "Down with Whalen's Cossacks" placard (Michael Whalen was the city's Commissioner of Police). I winced ineffectually as he wound up to make his throw.

"Hey, *jerk*," the frosty-nosed man called out. "Put it down. Now."

For a moment, the man appeared to contemplate the wisdom of throwing the rock in our direction. But a short staring competition with the rather muscular "human inspiration machine" convinced the would-be assailant to drop his weapon and wander back toward 7th Avenue.

"Yeah." The smile beneath the reddened nose was equally smug and sad. "We got the makins of a real friendly society here."

The crowd thickened exponentially as more and more New Yorkers deviated from their usual morning routes, drawn by the sounds of the commotion. Suddenly, a firm tap on my shoulder triggered dire visions of my mission's fate if those fingers were attached to the long arm of the law.

I eyed the time machine nervously.

"Isn't this fantastic, Douglass?"

The friendly voice only intensified my anxiety. "It's not going to be fantastic for long." I grabbed her arm, a little more protectively than I would have liked to. Lulu barked.

"What are you talking about?" Eileen studied the mostly placid faces in our vicinity. "Everything looks under control to me.... The dog woke me up early, and this was all they could talk about on the WOR News. I figured it couldn't hurt us to walk up here and show a bit of support."

"Normally, I'd agree with you." I spread my arms helplessly. "After all, I'm here too. But you aren't going to want to be anywhere near this place in a few minutes. Believe me."

She squinted at me. "Is this one of your hunches, Douglass?"

"'Fraid so." I started pushing my way toward the perimeter of the crowd.

Eileen sighed and pulled Lulu along.

Soon, the disconcerting sound of police sirens drastically altered the mood on the street. Everyone, regardless of their political convictions, retreated in the wake of the advancing paddy wagon caravan. Fortunately, our little party had managed to reach 7th Avenue before the stampede began.

"Oh my God." Eileen dropped angry tears. "I can't believe this is happening again. They're not even bothering to pretend that workers have rights."

"Oh, they've got rights," I argued. "They're just not allowed to start any conversations that matter."

"Are they actually going to arrest every single demonstrator?" Her tone was listless.

The wagons were filling up quickly. And the spectrally festive area outside the Dan Palter Shoe Company had been cleared of everything but a few brightly coloured banners and boldly worded placards.

"Pretty much." I tried not to sound too much like a guy who had read tomorrow's newspaper. "And some hapless bystanders in the bargain, no doubt. The women will be tried and sentenced at the courthouse near my place, but Mayor Walker's stylish new adjacent prison won't be ready to accommodate them for another year or two."

"I could easily have been arrested just for walking my dog...."

"Uh-uh." I shook my head. "For subjecting your dog to syndicalist propaganda."

"It's completely absurd."

I couldn't disagree with her there. "Yeah, but it's

not the kind of joke your producer would have appreciated. If it got around."

"Maybe I shouldn't care about that, Douglass. Maybe I should be in jail. Maybe you should be too. Maybe things would be different if everyone who understood how cockeyed things have gotten was willing to go to jail."

"Maybe. Or maybe there'd just be a lot more people in jail. Maybe you need to find yourself a soapbox that isn't set over a trapdoor chute to the hoosegow. Maybe you ought to be in pictures."

"Maybe." She paid no attention to my reference to a song that hadn't yet been written. "If the right chance comes along."

It was going to. Four days from now. As long as she didn't get arrested in the interim.

"Of course," I said. "That goes without saying. You don't want to wind up working for L.B. Mayer."

"What I want," she corrected me, "is to believe that those people are going to be treated fairly someday."

The police vehicles drove off, and ordinary traffic flow resumed.

Chapter Seventeen

I had never been so excited for New Year's. (I had never been excited for New Year's, period.) The December 31st *Times* carried a (very) short article on the recently widowed singer's expected return to *The Scandals* that evening, and, if the information Dorothea had fed me was correct (or still valid, in the brave new timeline I'd been helping to create), that little bit of show business news would soon pale in comparison to the momentous events that would envelop Eileen after the show.

There was certainly some cause for concern. After all, Dorothea's Eileen had been on a rather different trajectory than the person with whom I'd forged a fast friendship over the course of the past month. *That* Eileen had dramatically severed all connection with "domesticity" and a "conventional" female identity (at a considerable cost to her still-divided and somewhat traditional psyche, if her legendary descent into alcoholism was any indication) by obtaining an abortion two days after Pat's death. *This* Eileen had come through the ordeal in far better shape, and, as heartened as I was by my presumed effect upon her life, I worried that her more even-keeled state of mind might alter or nullify her prophesied chemistry with the producers of *King of Jazz*. The temptation to find some way of accompanying her to the party (to which she had not yet been invited) was immense, but I realized that any attempt on my part to micromanage the affair could only do more harm than good. A sober Eileen would doubtless impress the impresarios even more than an inebriated one had.

The singer gave me something else to worry about when she announced that, to go along with my complimentary ticket, she had landed me a date for the evening: Nora Kelly. Fortunately, I received this news via Mrs. Duncan's telephone, otherwise I'm pretty sure my face would have telegraphed far too much of the misery evoked by the unexpected reappearance of that blast from my now-erased past (and her never-to-be-realized future, since our first meeting had occurred in June 1930). With no choice but to try and make the best of a demoralizing situation, I put a smile in my voice as I consented to escort Eileen's "lifelong chum" to the show.

I met Nora at the corner of Bleecker and Bank at 7:30. (She was staying with Eileen, who had, of course, left for rehearsals at the theatre several hours earlier.) She had on a stylish green worsted wool coat that brought out her eyes (as if they needed bringing out), and her blonde hair was immaculately finger waved, as it had been the last time I'd seen her.

"One tip, Douglass." She extended a hand toward

mine. "Don't even try to live up to your billing."

"I promise you, I won't."

I hailed a checker cab, and the driver slammed on the breaks. I opened the door for Nora and jumped in after her.

"Apollo Theater," I told the man at the wheel. "Times Square."

"You got it," he coughed between puffs on his cigarette.

"I didn't mean you shouldn't talk at all." Nora smiled as we turned onto 8th Avenue. "Were you hoping for a brunette?"

"What's the matter with you, my friend?" the driver called back to me in a thick Greek accent. "This is a woman who should be talked to! If you do not talk to her, I will. An' my wife will not like this one bit."

"Ah, well." I stretched lazily. "If that's all it takes to keep your blessed union afloat, I'll do it."

"This is very good, my friend. I will not tell my wife what you have done for her. But I will give her a special treat when I get home, in your honour."

"You sure you wouldn't rather receive the special treat?" I asked Nora.

"I'll skip right to this." She lit a cigarette of her own, adding to the general toxicity of the atmosphere.

I rolled down my window as far as it would go. The cabbie turned right on 42nd Street.

"This is not very good talk so far, my friend," the driver seemed to feel entitled to remark. "I am afraid to leave you like this."

"Shows what *you* know." Nora handed him a pair of one-dollar bills. "I've already decided to fuck him tonight."

She hopped out and held the door open for me.

"Thank you, my friend." I saluted the perplexed kibitzer.

I heard Nora's laugh from somewhere within the penumbral neon haze. As my eyes adjusted to the hyper-real 42nd Street glare, I brought them to rest upon the Apollo's marquee:

NEW YEAR'S EVE!

GEORGE WHITE'S SCANDALS

10TH EDITION

ALL-STAR CAST

WILLIE & EUGENE HOWARD,
FRANCES WILLIAMS,
MITCHELL & DURANT,
EVELYN WILSON, MARIETTA,
AND GEORGE WHITE!

MUSIC AND LYRICS BY CLIFF FRIEND &
GEORGE WHITE

Of course, there was no mention of Eileen, but with any luck she was destined to outshine that entire "all-star" assemblage (not that any of the headliners other than impresario/dancer White ever achieved much in the way of lasting renown, but they were definite names to conjure with in 1929). Next door, the Times Square Theater was touting a play called *Many Waters* ("the season's comedy hit"–although it was closing this week), starring master milquetoast Ernest Truex, whose fame (as a Hollywood character actor, at any rate) *would* stand the test of time.

Nora sucked the remaining life out of her cigarette with vampiric aplomb and threw the butt into a puddle on the street. "You ready to go in, Douglass?"

I bowed and made the "après vous" gesture.

At the coat check, I realized that she was wearing the same "little black dress" she had so hastily thrown on to ring down the curtain on our last encounter. As I watched her smooth the fabric down her flanks, I was genuinely uncertain whether this new information would strengthen my resolve to keep my distance from her or weaken it.

The question gained urgency as she took my arm on our way to the stellar centre orchestra seats that Eileen had somehow contrived to obtain for us.

Nora whistled as we settled in. "My God, Douglass. They don't hand out comps like these to non-stars. Either this show is tanking or we're sitting here because Pat got killed."

The show wasn't tanking—the hall was filled to capacity.

"Pretty grim." I nodded.

"I'm in a grim mood." Her voice dropped into an uncharacteristically confidential register.

"You are?"

"Is that so surprising?" Her increasingly obvious desire to initiate a real conversation had taken me completely off guard. "What did Eileen tell you about me?"

Had she told me *anything* about Nora in this timeline? I was having a tough time parsing the memories.

"Just that you grew up together in Flatbush," I replied. "Why?"

"Because you're treating me like some combination of Theda Bara and the Fuller Brush man."

"I'm sorry." I owned up to my rudeness. "I've just... got a lot on my mind."

"Are you carrying a torch for Eileen?" She leaned toward me.

This was the last impression I wanted anyone to get, after I'd so heroically disabused my grandmother of the notion.

"No." I shook my head mildly. "Of course not. You sound like my landlady. Doesn't anyone around these parts believe that men and women can be *friends*?"

"Well"—she raised a darkish blonde eyebrow—"you haven't been very friendly with me."

"It's true." I shrugged. "Let's just say that my feelings toward you have already gotten...considerably more complicated."

"That's flattering, Douglass. Really. But right now I think I could use some of what Eileen's been getting."

"I think I can manage that." I smiled. And strangely enough, I meant it. I had imagined plenty of different outcomes to our evening, but not this one.

"How about skipping out on the first act of the show? Can you manage *that*? I came for the premiere in September, and believe me, there's nothing much to see before Eileen does her stuff after the intermission."

I might have begged to differ with her on that point. I would, in fact, be a little sad to miss the outrageously (during Prohibition) dipsomanic Harlem speakie first-act closer, set to Friend and White's "Bottoms Up."

Hold your glasses with bottoms up
Trouble passes with bottoms up
While you're swinging keep singing
Hallelujah Hallelujah Hallelujah
Go right to it with bottoms up
Overdo it, with bottoms up
While you're swaying keep saying
Hallelujah Hallelujah Hallelujah
[...]
Just make merry and drain the cup
Go through life with your bottoms up
You'll be forgiven for livin'
Hallelujah
If you do the bottoms up

On the other hand, I had already seen that number (and could see it again any time before the show concluded its run in February), while this fresh and fragile staging of the Nora Kelly story might conceivably close before the night's final chorus of "Auld Lang Syne."

"Yeah." I nodded. "Let's do it. I could use a bite anyway. I forgot to eat dinner." There was no sense in telling Nora that the prospect of seeing her had triggered that "forgetfulness."

We took another quick cab ride down to the Horn & Hardart on 6th Avenue just past 36th Street. I didn't see what made the place so special (other than its monumental vertical neon "AUTOMAT" sign), but it was apparently a sentimental favourite of Nora's. The large eating hall was doing a brisk business on New Year's Eve, but there were a few tables open, and Nora staked her claim on a spot that was reasonably close to the window.

I loaded our tray with five-cent cups of "French drip" java and two slices of pumpkin pie that tasted far better than anything fresh from a hole in a wall had any business tasting.

"Thanks, Douglass." She dropped a cube of sugar into the thick, aromatic brew and launched into an unwitting reprise (from my perspective) of her life story, with the twist that, this time, I detected a trickle of pathos within the mordant stream of her consciousness that had not been there in June 1930.

The portrait of her youth was essentially unchanged. Born into a lower-middle-class family headed by an Irish Catholic tobacconist and his German-Jewish wife, the gifted Nora had grown up pampered by her parents and practically despised by her siblings (two older brothers and a younger sister). Initially, the Kellys had envisioned a career in the arts for their daughter, but Nora took pains to emphasize that, despite the "pretty decent" voice lessons they were able to procure for her, her singing had never risen beyond the level of mere technical competence.

"And the funny thing is," she added, "they needn't have bothered scraping the money together. I'm glad they did, mind you, otherwise I probably never would have met Eileen, but it sure raised hell in our family. Anyway, I did so well academically (analytical essays, math championships, debating...the whole kit and caboodle) that I won my ticket out of Flatbush on a scholarship to study at Radcliffe.

"I majored in Classics. Greek and Latin, you know. I had a good time. Learned a fair bit. Met a platoon of men who were willing to pretend they were interested in listening to me talk. Screwed a good percentage of them just for putting in the effort, including one professor who could get me going just by whispering the name 'Gilgamesh' into my ear. Considered doing some graduate work in Assyriology, but then a classmate's dad offered me a job at Sears-Roebuck, and I took it the day after graduation."

"Very sensible." I felt the need to add *something*.

"Very sensible of you to *say*." She smirked. "That was about a year and a half ago. I served a three-month apprenticeship at the New York buying office and then accepted a summons to the corporate hub in Chicago! You don't turn down a promotion, do you? You'd *better* not."

"Aw, poor little high-powered executive! Or is that 'executrix'?"

"Oh, it's definitely executrix. At least when I'm talking under my breath." She smiled. "No idea whose will I'm supposed to be executing though.... Certainly not mine. Dead or alive, there aren't many things a woman can even strive to fail at in this world, except for being a woman."

The pie was nicely spiced and had a delicious golden crust, but I'd barely had the inclination to touch it since she had begun talking. Of course, she hadn't done much of anything with her own slice either.

"Nora...I'm afraid you're making way too much sense for your own good...."

"Yeah, that's what I told myself," she sighed. "Better fall in love, I decided. For real this time. So I did. There's always someone to fall in love with. He was a pretty nice guy. Good-looking. Attentive. Lived right near my house. Successful enough not to be too concerned about my achievements. Not particularly bright, and he didn't know anything about ancient Mesopotamia, but I figured I could teach him a few basic tricks. Even a parrot can say 'Gilgamesh.'"

"Sounds all right."

"It *was* all right. He asked me to marry him. I said yes. That's still technically on for the spring. But the crash threw him off his game, and he tried to asphyxiate himself in the garage the day after Christmas." She drove her fork into the pie.

"Does Eileen know about this?"

"No." She took a large bite. "*I* should bother her with this nonsense when her own man died legitimately last month?"

I nodded. "Do you think he'll try it again?"

"I'm not sure if it matters." She seemed to like the pie as much as I did. "With something like this, once is probably enough."

"I don't know if it would be for me," I said. "But I understand what you're saying. This guy was supposed to settle a few questions, not raise more of them."

"Exactly." She stood up. "And now he's going to be watching me like the stocks."

We made it back to the Apollo just in time to re-enter the theatre with the intermission crowd. Eileen was undoubtedly as good as she had ever been, and I clapped on cue, but I can't say that I paid too much attention to her rendition of "18 Days Ago," or to anything else that transpired on the stage. I was too busy attempting to reconstruct (or, I suppose, project) the first half of Nora's new year. The wedding would be cancelled, of course—along with any future possibility of conversations like the one we had just had. The woman I had met on that evaporated summer night had simply chosen to keep all of her questions to herself.

◆

We caught up with Eileen at the stage door after the show. She looked radiantly at ease as she clipped through the crisp air in an uncharacteristically snug-fitting (and intricately embroidered) cream-coloured dress, with tassels that tickled her knees and thighs.

"Did you have a good time?" She hugged us both.

"Absolutely." I smiled. "You were fantastic, Eileen."

"Thanks!" She hardly even blushed before dropping her voice a few decibels. "It may not be the greatest song ever written, but right now I'm pretty glad they gave it to me." She closed in for a second hug, whispering, "It's just a throwaway DeSylva, Brown, and Henderson tune, but it's the only one of theirs in the show. They used to write a lot of the music for George White, you know, before Buddy DeSylva left for Hollywood. Anyway, DeSylva was *here* tonight! With John Murray Anderson, the director (Nora, you might remember this) who wanted me for a little revue he was doing in the early fall...."

"Right." I felt Nora nod. "I remember."

Eileen's enthusiasm sent tremors through our confidential little huddle.

"Well, I had to decline Anderson's offer, 'cause I'd already won my spot in *The Scandals*. But he didn't forget me! And now he's shooting a movie. He just invited me to a party at Carl Laemmle, Jr.'s place on the Upper West Side. He's the kid (well, I guess he's about the same age as *we* are, Nora) who just inherited the big job at Universal!"

"Ah, yes." I came up for air. "I read about that. Sounds like a clear case of opportunity knocking."

"It does, doesn't it?" Eileen's teeth retreated behind a diffident half-smile. "What's the cure for that? Plenty of bed rest, I guess?"

"I withdraw the metaphor!" I yelped. "You're not going home, Eileen!"

"Oh, I don't know…. It just feels like…it's too soon for me to be grasping at the next rung on the ladder…. Don't you think?"

Nora grabbed her friend by the shoulders. "Honey, we're not thinking about this one. We're just going."

"But…I can't leave Lulu alone for another four hours. She must be climbing the walls."

"I'll handle the dog," I volunteered.

"Would you, Douglass?"

"Of course. You just take care of the moguls."

"Okay." She dropped the keys into my hand. "I wish you could come too."

"Ah, don't worry about that. It's probably for the best," I yawned (and I had definitely come around to believing it). "Happy New Year, kids."

Nora kissed my hand and then took Eileen's arm. "Shall we?"

Eileen took a deep breath. "I guess we shall."

"Don't wait up for us, Douglass," Nora called back to me as they disappeared up the steps into the theatre.

I hustled over to 7th Avenue and hailed a cab back to Eileen's. This driver was far too busy mocking the many sozzled revelers on the streets to bother making small talk with me, and I welcomed the reprieve. Despite my meddling, everything was proceeding on schedule (Universal-wise) this time, and I was breathing more easily than freak byproducts of temporal anomalies generally feel able to.

"Bleecker and Bank, buddy." The cabbie's harsh voice woke me.

"Ah...thanks." I wiped the existential drool off my chin and paid the man.

Lulu had some choice barks for me at the door, but she changed her tune when I grabbed her leash and hitched it to her collar. The big German shepherd generally took a brief constitutional around Abingdon, but I'd lost my fondness for that place on a pair of November 28ths, and besides, I figured she had earned a longer stroll down to Washington Square. As the cabbie had noted, public drunkenness was very much the order of the Eve, especially in the parks, but everyone we met was quite friendly. Or perhaps they were just a little bit scared of Lulu, who didn't really behave as if she intended to make a habit of obeying my commands. I certainly didn't have much luck talking her out of pissing on the base of the monument to Giuseppe Garibaldi.

On our way home, I peeked in at Risotto Voce, where they'd finished serving customers for the night and switched over into staff party mode. The group had ample cause for celebration, given Eileen's plan to make the place an employee-owned cooperative, and they were happy to exchange New Year's greetings with me (and the Corelli family dog), even though I really hadn't gotten to know any of them in this timeline. After one quick glass of Chianti, I cajoled Lulu back upstairs to the flat, refreshed her water bowl, and passed out on Eileen's couch.

"Well, Douglass, it worked!" The lady of the house passed a steaming cup of coffee under my nose.

I sat up.

"What time is it?" I took a grateful sip.

Eileen settled in near my feet at the other end of the couch. The party dress was gone, replaced by her gingham housecoat. Her movements were calm, but her pupils had completely dispossessed her irises. "Oh, it must be nearly eight. The sun came up just before I left the party."

"Good party."

"Very good."

"You met Carl Laemmle, Jr.?"

"Laemmle, Paul Whiteman, Frankie Trumbauer, Mildred Bailey.... It was amazing. And no one seemed to notice how fat I am.... The only thing missing was

Bix Beiderbecke. Apparently, he isn't doing so well."

From what I remembered, the original "Young Man with a Horn" would be doing a lot worse before too long.

"That's too bad," I said. "He's nearly as good as Louis Armstrong."

She nodded. "It would've been great to do a song with him."

"You sang with Whiteman's orchestra?"

She jumped up. "Yes! Well, not the whole orchestra but a lot of them." She put her hand on my shoulder. "Douglass, they were supposed to do a live New Year's Eve show from Los Angeles tonight, but instead they rushed back to New York in time to broadcast it from here. And it seems like they did it all for *me*!"

"What?"

"The party was actually more of an audition. Well... no...that's not true either. It was definitely a party. But Anderson invited me because he thought I'd be perfect for a spot in *King of Jazz*, the big musical picture he's been working on. They're nearly done shooting, but Whiteman wants to add one more number, and of course he's the star, so they're giving him what he wants. But apparently he didn't know exactly what he wanted until he heard me sing 'Body and Soul' with the band."

"'Body and Soul,' hunh?" I spliced my vision of Eileen's performance into the version of the film that I was familiar with. "That's good. That'll work beautifully."

"God, Douglass." She gave me an ironic little

smile. "You don't sound very excited about any of this. Maybe I should have made that coffee a little stronger."

I looked up at her. "Excited? Of course I'm excited. I'm just not very surprised, that's all. You deserve this, Eileen. And it's only the beginning."

"Well, we'll see about that. What do I know about performing for the camera?"

"You'll be a natural."

"We'll find out soon enough. My train leaves this evening. Can I saddle you with Lulu for a week or two?"

The dog brought me the rawhide candy cane I'd gotten her for Christmas.

"With pleasure. I'll bring her to the office. Scare Tom Katz out of his mind."

"You're amazing, Douglass. I don't know where I'd be without you."

"Exactly where you are. Minus a few kennel expenses."

Her smile broadened. "You want to get some breakfast?"

"Sure." I stretched. "Is Nora coming too?"

"Oh." She turned away shyly. "I...don't think so... Douglass. I'm...not exactly sure where she is. I really don't know what got into her last night. Did she tell you she's engaged?"

"She did. But she didn't make it sound like a permanent thing."

"Nothing ever is, with Nora."

"Oh, I don't know. She seems like a pretty solid friend."

"She is. The best."

"Well." I stood up, famished. "That's not nothing."

Chapter Eighteen

I moved in to Eileen's place for the duration of her trip. I had no desire to drag Lulu away from her favourite spot in front of the Corelli family fireplace, and in fact I quite relished the prospect of joining her there. New York gets pretty chilly in January, and the radiators at Mrs. Duncan's boarding house couldn't match her chicken soup for warmth. It was also kind of a nice change to have such immediate access to a phone after having lived without one for a while. In my "modern" existence, I had all but given up on that telemarketer-haunted device, preferring to communicate chiefly via email, but I actually got kind of a kick out of talking to 1930 operators and asking for telephone exchanges by name.

I even started answering the damn thing, more often than not. After enduring a few days of gruelling cross-country rail and air travel, Eileen called to check in with me on the evening of Saturday the 4th. She didn't have a whole lot to report, other than that Southern California was paradise, Paul Whiteman was a lamb, and Universal had asked her to change her name to "Cynthia Ward."

"What the hell's the matter with Eileen McWade?"

I tried to sound as shocked as I had been the first time Dorothea had sprung this information on me. "It was good enough for Broadway."

"Sure, but apparently it's just a little too 'ethnic.' And not the 'exotic' kind of ethnic either, like Garbo or Novarro. It's not the kind of name that winds up at the top of a bill."

Only fourteen months after New York Democrat Al Smith's disastrous campaign for president, "Irishness" remained a very hard sell in America outside of the major metropolitan centres.

"Well, it's a shame."

"It is. But what can you do? I don't have any family left to offend." Her tone was glum but self-assured. "I'll take my stands later, when I've got a little leverage working for me."

"Sounds like you've been talking to an agent."

"Constantly, Douglass. I didn't even get to play cards once during the whole trip."

"You'll be an easy mark when you get back."

"I'm looking forward to it. Everything going okay with Lulu?"

"Absolutely. I haven't mustered up the nerve to bring her into work yet, but the restaurant people kept tabs on her during the daytime this week."

"I can't thank you enough, Douglass."

"Don't be ridiculous. My place is too cold right now anyway."

"Well, I'd better get to bed. More shooting tomorrow."

"On a Sunday?"

"I'm afraid so. We're squeezing this one in under the wire. Good night, Douglass!"

"Good night, Cynthia."

I heard her laugh as I hung up the phone.

I had established my quarters in the guest room, where I had convalesced after the beating that kicked off my first sojourn into the past. It remained absurdly cozy, and of course it had its own little fireplace (which I hadn't lit that day, much to Lulu's chagrin, because the temperature had actually reached the mid-50s).

I had been reading Vernon L. Parrington's *Main Currents in American Thought* when the telephone rang. Regarded as nothing more than a Progressive Era curio by the time I got to university during the '90s, the recent Pulitzer Prize–winning study seemed fresh and ground-breaking now that I was encountering it in its proper cultural context. I finished the chapter on Margaret Fuller (whom Parrington describes as "a ferment of troubled aspiration [and] an enthusiasm for a more generous culture than New England had known") and then hopped out of bed to fix myself a snack. While spreading jam on my toast, I actually considered setting the watch back to 1840 and asking Ms. Fuller how she liked being described as a "ferment" and an "enthusiasm."

A fire engine screamed by on Bleecker, and Lulu dashed to Eileen's bedroom window, determined to get the last word. I went in to calm her and realized, with a start, that I had never before entered that room. Very simply furnished, with sombre browns and blacks predominating, the chamber contained only the most unobtrusive decoration. The crisply made king-sized bed had a dark cotton blanket folded back upon itself near the head and, just beyond that point, a pair of plain flat pillows lying side by side. The two bedside tables, probably made of mahogany, matched perfectly, and each one held an identical brass lamp with a sloping white shade. Two large dressers dominated the wall opposite the window, and the apartment's third small fireplace faced the bed. The mantelpiece contained a lone miniature bust of Julius Caesar. There was no trace of a mirror.

At the foot of the bed, nestled against the dark blanket, I noticed a thin black photo folio. Well, actually, first I sat on it. Then I noticed it. For at least five minutes, I ran my fingers over the smooth leather cover without opening it. Eventually, though, my desire to leaf through what simply had to be my grandparents' wedding album got the better of me.

But that's not what it was.

Instead of a dull procession of full-dress stills taken at various likely Central Park locales, the book contained about twenty frankly sensational shots of Pat Corelli (on the beach at Coney, valiantly defending a sand castle against Lulu's ungovernable wag; leaping off the 6th Avenue El at the Bleecker Street station, looking about two-thirds in the bag; making pasta with his shirt half undone in the Risotto Voce kitchen after hours; sitting in the stands at Ebbets Field, peering back over his shoulder with a sun-induced squint and a smile that is somehow both tenderly bemused and rivetingly carnal; etc). Clearly taken by Eileen herself, these photos composed a mosaic of ironic yearning which expressed a part of her being that I had never understood before (in any of the three timelines we'd crossed paths in so far). She had been deeply in love with this man whom I had allowed to die. This was no rote romance, no unthinking slouch onto the gender treadmill. As limiting and as ultimately unfulfilling as the relationship had most definitely been, Eileen's brilliant album robbed me of the luxury of pretending that her feelings for Pat had somehow been less "true" to her psychological core than the extraordinary films I hoped she was on the verge of making.

I returned the book to its station at the foot of the bed and crept guiltily out of Eileen and Pat's room.

I reluctantly skewered the last ember in the guest room fireplace and urged Lulu out into the bright, cold Monday morning air. Normally, the walk from Eileen's place to the office took about twenty minutes, but the dog's inexhaustible curiosity and intermittent intractability nearly doubled my commute time that day.

Tom Katz looked up from his coffee and cigarette buffet as we paraded into the editorial office. "You show up for work in the *afternoon* and you got with you a grizzly bear? This ain't how people get ahead in business, Douglass."

"Maybe not." I smiled. "But we made a big hit with your niece out there."

"All right, kid." He tossed a manuscript at me. "Park that yeti somewhere and see what you can do with this story. It ain't much more readable than hieroglyphics, but it's got a terrific hook: This scientist builds a turbine that can harness the flow of *time*. He calls it chronoelectric power. Of course, it causes some problems with the Earth's rotation and the seasons and that kinda stuff, but they get everything straightened out in the end."

I remembered this story very well. There were, to put it mildly, a few problems with the writing. At one point, the embattled protagonist tells his detractors: "You think me a fool and a maniac. A meddling frayer of the universal fabric. But *I* say that, in the end, time will finally be on our side at last." It would be tedious to edit this monstrosity again, but at least this time I wouldn't waste any breath trying to sell Katz on my revised ending in which the entire past gets cancer.

I settled into my chair and brandished a blue pencil, luring Lulu to my side with a fresh rawhide candy cane. I was about four pages into the job of terraforming author Archie Mead's alien writing when Doreen, our receptionist for the day, tapped me on the shoulder.

"I'm sorry to bother you, Douglass," she whispered,

"but...there are two men here to see you." She paused dramatically. "I...I think they might be from the police."

"Really?" I tried not to sound unduly concerned. "Hmm...well, I guess I'd better see what they want."

"I guess so." She flashed a weak but encouraging smile.

"Come on, Lulu." I picked up the leash. "It's time for your walk anyway."

Out in the vestibule, I found Fredericks and O'Meara scowling at poor Jimmy Kushner, the fidgety kid with the sketchbook who'd been waiting to see Tom Katz since before I had arrived that morning. Every week, the gawky red-headed teenager made the rounds of the New York pulp mills, armed with a satchel full of thrilling illustrations in the hopes that one of them would line up well enough with a soon-to-be-published story to wind up on the cover of a magazine. I'd looked through his catalog many times. He had a real flair for art deco futurity and pathos-stricken robots. He would actually manage to sell a piece to *Corking Tales* in April. I couldn't tell him that, but I could throw him a lifeline.

"Hey, Jimmy, Katz'll see you now."

"Thanks, Mr. Infantino!" He leaped out of his seat and didn't look back.

The police detectives eyed him with moderate disdain.

"Nice business associates you got, friend," the younger cop grunted at me. "That kid was drawing us like Cossacks."

"Blame it on the papers, O'Meara," I grunted back. "They did it first."

The stocky man aimed his chin at Lulu. "Isn't that Corelli's dog?"

"Yes, it is." I nodded.

"You aren't wasting any time are you, friend?"

"No, but you are."

I caught a brief glimpse of his teeth. Lulu growled. Behind me, Doreen exhaled theatrically.

Fredericks put a cauliflowered hand on his partner's tensed shoulder. The senior detective's knuckles had taken, and almost certainly dished out, a beating since I'd last seen them. He pointed a warped index finger in my direction. "You'll have to leave the dog here, Infantino. You're wanted for questioning."

"In what connection?" I demanded to know. "You still think I had something to do with Pat's death?"

"Ah, so it's Pat now, eh?" Fredericks raised an eyebrow. "You two have gotten awfully chummy since he died. I thought you didn't know him."

"While we're on the subject of thinking," I fired back, "I thought you two had given up on this delusion a while ago. Is this really why you're interrupting my workday? More questions about my relationship with the Corellis?"

"Hey, you can't hang a guy for being curious," Fredericks laughed. "But don't worry. What we think doesn't really matter in the grand scheme of things. The department doesn't figure you for the murder. End of story."

"Yeah." O'Meara gave me his dead-eyed smile. "This is a brand new adventure. A 'corking tale' even."

I sighed and looked back at Doreen. "Can you handle Lulu for a bit? I shouldn't be gone long."

"Sure thing, Douglass."

I followed the detectives to their squad car parked a little farther west on 29th Street. The pair remained uncharacteristically silent during the ten-minute drive down to the 8th Precinct police station on Mercer Street, near Washington Square.

As we came to a stop outside of the decrepit building, O'Meara squinted back at me over the top of his seat. "Better settle on an alibi, friend."

"An alibi for *what?*" I had trouble concealing my alarm. I knew the matter couldn't concern Eileen. She was safe in California. And Nora had returned to Chicago for the time being. Whom else did I even know, aside from the people at the magazine? Had someone attacked Mrs. Duncan while I was off housesitting in the lap of multifireplaced luxury? An unsettling thought.

Fredericks switched off the ignition and turned his own inscrutable eyes on me. "You have any relatives, Douglass?"

"Relatives? What do you mean?"

"People who are related to you. A sister maybe? A brother?"

"No." I shook my head. "I'm an only child. Of

course, I had the standard mother and father setup, once upon a time. But they're gone now."

"How about a really close cousin then?"

"No. No first cousins. My mother was an only child, too."

That last part was true. I saw no reason to add that I did have a few seldom-seen cousins (and a couple of half-siblings) on the Infantino side. Unless they too had stumbled onto time machines, they wouldn't be showing up around here to refute my testimony.

"Looks like he's telling the truth," O'Meara concluded reluctantly.

"Yeah." Fredericks ran those misshapen fingers across his well-lined forehead.

"What's going on here? You said you were bringing me in for questioning. Are these the goddamned questions?"

O'Meara lit a cigarette. Fredericks swivelled back to the wheel and started the engine, taking a northeasterly route through the noontime traffic. They weren't driving me back to work. Or to my house.

As we neared the East River, travelling on 23rd Street, I realized we were on course for Bellevue.

"Jesus, are you guys gonna have me committed?"

"Relax, Infantino," Fredericks sighed wearily over his shoulder. "We just want to show you something. That's all."

"Show me something at the hospital? No, thanks. I already know that cigarettes and red meat are bad for me."

"We're not asking, friend," O'Meara snarled.

"You know, I'm worried that certain aspects of friendship have eluded you."

Fredericks turned off 1st Avenue and parked the car on East 29th, outside of the "Pathological Building." Pretty much the definition of *ominous*.

We entered the red brick structure through a side door and took the first staircase down to the basement. Before I knew it, we stepped into the gloomily officious admittance room to the New York City Mortuary. Fredericks gave a perfunctory half-wave to the sallow-faced man at the desk and pushed on through a pair of heavy doors. These opened directly into a clinically lit octagonal chamber occupied by the day's grim harvest: six bodies lying under sheets on beds arranged in a circular pattern.

"Where is he?" O'Meara barked at the nattily smocked bon vivant who presided over the place.

With stylishly coiffed black hair and an O'Meara-proof smile, the tall morgue attendant seemed imperfectly fitted to his situation, but he knew his business, pointing immediately at bed number five. Fredericks sauntered over to the spot and finessed the cadaver's left arm into the light.

I recognized the gold watch on its wrist immediately. Could this be Dorothea, I worried. But, no, the amount of hair on the arm ruled out that possibility. A new agent from the future, then? Sent to spy on me or derail my entire project? Or maybe it was just some poor guy who'd broken into my room at the boarding house and stolen the surplus time machine I'd stashed in the medicine cabinet. A dizzying succession of possibilities ambushed my mind.

"That's Exhibit A," Fredericks deadpanned.

He swept the sheet aside with a magician's practiced touch.

The body was *mine*—with a lot of water damage and a gaping hole in the chest where the heart should have been.

"Ain't that a corker?" O'Meara breathed smoke in my face.

"Is Ford making Infantinos now?" Fredericks smirked. "Too bad this one spent a week in the East River. I'd have liked to have seen how closely the fingerprints matched."

"All right." O'Meara looked just the slightest bit uneasy as he covered the body. "That's all for now. You can go. Friend."

My legs felt weak. I let them accordion to the floor. "I can go?"

"There's no law against *being an exact duplicate of a stiff*." Fredericks extended a hand. "We just thought you'd be interested."

"Interested?" I declined the offer.

O'Meara patted my shoulder with mock solicitude. "If you think we did wrong, write your local assemblyman."

Then they were gone.

I sat there for a while, thinking about the man under

the sheet. He had to be the me who'd stolen the watch and made the first leap back to 1929, the one I'd spotted lurking in Abingdon Square on Thanksgiving. But wasn't he *me*? I had done those things, too. Well, no, that wasn't true. I had saved my grandfather the first time, while this Douglass had taken my cue and likewise washed his hands of the murder. Then he had apparently disappeared into the metropolis, only to be ripped apart by bullets and tossed into the river within a month of his arrival. But if he was dead in January 1930, how had *I* been alive in June to set my watch back for a second kick at the can?

It didn't seem to add up.

But of course it had to add up. No matter how dead *he* was, I *did* exist. The inescapable conclusion was that time travel just didn't work the way they'd always claimed it did in science fiction magazines. My experiences had exposed the brain-teasing paradoxes which had fuelled the genre for more than a century as nothing more than literary shams. I had met myself in the past without any serious repercussions (other than psychological shock). I had also met two distinctly different *Dorotheas* (and even robbed one of them a second time) before either of them had leaped back to 2010, thereby eliminating the physicist's entire rationale for contacting me at random in the first place. And yet here I was: a living, breathing insult to every law of cause and effect.

The thought was cheering enough to stop my brain

from spinning like a top. I steadied myself against a cold gurney leg and stood up.

The affable attendant looked up from his clipboard and said, "Don't let those boys get you down. They're just not very good people. That's all."

I took the crosstown 34th Street bus back to Chelsea and asked Tom Katz for the rest of the afternoon off. I must have looked even more depleted than I thought, because he barely put up a fight, asking only that I finish editing the chronoelectric story at home. I thanked Doreen for taking care of Lulu and set forth down 8th Avenue with the dog at my side.

For some reason, I felt like being in my own place that evening, even though it was one of the coldest nights of the winter thus far. I had a stash of dog chow and Milk-Bones there, so I knew Lulu wouldn't mind too much. As we climbed the stairs to the room, an ebullient Esther Duncan burst out of her sanctum.

"Douglass! You're all right!"

"Sure, of course I am."

"When the police came here this morning, every question they asked made it sound like you were dead."

I smiled. "Well, I'm not."

She gave me a quick hug before pulling back down a step with an intense look. "Are you in trouble, Douglass? Do you need me to hide you?"

"*Hide* me?" I relapsed momentarily into anxiety. Was I in danger? Had someone (maybe even Dorothea?) out there declared open season on renegade time travellers? That seemed unlikely, given that my counterpart had not been stripped of his waterlogged watch. I decided to let that be my answer and push on with my plans. "No, Esther, I'm not in any trouble. But I'll tell ya, I could sure use a crossword and some chicken soup right now."

Her eyes brightened immediately. "Are you kidding? We got enough down there for you and *ten* dogs! Come on, Douglass. The *Loew Featurette* is just about to start. That's always so interesting. Then we've got the news and some nice music programs. And maybe you'll even wanna stick around for *Amos 'n' Andy* for a change?"

Maybe I did.

Chapter Nineteen

Eileen returned to New York two weeks later, aglow with enthusiasm for the filmmaking process.

"It's absolutely incredible," she told me between quick sips of coffee on her first morning back. "What they can *do*! I mean, performing for the camera isn't as immediately satisfying as hitting a live Broadway audience with everything you've got, but I think I started to find my rhythm with it, near the end. And the results, Douglass! The *intimacy* of it! To sell a song with a look instead of a gesture. To get the whole complex feeling across for a change. To slip into another world, created by light and a director's imagination, and discover that it's your world too, if you know what you're doing.... I'm going to learn everything I can about movies."

"Yeah, movies are good," I mumbled inanely, still more than half asleep. It was about 7:00 a.m. on Sunday, January 19th, and I had been hunched over Eileen's Underwood until 5:30, pounding out an "alien invasion" story to fill a gap in the next issue of the magazine. (My "invaders" were actually "cosmic social workers," sent to talk the Earth off the ledge of militarism. Naturally, the League of Nations chooses this inopportune moment to act vigorously for the first and only time in its sorry career. The aliens are either executed or squirrelled away in labs for future delectation, and the countdown to 1939 resumes.)

Eileen had burst into the cozy guest room, armed with redolently steaming paper cups from the deli. Fresh off a night flight from Chicago, her jagged fervour would certainly have been contagious if I'd had the slightest bit of energy to catch it. Fortunately, Lulu's jubilant bark aria more than made up for my sluggish reception.

"'Movies are good'?" She tweaked my nose gently. "Douglass, those cold-blooded kudos would get you burned at the stake in L.A. I've been running with the bull in the land of ballyhoo, remember?"

I sat up. "I'll refill my Benzedrine prescription immediately."

"That's the stuff." She smiled. "You'll do fine out there."

I sipped my still-scalding coffee. "*I'll* do fine?"

Eileen smiled. "Well, of course I'm going to get you a job at Universal too." Her voice dropped an octave. "Douglass, you'd come, wouldn't you?"

"Me?" I yawned. "Ride a woman's coattails into Hollywood?" Sheer contentment overwhelmed my mock frown. "What do *you* think?"

She took my cup and hit me with a pillow. "Good. Back to sleep with you then. I'm taking Lulu out on the town."

The dog raced toward the door, and I went out like a light.

❖

A little while later, the sound of violent shouting drove a final stake through my morning's repose. I practically crawled to the half-open door, dreading to hear the argument more clearly.

"We come ta see you on your first day back and we fin'a *man* sleepin' here?" Laura Corelli's shrill voice reverberated down the hall from the living room. "It's not enough you're gettin' rid'a Pat's business? You gotta give away everythin' else too?"

Lulu's barking took on an irritated edge.

"I'm not going to discuss this with you, Laura," Eileen said flatly. "I don't *have* to discuss this with you."

"If you tink we gonna let you raise our gran'kid in a sichuation like dis, you're crazy," Francesco fired back.

Laura's next jab seemed to come from a little farther away. I pictured her standing at the window, addressing the sky. "I *tol'* him not ta get involved with a showgirl! I *tol'* him!"

I considered going out there and throwing my two cents in the ring. After all, my friend was outnumbered (unless you counted the dog) and probably completely exhausted from her cross-continental trip.

"Who *is* dis guy, Eileen?" Francesco pressed the attack. "One a' dose gangstehs dat hangs out by de stage doah? Mebbe he liked ya 'pehfohmances' so much he had our boy killed?"

"*Miseria!*" Laura began to cry.

I took a deep breath and stepped into the hallway, but Eileen's tone stopped me in my tracks.

"Close that window, Laura."

"I'm swelterin' in heah," the older lady sobbed. "How many fiyuhplaces you got goin' in dis place anyway?"

"If you need some air," Eileen continued, "there's the door. I don't want my neighbours hearing a syllable of this disgusting conversation."

"Don' chu talk ta my—" Francesco started to yell.

"I'll talk any way I like in my apartment, Frank. *My* apartment. That means *I'm* the only one with keys, understand? I don't want any more of these goddamned ambushes. You're not my parents. My parents are dead. My husband is dead. That's a lot for one person to take. And one thing I don't have to take is you. If you want to see my son or daughter someday, if you even want to find out whether it's a boy or a girl, you'll get the hell out of my house. Right now."

The front door opened and closed without any further comment. Not even from Lulu.

Eileen came down the hallway with clenched fists and the beginnings of a very big smile. "It worked!"

"Are you telling me that was an act? I'm still picking shrapnel out of my ears."

"Oh, the anger was real enough," she laughed. "*Is* real enough. But I decided to channel it and play things your way."

"Nicely done."

"Thanks. I'm sorry you had to hear any of it though. I wish I could tell those lunkheads how things really are between us, but there's no chance they'd ever understand it."

I nodded and started shuffling toward the kitchen. "Hey, can we break out that waffle iron?"

"Of course." She skipped ahead of me. "Although I guess there aren't any fresh blueberries in the house?"

"Wrong guess." I grabbed a huge container out of the icebox.

"Fantastic!"

I plugged in the machine and set it down on the spacious marble counter next to the sink. Eileen cracked the eggs, and I measured out the rest of the ingredients.

Soon, the first batch of buckwheat batter was sizzling on the griddle.

"Did you confiscate their keys?" I watched the steam rise. "Really?"

"You bet I did." Eileen lit a cigarette and settled into a chair. "And I'm changing the locks, too."

The last bit of steam evaporated. The waffles were ready. I slid them onto plates and drenched them in syrup.

"Of course," she added, "I'll cut a new set for you."
We dug in.

A little later, after we'd dispensed with the dishes and moved onto the velvety dark purple couch in the living room, I prodded Eileen for more details about her trip.

"Well, they seemed to like the way I handled myself," she replied. "Whenever I wasn't trapped in a makeup chair or standing in front of a camera, men were talking to me about contracts. Or, anyway, the possibility of a contract. Pretty tantalizing stuff. But they're not making any promises until after the public sees my number in *King of Jazz*."

"When'll that be?" I figured I should ask, although of course I knew the answer better than she did.

"In New York? I think they're aiming for early May. At the Roxy. Whiteman's orchestra's gonna do a live show, too. With George Gershwin. ("Rhapsody in Blue" is the biggest song in the show.) You should come with me, unless you've got an aversion to being seen in public with seven-month-pregnant starlets."

"Not at all. I'd love to come."

"Good." She smiled. "I'll introduce you around. If anyone's still talking to me by the end of the movie, I should be in a pretty strong bargaining position, strong enough to politely suggest they consider hiring my brother, who already writes for the pulps, as a junior screenwriter."

"Your brother, hunh?" I scratched my chin. "You think that'll fly?"

"Sure. You're my half-brother. From Canada. Why not? No one but Nora would be wise."

"What about the Corellis?"

"The Corellis don't know anything about my family. They never cared enough to find out. And besides, they're delusional. They think you're some hopped-up gunslinger from the Mineo gang. This story's a lot more plausible than that."

"Are you saying I lack 'menace'?" I delivered my impression of a harrowing squint.

"And besides"—she shrugged my feeble joke aside—"it's pretty much the truth."

Pretty much.

Nothing else needed to be said.

"Shouldn't I have some scripts, then?" I pursued her scenario. "Some treatments at the ready?"

"Absolutely, Douglass." She nodded. "Three months from now."

"Right, but who knows how long it'll take me to get the hang of that kind of writing? It's very specialized. Maybe we should work on something together?"

"Well," she laughed, "my days are going to be pretty booked up with swelling, backaches, and retching for the next few months, but I think I can squeeze in a little hack writing, on the side...."

After accepting the *King of Jazz* gig, Eileen had cheerfully surrendered her song spot in *The Scandals* (which would close in early February anyway) to her understudy, Jessie Kassel, who had performed it (capably, by all accounts) every night since Pat's death, except on New Year's Eve.

"Great!" I retrieved a notebook and a pen from the guest room. "What genre of movie are we talking about here?"

"A musical, of course." She pulled her legs up into a crossed position on the couch. "I'll leave the space alien and time travel stories to you."

I got up and tossed another big log on the fire. "Fair enough."

"But"—she turned her mind seriously to the question at hand—"I'd want to do something a little bit different, you know? If I'm going to bother writing one."

"Different in what way?"

"Well, less frivolous somehow. I mean, don't get me wrong; Anderson did a wonderful job of staging my 'Body and Soul' number in the movie. You'll see—we'll both see—the finished product in May, but I got a peek at some of the 'rushes' and all of the storyboards, so I know exactly what they were going for. It's very modernist or expressionistic or whatever you want to call it, with my form splitting into duetting physical and spiritual halves and recombining when I finally kiss the object of my affection...Paul Whiteman...which is kind of ridiculous, if you know Whiteman, but of course that's on purpose. It's about as far from Broadway as you can get, without scrapping the show tunes."

"Sounds really fun," I said, noting with private satisfaction how seamlessly the number would mesh with the version of *King of Jazz* that I was familiar with.

"Oh, it's going to be a great musical," she agreed. "But still, it doesn't have much to say about...well, the people who were arrested outside of that shoe factory, for instance."

"Or even," I added, "the millions of people whose lives seemed to be improving who are about to discover just how bad things can get under capitalism."

"Is this pessimism or prescience talking?"

"A little of both, I guess." I had decided to distance myself from the old fortune-telling sideshow identity, except in my *Corking Tales* work.

"I'm afraid you're probably right," she sighed. "They're already saying that half the houses on Broadway will be closed by next Christmas. Maybe that's alarmist. I don't know. Either way, it's not exactly the Irish Potato Famine, but I guess we could get there if this goes on long enough. The people who still have money—and there are lots of them—just aren't spending it."

"It's an insane way to run a country." I got up on my soapbox. "Relying on a bunch of con men, who've already made their millions, to keep the rest of us off the breadline? Every piddling drib of 'prosperity' that we get is just come-on money, a ploy to suck more societal energy into the pot; and if these guys ever decide to stop being 'greedy,' cash in their chips, and run away to Tahiti, it's game over for everybody else."

I could have made the exact same speech in 2010, and I would've had to have gone back a lot farther than 1930 to find a situation it didn't describe.

"Good Lord, Douglass! In the old days, if any mouth other than mine had dared to profane this room with that kind of talk, Pat would have knocked every tooth out of it."

"Any mouth *but* yours?"

"Well, I guess mine was too pretty to punch."

"That's pretty condescending."

"Very." She smiled a little too wistfully for my liking. "I used to tell him that his weakness for the *prolegtariat* would trip him up in the end."

"The prolegtariat, hunh?" I seized my moment. "That's exactly what this script should be about...."

By the time I left Eileen's place that evening, we had completed the first draft of a treatment for *Chorines in Arms* (although she didn't come up with the title until about a month later).

Chapter Twenty

My first trip through the winter of 1930 had been a blur of discovery and frustration. That pace slackened considerably the second time around, but my experience of this once-dead world remained profoundly jarring and conflicted. Perhaps even more so. As the days slogged by, I was increasingly torn between the maddening urge to analyze every timeline repetition and deviation I observed and the impulse to simply fast-forward myself to the May 2nd premiere.

Of course, I never seriously considered the latter option. For one thing, my uncanny encounter in the morgue had confirmed that I had no idea how this time travel business actually worked. Any recourse to the watch now seemed like a very risky proposition indeed. If I wasn't careful, I was liable to bring down a plague of Infantinos upon the early 1930s. And even if I had managed to recapture some of that lost chrono swagger, I didn't dare abandon Eileen now that she had severed her ties with the Corellis and adopted me as a virtual sibling.

The friendship continued to gather momentum, as did our screenwriting partnership. Eileen made a wonderful collaborator, maybe too wonderful. I lost a lot of sleep worrying about the potential consequences of my bungling intrusion into her creative process. I deferred to her historically proven ideas whenever possible, but she insisted on letting me write nearly half of the dialogue for our spec script of *Chorines in Arms*. I did the best I could, but only time would tell how many of my lines would actually make it into the finished film—and what effect they would have on its all-important reception at the box office.

Those concerns were nerve-wracking, but at least every Eileen-centred minute of this second tour of duty felt completely fresh and unrehearsed. For better or worse, Pat's death had reshuffled the chronological deck with regard to that relationship. Instead of the "friend of the family," I had *become* her family—and this time I participated far more fully in the drama of her gradual acceptance, and even embrace, of the biological changes that she had been dreading. (In early March, she interrupted a writing session to put my hand on her belly, which my mother was busily assaulting from within.)

On the other hand, I could certainly have done without the tedious shot-for-shot remake of my daily grind at the *Corking Tales* office. I'll admit there was a certain fascination in being the only self-aware variable in a room full of constants, but that novelty wore off pretty quickly. I remembered the punchline to every one of Katz's jokes (very few of which had been funny the first time around). I knew exactly how badly our circulation numbers would fall off in March. I edited each new batch of stories with a mental mimeograph.

This endless déjà vu could be dull and a little maddening, but I never considered quitting the magazine. After all, I had a reputation as a hack writer to build, and besides, I liked Tom Katz. I just didn't like seeing him in the role of fate's caustic automaton.

So I did what I could to keep things in flux. I came in late on a regular basis, hoping to land slightly different assignments. No dice. I just wound up working a lot of evenings. I asked Doreen out in an effort to get her uncle's patriarchal goat. That got me nowhere, as the receptionist made a pretty convincing show of her utter indifference to my charms. We did grab a few platonic lunches though—and even went to a couple of Yankee games in April. (Babe Ruth and Lou Gehrig were still at the top of their respective games in 1930, but the team was destined to be overshadowed by Lefty Grove's Philadelphia Athletics this season.) I called in an anonymous tip about fire code violations in our building. (That kind of backfired, as Katz ordered me to clean out the archive with his nephews.) And I turned in some truly outrageous stories, just to generate a little controversy around the office.

The last tactic bore entertaining fruit one sunny mid-March morning, when Katz dropped a few agitated fingers on my shoulder as I settled in at my desk.

"What the hell is this story, Douglass?" he asked.

"This 'Cream of the Crop'?"

"Ah, yes." I sipped my coffee and flashed a self-satisfied grin. "That one's a keeper."

"A keeper?" He stooped closer, peering into my eyes. "Maybe as evidence at your *insanity* hearing it's a keeper."

"Are you kidding?" I stood up, returning his bewildered glare. "That piece is *textbook* scientifiction."

In fact, I stand by that assertion, although I prefer to call the genre "speculative fiction" when I'm out of earshot of 1930s types. "Cream of the Crop" is narrated by an acerbic H.L. Mencken–worshiping reporter who lucks into covering a wild and woolly sequel to the infamous Scopes Monkey Trial of 1925. This second coming of fundamentalist fury takes place in Jackson, Mississippi, during the imminent presidential election year of 1932. I started writing the story after learning that Mississippi had in fact passed anti-evolution legislation the year after the real Mencken and lawyer Clarence Darrow had dragged the State of Tennessee kicking and ranting through the national headlines. Unlike the Scopes affair, which was a test case choreographed by the American Civil Liberties Union, proceedings in my fictional trial are initiated by a demagogic Baptist preacher (the Reverend Timothy Barker) who claims that the Great Depression is the Lord's judgment upon an increasingly "pagan" America.

The sacrificial target of this crusade is the Jackson Board of Education, which tries to slip a pre-university biology elective into the curriculum of its two most prosperous high schools. After some meticulous scene-setting by my narrator, the trial is about to commence. With the eyes (or, at any rate, the ears) of the nation upon this arena for cultural conflict, observers and antagonists on both sides are all set to savour another round of wrangling over the origins of humanity. But before anyone can launch a single sanctimonious salvo, a large polka-dotted and multitentacled creature appears on the steps of the courthouse, hovering at the heart of the media circus. The thing ignores all interview requests and makes its way inexorably toward the witness stand.

"Hello, there." The squidlike being introduces itself (although no one is quite certain where the sounds are coming from, since the alien does not appear to have a mouth). "In the Alpha Centauri system, where I am from, we do not use names, but I would be delighted if you would call me Farmer John."

The courtroom erupts into hysterical laughter, which patrician Judge Ambrose Boynton manages to gavel down after a few minutes. One hooligan brandishes a gun and takes a potshot at the alien, but the bullet travels wide of the mark, and deputies drag the would-be assassin off to the hoosegow.

Farmer John then apologizes for missing the big 1925 trial, explaining that it takes a long time (in human years) to reach the Earth from Alpha Centauri. He laments that the State of Mississippi has been put to the unnecessary expense of yet another legal confrontation on the subject of evolution.

"I was sent here to settle this matter once and for all." The alien spreads its tentacles earnestly. "It would be cruel of us to allow you to go on bothering your brains about these things."

At this point, Judge Boynton warns the alien that such patronizing language is grounds for a contempt of court charge. Suitably chastised, Farmer John adopts a very respectful tone as he reveals that his people live for billions and billions of years. The Alpha Centaurians are a peaceful, prosperous race, with no natural or political enemies and a real talent for enjoying their extravagantly long lives. They're also quite fond of interstellar travel. In fact, Farmer John had visited the Earth as recently as four billion years ago—although this had been no mere sightseeing trip.

"I had a batch of pre-ionized carbon seeds in my trunk," he tells the crowd, "and I tossed them onto the lake of fire that still covered this planet at the start of the growing season. I was just doing my job. I am not, despite the strident claims made in so many of your books and political documents, a 'god.'"

Here again the courtroom swells with the sounds of panic and nervous amusement, and again Judge Boynton exerts his calming magisterial influence.

"Can you please clahrify that statement, suh?" the stern-visaged official asks Farmer John. "Are you tellin' this court that *you* are our Divine Creator?"

"Certainly not!" Farmer John protests. "If anyone can lay claim to that title, I suppose it would have to be the agricultural biotechnology company that designed the seeds. All I did was plant them in an appropriately molten environment and let your sun do the rest. I spent the rest of the growing season on a nice vacation with my family in Andromeda."

Judge Boynton scratches his silvery hair. "The growin' season? What on Euth are you referrin' to, suh?"

"Well, it takes a certain amount of time, about four billion of your years, in fact, for those seeds to develop into the crop my people prize above all others."

"*Develop*, suh? Do you mean to hover there and tell us that this diahtribe of yours has been submitted in defense of a mohrahlly dubious scientific theory which has been outlahwed from this state's educational institutions?"

"Oh, I suppose I am." Farmer John doesn't nod because he doesn't have a head. "Although *evolution* is a pretty ostentatious term for a process that was predetermined from the start. These seeds have been around for thousands of seasonal cycles—and they always produce the same wonderful fruit."

"Preposterous!" the judge ejaculates. "The very idea that our beautiful green Euth is just an Alpha Centaurian gahden patch!"

"I am afraid you have described the situation perfectly, Judge Boynton. Moreover, the produce is just about ripe."

"Well, suh, you might have us beat in the tentacle depahtment, but I do believe we've got a considerable edge in fireahms!" The judge gestures for a bailiff to take the alien away. "We aren't goin' to give up our veg-etation without a fight, suh, I can promise you that!"

"No need to worry." Farmer John wraps a tentacle around the judge's head. "We are not here for the 'veg-etation.'"

The lifeless magistrate slumps face first onto his gavel.

"Ah." The alien smacks non-existent lips. "Upper-crust, bourgeois, democratic brains! Delicious!" He ad-dresses the petrified onlookers: "By the way, I'd like to retract my statement about evolution. That brain *was* qualitatively better than anything I've ever tasted be-fore. There appears to have been some unforeseen im-provement on this planet after all."

THE END

"Yeah, Douglass." Katz knocked on my forehead. "It's a good yarn. But I can't publish it this way. We got *readers* in the South, fer Chrissakes!"

"So what?" I countered. "They're not fundamental-ists, are they?"

"I dunno." He shrugged. "Probably not. That's not our crowd, Douglass. But I don't like this pokin' fun at a respecktable Southern judge. We'll have crosses burnin' on 29th Street! Rewrite it so's it's set in Canada, and I'll make it the cover feature next month."

I spent the rest of the day happily reworking the story to suit the magazine's needs. Later on, while strolling home, I remembered with a twinge of remorse that this new twist in the timeline would rob little Jimmy Kushner of his April cover sale.

Chapter Twenty-One

Doreen poked her head into the editorial office.

"Douglass." Her eyes narrowed as they hit the wall of cigarette smoke. "Your sister's on line one."

"My sister?" I looked up from a particularly incoherent giant ant attack story that I'd been jabbing with the blue pencil all morning.

"That's what she claims."

I picked up the phone. "H'lo, sis."

"Did you pick up your suit?" Eileen asked nervously.

"Not yet." I turned around and consulted the small black clock on Tom Katz's desk (it was nearly 1:15 p.m.). The editor's big armchair was empty, but the half-cigarette on the rim of his ashtray was still very much present. I crushed it out. "I'm taking a late lunch today. I'll run over to the tailor's as soon as Katz comes back. I get a lot more work done when he isn't here."

Sam, the lone nephew on letter-opening duty that day, snickered from his corner of the room.

"All right." Eileen's voice sounded anything but all right. "Just don't forget about it. This is a big night."

There was no question about that. It was Friday,

May 2, 1930. The premiere was at hand. A white-tie event if ever there was one. (And there never had been one, in my life, before this moment.)

"I'm not going to forget. Will you be able to nap?"

"I hope so."

"Me too. Just think of it this way: The hard part's over. The performance is already in the can. All you have to do tonight is bask in their adulation."

"Ah, Douglass, you don't understand the performer's soul. I don't get nervous before a show. The basking's the trouble, especially when I'm carrying this much ballast."

"You look incredible, Eileen. Get some rest." I hung up before she could go any further down that oft-travelled road.

Doreen reappeared in the doorway. "Nice pep talk, Douglass. You really know how to reassure a woman." She left again.

I looked at the manuscript on my desk. The big ants were raiding dairy farms, searching for big aphids. I put down the pencil and retrieved my hat from the rack.

I picked up the suit.

◆

Located just a bit north of Times Square, on West 50th Street, the Roxy was the Chrysler Building of New York film palaces—the biggest name in town for about two seconds, until Radio City Music Hall stole its thunder in 1932. Built just a couple of years before my arrival, the theatre's colonnaded rotunda-style "Grand Foyer," golden 6,000-seat auditorium, regimental ushers, 110-piece symphony orchestra, and Broadway calibre stage shows had already achieved legendary status. Owned by Fox, a major studio that would soon fall prey to Depression woes of its own, the Roxy was *the* place to premiere a big movie in the spring of 1930, and booking a film there can't have been cheap. After launching soon-to-be Best Picture–winner *All Quiet on the Western Front* at the much smaller Central Theatre in late April, Universal was pulling out all of the stops with *King of Jazz*.

The public responded accordingly, with reporters and other enthusiasts thronging the 50th Street sidewalk outside of the theatre and the adjoining Manger Hotel. There wasn't enough runway out there to accommodate a proper red carpet, but the event's promoters had compensated for this by transforming the imposing lobby, which boasted "the world's largest oval rug," into a perfect media echo chamber.

Every moment of the affair was carefully orchestrated. Stars and other studio personnel arrived in a prescribed order, generally in an alternating pattern between major and minor celebrities. Our limousine pulled up just as Laura La Plante was bidding adieu to her fans across America, so I suppose that placed Eileen firmly in the "minor" camp. However, any viewer who paid attention to "Cynthia Ward's" mini-interview when the newsreel hit the theatres would certainly come away from it with the impression that this young woman was being groomed for greatness.

Photographed from the collarbone up, she looked incredible in a diaphanous white wrap that set off her dark hair and pert hazel eyes in striking fashion, while hinting subtly at voluptuous curves just beneath the frame. Despite this visual gambit, there was no attempt to conceal the fact of Eileen's "delicate condition," not when it offered such exploitable pathos. The announcer, a mustachioed and bespectacled man with one of those clipped '30s voices that simply don't exist in the 21st century fed her a leading question about Pat's tragic absence from the event.

Eileen's reply came direct from a press agent's pen: "I miss him so much, but I know he'll be watching from the best seat in the house tonight. And soon I'll have Pat, Jr. beside me."

Of course, she had no intention of naming the baby after Pat, even if it did turn out to be a boy (which it wouldn't), but America didn't need to know that. The movie magazines, and even the legitimate press, had been pushing her sob story all week, obviously at Universal's behest, and Eileen's treacly little offering was intended to supply the star-making catharsis.

I even got to contribute a little fake smile to the cause in my role as the supportive brother on her arm. Then a studio operative led us into the vast, gilded

Spanish-style theatre, seating us in the front row (a considerable distance from the centre-stage preserve of luminaries such as the Laemmles, Bing Crosby, La Plante, John Boles, Jeanie Lang, John Murray Anderson, Mary Nolan, Joseph Schildkraut, Pál Fejös, and their dates). Paul Whiteman, the star of the movie, began the evening in the orchestra pit, conducting a rousing version of Gershwin's "Rhapsody in Blue" (with the composer himself at the piano).

King of Jazz was a revelation. The two-strip Technicolor, so dull and washed out on my early-'90s VHS copy, fairly glowed in its original presentation. It didn't look remotely "real," but the process lent a warm storybook quality to the unusual images (ostensibly drawn from "Paul Whiteman's scrapbook") paraded across the screen by first-time film director Anderson.

The show gets off to a fascinating start with a politically noxious but beautifully animated (by Walter Lantz, later of Woody Woodpecker fame) cartoon fable in which Whiteman hits upon the "hot" notes that will make him "King of Jazz" while eluding predators on safari in Africa. Then, in an expertly crafted double-exposure sequence, the jovial bandleader unpacks the miniaturized members of his orchestra from a small satchel, to the astonished delight of MC Charles Irwin. When these shrunken soloists and sidemen blossom into fully fledged performers, the movie kicks into high gear, running through a succession of breathtaking pop numbers, all glimpsed through the lens of a surprisingly (for 1930) agile camera and underscored with Easter egg pinks and blues.

I enjoyed nearly every minute of it, from the Rhythm Boys' (a "hot jazz" vocal trio led by emerging superstar Bing Crosby) renditions of "So the Bluebirds and the Blackbirds Got Together" and "Happy Feet" to John Boles' anthemic "Song of the Dawn" to Jeanie Lang's Betty Boop–ish "I Like to Do Things for You" to the on-screen orchestra's surreal reprise of "Rhapsody in Blue" (delivered from within the confines of a gigantic, and appropriately azure, grand piano).

There were a bunch of vaudeville-style comedy skits sprinkled throughout the film's running time, none of which came very close to making me laugh, but the director wisely cut each one short just before gangrene set in.

Eileen's spot came on the heels of a particularly silly World War I sketch called "All Noisy on the Western Front," in which doughboys Whiteman, Slim Summerville, Walter Brennan, and half the rest of their battalion all show up on the doorstep of lovely French peasant girl "Marie," who tells each one in turn how devoted her love is before pushing him into a closet at the sound of the next paramour's knock. The "Body and Soul" number was considerably more inspired, with a lilting orchestration that complemented Eileen's sweet jazz voice perfectly and more double-exposure trickery to create her astral duet partner. She even sparked up a playfully amorous chemistry with the portly, avuncular

Whiteman, the supposed object of her physical and spiritual affection.

The production's only real misstep, from my perspective, came during the "Melting Pot" finale, which brought together most of the show's songs in a pitched sound collage against a backdrop of multicultural fusion that somehow failed to include any non-European elements. Not a very convincing "Origin of Jazz." However, by that point in the evening, my attention had shifted pretty decisively away from the screen. I sort of lost the plot once I spotted Helen Chandler sitting just across the aisle.

Chapter Twenty-Two

Some classic Hollywood legends have entered the general cultural lexicon: Selznick's search for his Scarlett, the Kennedys and Norma Jean, James Dean living fast and dying young. Many slightly more esoteric tales will be familiar to casual film fans: Hearst's war on *Kane*, John Gilbert's mic and bottle troubles, Judy Garland's diet pills. And then there are the stories that only the most obsessed aficionados ever get wind of. The Helen Chandler saga falls pretty definitely into the third category.

I first encountered this unique actress as Mina in the Bela Lugosi version of *Dracula* (1931)—the only one of her films that attained anything like "classic" status. It was the lead feature in a PBS "Scare Up the Pledges" drive one late-'80s Halloween. Made by director Tod Browning at Universal, the movie has a lot going for it, from Lugosi's iconic performance to Karl Freund's eerie cinematography to Dwight Frye's deranged turn as realtor-turned-henchman Renfield. However, that first night, I paid more attention to the bizarre possums roaming the Count's Transylvanian crypt, the fake bat hovering flimsily over the balcony, Jonathan

Harker's po-faced exclamation "*my that's a big bat*," and the mischievous blonde actress who seemed even more amused by these things than I was.

Some might argue that Chandler's skewed performance in *Dracula* throws the entire film off-kilter. And perhaps it does but in the best way possible. Quite simply incapable of playing the simpering ingénue role as written, she wafts through the narrative on the evanescent wings of a smirk: delivering the world's first Lugosi impression (for the benefit of her infatuated friend Lucy), matter-of-factly discussing her vampiric possession with Professor Van Helsing, staring wanly into space at the behest of that big plastic bat, and erupting out of her pallor to sink wide blue-eyed daggers into David Manners' neck.

I treasured Chandler's Mina, revisiting the film every Halloween, but it would be more than a decade before I'd get a chance to see her in any other role (Turner Classic Movies eventually obliged me). By then, I'd read every scrap of material ever published about the actress and had forced those ill-matching puzzle pieces to yield a very unsatisfying portrait of her life.

Born in New York in 1906, she spent most of her earliest years in Charleston, where her father raised racehorses until South Carolina outlawed the "sport of kings." The Chandlers returned to Helen's native city sometime around her tenth birthday, and they promptly enrolled their precocious daughter at the Professional Children's School, in the Entertainment

District. From there, she made a quick leap to the Broadway stage, playing a number of key roles, including Hedvig in Ibsen's *Wild Duck* at the age of seventeen. A few years later, she got a yen to crash the film industry and talked her way into a contract at Fox, after barging unannounced into the studio's New York HQ on 10th Avenue. Unfortunately, Fox had no real idea what to do with the unorthodox contract player.

Prone to jerky movements and a little bit strange-looking, with a jagged-nosed profile that prompted her to tell an interviewer "when they turn me sideways to the camera, I look like the edge of a Bible," Chandler brought a disconcertingly "flavourful" quality to even the smallest, most innocuous roles. She did have remarkably "starry" Lillian Gish–type eyes and the petite build to play the latter's "soulful waif" parts, but producers were reluctant to unleash her wry insouciance in such solemn contexts. She spent most of the late '20s on the stage, waiting for Hollywood to create the proper cinematic niche for her talents.

Things finally began to break her way in 1930, when she was cast opposite Douglas Fairbanks, Jr. as one half of a suicidal romantic couple in the otherworldly *Outward Bound*. Based on a popular play, the atmospheric drama concerns the adventures of several confused passengers aboard a mysterious fog-enshrouded ship, later revealed as the ferry to the "other side." I couldn't remember exactly when *Outward Bound* was due to appear in theatres, but as I watched

King of Jazz's end titles bounce off Chandler's eyes, it occurred to me that she had probably just finished filming it.

I did recall reading that she had married the film's screenwriter, Cyril Hume, in February. Latter-day commentators described the union as unstable from the words *I do*. In any event, that night at the Roxy, a mere three months after their wedding, I saw no evidence of the groom. What I did see was a long-admired classic film actress on the cusp of the period of her greatest success. In 1931 alone, she would star in *six* movies, including *Dracula*, *Daybreak*, and my personal favourite, *The Last Flight*.

The Last Flight plays like a more whimsical, but still very emotionally charged, adaptation of Hemingway's *Sun Also Rises*, complete with drunken World War I vets and bullfighting but with the crucial addition of a distractedly comradely lady named Nikki, apparently based on Helen herself.

Unfortunately, it would all be downhill from there. Critics (especially *The New York Times*' Mordaunt Hall) would champion the actress' work and embrace her quotable persona, calling her "The Chandler," but the public would never warm to her. By 1933, she'd be reduced to supporting roles, and soon even those would evaporate. Her erratic behaviour, considered charming during the early '30s, would intensify to the point of impossibility—as would her drinking. Marriages and divorces would pile up, until terrible burns suffered in a 1950 apartment fire would drive her even further into herself. She would live on for another fifteen years, spending many of them in mental institutions, before succumbing to a heart attack and a very sparsely attended funeral at the age of fifty-nine. Her fate wasn't so different from the one that might have claimed Eileen—except that Helen's luck would give out before her liver did.

The lights went up at the Roxy.

"Who's that?" I poked Eileen.

"That?" She followed the line of my surreptitious gaze. "That's Helen Chandler."

"You know her?"

"Well, I've met her. She seems worth knowing, though. A real screwball, in a good way. You want me to introduce you?"

I almost said yes, but the actress' cock-eared body language convinced me that I could just do the job myself.

I stood up and stepped into the aisle.

She saw me coming a mile away.

"Hello, Cynthia's brother." She smiled.

"Hello." I extended a hand.

She took it. "No matter how full the room is, when I hear the word *screwball*, I know somebody's talking about me." She delivered the line with enough volume to catch the attention of the "somebody" in question.

I turned in time to see Eileen's bashful shrug, before she plunged into some kind of a conference with her agent.

I sat down next to Helen.

"Did you enjoy the movie?" I asked her.

"Delightful!" Her eyes lit up. "Although I'm a little cross that no one wants to film *my* scrapbook."

"What's in it?"

"Oh, the usual assortment of dried leaves, theatre tickets, and spelling bee ribbons. Wouldn't you like to hear a Gershwin song about those things?"

"I like to hear Gershwin songs about anything."

"Exactly."

I felt comfortable already. "Are you here alone?"

She nodded. "Aside from all these people."

In fact, many of those people, including my "sister," were now filing out of the auditorium. I waved at Eileen, but the intervening swarm of studio types kept her from noticing. There was no question in my mind that she was well on her way to signing that seven-year contract.

"Shall we join them?" I stood and offered her my hand.

Helen looked around quizzically. "You want to go where they're going?"

"I'd like to go where you're going."

She rose and smoothed down her silky black dress. "So where are we going?"

It was that simple.

We walked up 8th Avenue to Columbus Circle, where we ducked into Central Park despite the lateness of the hour. Helen wasn't the kind of person who feared, or even thought about, the possibility of a midnight garroting, and I did my best to keep pace, although I am exactly that kind of person. It was a warm, clear night, and my companion seemed to know just what to do with it. She led me deep into the park, toward the Sheep Meadow, which I had always known as a place to fly kites or sunbathe but which actually was a sheep meadow in 1930.

"Of course." She tossed her heels over the fence and clambered after them. "At the moment, the sheep are all tucked away in their fold, on the other side of West Drive, which is too bad because they're quite personable." She planted her bare feet in the fresh spring grass and urged me to follow suit. "Come *on*, Douglass!"

I complied with far less reluctance than was customary with me. We settled under an old elm tree on the cusp of the lawn.

"She's my favourite tree in the park." She patted its bark. "I've been visiting her since I was a kid."

I studied the trunk carefully. "What, no initialled heart?"

"Shh!" She cupped a small hand over my mouth. "I rarely carve anything in my friends."

"Point taken," I mumbled through her cool fingers.

"Good." She relaxed her grip.

"Do you come here with your husband?" I felt obliged to ask.

"Oh, Douglass, please." She grinned. "You're not stuffy, so why behave as if you were?"

"You make a compelling argument."

"I also make a compelling pumpkin pie. Is that the kind of conversation you're looking for?" Her eyes made you feel that you could say and do things that no human being ever had before.

"Definitely not," I said. "I...want to know how you knew that this tree was the one."

"Oh, I didn't know." She slid her head down onto a gnarled root pillow. "I just decided."

"Isn't that the same thing?"

"No."

I got as close to her as I could. "How long are we going to stay here? Until the sheep reclaim the meadow?"

She shook her head and brushed my nose. "Until the shepherds drive us off."

Chapter Twenty-Three

The next morning, Esther Duncan caught me halfway up the stairs.

"You have a good night?" she asked with her trademarked insinuating benevolence.

"So it would seem." I groped sleepily for the bannister.

"What's this?" She pinched the hem of my trousers. "Grass stains?"

"Yeah." I surveyed the extent of the damage, which was by no means limited to the pants.

"You're coming up in the world, Douglass. Not many people can afford to ruin such a suit."

I pulled a crumpled piece of paper out of my pocket. There was a number written on it. "But I still don't have a telephone."

"You wanna call somebody?"

"Sure." I smiled. "You'll like this one."

"All right then." Her excitement was palpable.

She put on a pot of coffee, and I reached for the phone.

"Medallion 2893," I told the operator.

"Is that the New Yorker Hotel?" Esther whispered at me.

I put my hand over the transmitter. "How could you possibly know that?" I asked her with genuine awe.

"Douglass," she said matter-of-factly, "it's *only* the biggest hotel in town."

"You never leave this building!"

"Best place in the world to hear about a grand opening."

"I guess that's true."

The 2,500-room art deco hotel on 8th Avenue had launched its illustrious career just after New Year's.

"New Yorker Hotel," a cultured desk clerk enunciated on the other end of the line.

"Ah, hello," I greeted him, "can you connect me with room 304? Ms. Helen Chandler."

"Helen Chandleh?" Esther poked me. "From *The Sky Hawk?*"

I knew that Helen had done a few inconsequential films before *Outward Bound*, but it had never occurred to me that they actually had names.

"I bow to your outrageous omniscience."

"Ah." She patted my arm. "You're a sweet kid."

"Hello, Cynthia's brother," Helen answered.

"Hey," I said softly, turning toward the wall, "what if I was someone else?"

"You'd be confused."

"I think I am anyway."

"It's perfectly natural. These are confusing times. Everybody says so."

"You said it."

I peeked over my shoulder at Esther. She went to check on the coffee.

"So when will I see you again?" I asked in as unmelodramatic a tone as I could muster.

"I'm going back to California this afternoon," she replied in her wistful deadpan. "It'll have to be there."

"Then that's where it'll be. Travel safely, Helen."

"I'll convey your request to the engineer."

I hung up and dialled Eileen's place.

She answered on the first ring. "Hello?"

"Hi."

"Where on Earth did you disappear to?"

"Oh," I dodged, "we can talk about that when I see you. What happened with the contract?"

"It's all signed," she replied. "I'm theirs for seven years, starting October 13th. I've got to be filmworthy by then."

"Amazing!"

"Yes, but, Douglass, I was supposed to introduce you around, remember?"

"Aw, I'm sorry," I purred, "but that newsreel stuff really spooked me. I'm strictly a behind-the-scenes kind of guy."

"Well"—her tone softened—"not to worry. I spent half the night talking to Carl, Jr. and E.M. Asher, an associate producer on the lot. They asked me what kind of a film I'd like to star in. I don't think they expected anything too definite from me, but they asked for it. So I brought them back to my apartment, handed them our script, and told them: '*This* kind of a film.'"

"What'd they say?"

"Oh, you know how producers are. Asher said he'd give it his 'full attention.' But the gag'll be on him because it is the perfect vehicle for me, and it's so timely!"

History, I knew, would prove her right.

"Oh, and I told him that you wrote the whole thing," she added. "So if they want to make the movie, they'll have to sign you."

"Eileen, *you* wrote the whole thing! And it's really good. Don't you want people to know it?"

"Don't be silly, Douglass. They don't give writing credits to actors. Unless they're Noel Coward. And people will know everything I need them to know when they see my performance."

"Eloquently put," I conceded. "But it's still a damned shame." A burst of panic overwhelmed me. "Hey, wait a minute! Are you sure he hasn't just tossed the whole thing in the trash? That's what I'd probably do with some nebbishy brother's script."

"This is Universal, Douglass. They understand nepotism. He'll read the first page. And when he does, he'll read the rest."

"I hope you're right." I understated my feelings dramatically.

"Trust me. I am."

"You're a paragon of confidence this morning, aren't you?"

She laughed. "If you'd stuck around last night,

you'd know why."

"I'm really sorry about that. It couldn't be helped. The movie was incredible though. Well, your number was. And the Rhythm Boys stuff. And the 'Rhapsody in Blue' segment. I loved the way Anderson shot 'Song of the Dawn,' too. It's just too bad Bing didn't sing it."

"Oh, they wanted him to, but a judge gave him forty days for drunk driving right before they were scheduled to shoot. So they brought in John Boles— who's a lot more fun in person than he looks on the screen, by the way."

"Really? I don't think I ever heard that story."

"About John Boles?"

"About Bing's sentence."

"Well, why would you have, Douglass?" She sounded mildly unsettled, as she did whenever I made one of my anachronistic slips. "It just happened."

"It just sounds like something the gossip columns would have printed, that's all."

"Ah, Douglass"—her voice relaxed—"you wouldn't believe what a studio publicist can do."

"Oh, I think I know, after that red carpet family re-union last night."

"I'm really sorry about that. I guess it was just another one of those things that couldn't be helped."

"*Touché*, mon amie."

"You're welcome."

"I'll talk to you soon."

I cradled the receiver.

Esther gave me a lukewarm cup of coffee and a police detective's squint. "Is she *really* your sister?"

Chapter Twenty-Four

The spring sped swiftly by. I worked hard on my scientification, pitching the new stories in an especially horrific key in the hopes of reselling them to Universal, which was just on the cusp of its monster movie phase. (*Dracula* would premiere in early 1931.) But I didn't hear a peep from the studio, or from Helen for that matter.

"I wouldn't worry," Eileen counselled as we strolled in Hudson Park with Lulu one evening in mid-June. "About the script, I mean. I'm sure they're just playing cagey with us. I would worry *a* lot about Helen, though, if she ever calls you again."

I had broken down and told her everything about my night in Central Park, against my better judgment. So far, widowhood had only reinforced Eileen's rather prim view of sexual relations.

I nodded. "Maybe, but that's not going to keep me from picking up the phone. A night like that has to lead somewhere."

"Do you have any idea how ominous that sounds?"

The dog exerted all of her might to divert us toward the St. Luke's Place entrance to the park, where she continued her reign of vandalism by pissing on a marble sarcophagus dedicated to three fallen members of Eagle Fire Engine Company No. 13.

"Are you sure you don't want me to take the leash?" I asked.

"Don't try to change the subject, Douglass."

"I'm not," I protested. "I just...."

"Don't think an eight-and-a-half-month pregnant woman can do anything by herself?"

"Okay." I grinned. "I was trying to change the subject."

"I don't fall for that stuff anymore. I'm practically a mother. We're pretty hard to fool."

"Sure. But don't forget: You're not my mother. And you wouldn't be my older sister either, if you actually were my sister. I've got more than ten years on you."

"Ten years of bachelorhood? What's that worth, really?"

"You'd be surprised."

"I imagine you'd get so cynical that you'd mistake any stray spark of romance for the Greatest Love That Ever Was."

"Okay, maybe you wouldn't be surprised."

"I'm sure it was a fascinating date, Douglass. But she's married. Also, she's a little bit crazy, from what I gather."

Now it was my turn to step up to the lectern. "That reputation isn't so hard to come by in a patriarchal culture like ours. All it takes is the right kind of crisis and the wrong kind of interested observer."

"Patriarchal?" she laughed. "We aren't living in the Old Testament, Douglass."

"We might as well be. How do you think people would have reacted if you had gone through with your plan last November?"

She grew quiet. "You're the one who talked me out of that."

"Yes, but not because I thought it was wrong or in any way immoral; I just wasn't sure you'd really thought it all through."

"No." She smiled slightly. "I hadn't. But I guess you're right. I could easily have done a lot of things that might have started tongues wagging, after Pat died."

"Exactly."

"Doesn't change the fact that she's married."

"No, but that's not an irreversible condition."

"Are you going to wait until she reverses it?"

"Well...I'll try."

"Fair enough." Eileen steered the dog toward Leroy Street.

"Homeward bound?" I asked.

She nodded. "Nora's coming in on the 20th Century Limited tonight. Did I tell you?"

I shook my head. "How's she doing?"

"I'm not exactly sure. She did say she had a surprise for me. Want to come see it for yourself?"

Of course I said yes.

The news from Chicago had been rather sporadic since Nora had returned there in January. We knew that she had broken her engagement and that she had not succumbed to any fatal diseases. That was it. I wondered how this version of Eileen's friend would compare to the one I had first met at the bridge game, in that now-discarded version of June 1930. Had our New Year's Eve talk changed anything (aside from the timing of her mid-year New York visit, which had definitely occurred a little earlier in the month the last time around)?

Nora pulled up in a cab around 10:00 p.m., looking radiant, as usual, in a silvery evening gown that she certainly hadn't worn all the way from Chicago. A well-dressed man toddled after her, lugging a pair of red alligator suitcases.

Lulu barked maniacally.

Eileen joined me at the windowsill. "Well, this is interesting."

The doorbell rang.

Eileen went to let them in.

A tumult of hugs and hellos swept the vestibule while I listened from the parlour. Amid this happy clamour, several crucial facts emerged. For instance, the man's name was Tom. He was a real estate developer in Kenosha, Wisconsin. He had a pleasant laugh. And he had married Nora just before boarding the train in Chicago.

"This is our honeymoon!" Nora exulted as she

stepped into the parlour. "Oh! Douglass! Eileen didn't tell us you were here." She latched onto my shoulders and reeled me in.

"Good to see you, Nora," I mumbled into perfumed blonde hair.

"You haven't met Tom yet." She beckoned toward the man in the dinner jacket. "Tom, this is Douglass. Eileen's brother. From Montreal."

I shook Tom's hand. "Pleased to meet you."

The tall, dark-haired swain grinned. "Douglass, there's a rumour going round that you're some kind of a saint."

Nora whacked him in the back of the head. Gently.

"I've always thought of myself as more of a bodhisattva," I replied.

"A body-what-va?" he laughed.

"I never know what he's talking about either," Eileen chimed in.

"It's Buddhist," Nora explained. "A bodhisattva's just an enlightened person who sticks around to help the rest of us out of jams."

"Sounds about right." I sat down on the couch.

"A regular guardian angel." Tom joined me.

"A most irregular one, I'd say," Nora qualified. "Unless clairvoyance is standard issue with bodhisattvas."

"I can't believe we're talking about me when there are newlyweds in the room," I protested.

"You're a lot more interesting, believe me." Nora cuddled up to her husband. "What do you do, sweetheart?"

"I build apartment houses," he said proudly.

"Pure conversational homicide." Nora smiled.

Eileen settled into the armchair on the other side of the marble coffee table. "Maybe so. But not deadly enough to get you out of telling us how you met."

"Oh, that," Nora laughed. "It was at the Field Museum. In April. The Sumerian exhibit. They had a lot of great stuff, including the Deluge tablet of the Akkadian version of the Gilgamesh story...."

"I was there for the dinosaurs," Tom yawned.

"I asked him if he knew where they were keeping the newly unearthed Kish ceramics," Nora continued.

"And I said, 'It's all Gilgamesh to me.'" Tom savoured his inane punchline.

Nora shot me a deadpan sidelong glance. "A recipe for modern romance," she concluded.

"Oh!" Eileen's spine straightened. "Would you excuse me for a moment?" She didn't wait for a reply.

"You think she saw Hamlet's ghost?" Nora asked slyly.

"Maybe she bought us a gift?" Tom mused.

"Tommy," Nora doted, "she didn't even know you existed until twenty minutes ago."

"I guess you're right."

"Nora?" Eileen's voice echoed weakly from the direction of the bathroom. "Could you come here for a minute?"

Nora got up and shrugged contentedly. "She needs me."

I turned to Tom. "So, you got married yesterday?"

"Yessiree," he beamed. "I guess you'd call it an elopement. We decided kinda quick. But we'll do something more official next year. On our anniversary: June 14th."

The letters and numbers somersaulted through my brain. "Do you mean tomorrow's the 16th?"

"Sure. Is that some kind of a Canadian holiday?"

"Yeah." I got up. "Sort of."

Nora sprinted back into the room. "You'd better call a cab, Douglass."

My mother was about to be born.

Chapter Twenty-Five

After an anxious cab ride down 14th Street and 1st Avenue, I found myself back at Bellevue Hospital for the first time since my harrowing encounter at the morgue. Thankfully, the maternity ward was in an entirely different pavilion. Eileen showed no outward sign of alarm, but as we waited together on uncomfortable wooden chairs in the admittance area, I remembered a pertinent scene from my childhood. It took place during one of my frequent overnight stays at Grandma's place in Turtle Bay.

I was probably about nine, and thrilled to be watching a Betamax tape of Ridley Scott's *Alien*, which my mother had repeatedly refused to rent for me. We were cozily installed under blankets on the beaten-up old plaid davenport in the den. I was halfway through a huge bowl of Neapolitan ice cream, and Grandma had downed a good many sherries. As the grim spaceborne tension reached out from the screen, I was beginning to suspect that my mother had been right for a change. I was scared as hell. And then, just as things seemed to be calming down a bit, John Hurt's chest blew wide open, taking what was left of my courage with it.

But before I could completely lose control, my laconic guardian put down her glass, pulled me tight against her miraculously intact torso, and said, "Believe me, Douglass, that's nothing compared to what your mother put me through."

I put my arm around Eileen's shoulder. "How are you feeling?"

"It could be worse." She patted my forearm. "I guess it will be worse."

"Maybe it'll go quickly?" I really had no idea what to say.

"Somehow, I don't think so." She smiled. "You've infected me with your premonitions.... On the bright side, I'm pretty sure it's gonna be a girl."

"Yeah?"

"I'll call her June."

"After the month?"

She dropped her face into her palm. "Oh, God. It *is* June, isn't it?"

"The 15th." I consulted my watch. "It'll be the 16th in about twenty minutes."

She straightened her back against the unforgiving chair. "Well, I'm naming her after June Mathis. The most important woman in Hollywood. Before me."

A nurse arrived with a wheelchair and helped Eileen into it.

"Stick around, Uncle Douglass." She waved as they rolled her away, leaving me to ponder the implications of this new bit of family trivia.

I had, of course, never doubted that my mother's name had derived from the date of her birth. She herself believed this to be the case, and it was a perfectly logical assumption, given the banality of life under Pat Corelli's regime. It was quite a revelation to discover that, even in my own timeline, Eileen had seen herself, if only for a very short period, as a person fit to carry the mantle of the silent era writer/producer of milestones such as *The Four Horsemen of the Apocalypse*, *Blood and Sand*, *Greed*, and *Ben-Hur*—a pioneer who had risen through the ranks at Metro to win what the *Los Angeles Times* had called "the most responsible job ever held by a woman," only to die of a heart attack in 1927 at the age of thirty-eight.

"Everything all right?" Nora's voice interrupted my dimension-spanning query into identity and film history.

"Oh." I looked up, probably a little distractedly. "Yes, I think so. She's with a doctor now."

"This is so exciting!" Tom chirped from somewhere behind her.

She turned and touched his shoulder. "Honey, do you think you can track down some coffee for us? There must be an all-night cafeteria in the building somewhere."

"I'll find it." He winked. "Don't worry about her, Douglass. She's gonna be fine." He wandered back to the admission desk to charm the nurse on duty.

"What do you think of him?" Nora settled into

Eileen's vacated chair.

"He's a ray of brawnshine."

"I know. It's ridiculous, isn't it?" She smiled.

"Oh, I wouldn't say that. I think it's pretty great. I wish I had his outlook."

"You wish you had his *shoulders*."

"Those too." I nodded. "So I guess this means you're staying in Chicago?"

"Yup." She lit a cigarette. "For the time being. It's a pretty great town, if you know the right speaks and keep out of garages on St. Valentine's."

"Love that municipal pride! Next you'll say the wind is bracing."

"It's been a bracing year."

"It sure has."

A little while later, Tom returned with a tray full of caffeine, setting it down on the little end table at my elbow. He handed a sugared and creamed cup to Nora.

"I wasn't sure what you take in yours, Douglass." He looked at me apologetically. "So I just left it black. Is that all right?"

"That's exactly right, Tom. Thanks."

"Ah, good. I had a feeling that'd be your speed."

I took a sip. The coffee was no better than its 2010 hospital counterpart would have been, but I welcomed it all the same.

"What do we do now?" Nora wondered.

Given my grandmother's future description of this birth, I assumed we were in for quite a wait.

"I guess this is a pretty strange way to kick off a honeymoon," I mused.

"Not at all." Tom grinned at Nora. "It's a preview of coming attractions."

That seemed to make her a little bit uncomfortable.

"How about a game of bridge?" I suggested quickly. "You play, don't you?" I took care to add, since our one and only partnering had been unceremoniously erased from the continuity.

"Are you kidding?" Nora's smile returned. "We've struck fear into the heart of the Midwest. But we'd need to find a fourth."

"I don't think that'll be hard." I gestured to the room full of expectant fathers, one of whom had been chain-smoking and playing solitaire the whole night.

"Looks like our man." Nora beckoned toward him. He was.

"My name's Sam Brodsky." The mildly dishevelled thirtysomething removed his porkpie hat. "I been here since ten in the mornin'."

"Everything all right?" Tom asked.

"Sure, they say this ain't unusual with a first birth. Especially since my wife's a little older. But, jeez, I don't think I ever wanna go through this again."

"What's your wife's name, Sam?" Tom seemed genuinely concerned. It made me wish I was too.

"Rosie," the man replied proudly, as if that said it all. And perhaps it did.

Sam dropped the cards onto the coffee tray and pulled the end table into the centre of the aisle. "What're we playin'? Poker?"

"Actually," Nora pounced, "bridge. Do you know it?"

"Yeah." He nodded. "I played a couple times. With my sister 'n' her family. They're sorta smart set types."

"Great!" She started shuffling.

Sam made a pretty decent partner, although he had a bad habit of doubling as a bluff. I hoped he had more luck with that at poker. We played six rubbers, and lost five, before a nurse brought the news of Rosie's triumph: A baby boy named Saul. Seven pounds and three ounces.

There were hugs and handshakes all around. Then Sam went on his merry way, leaving the cards behind as a gift.

We switched to three-handed hearts after that, with breaks for cafeteria runs. I drank even more coffee than I had downed on my last night in 2010.

Finally, just before noon the next day, June Corelli arrived safe and sound. I caught my first glimpse of her through a window, twitching redly in her cradle, just two newborns to the left of baby Saul.

Nora and Tom weren't permitted to visit the mother so soon after her ordeal, but as the "nearest living relative," I qualified.

Eileen welcomed me with open, if exhausted, arms. "I've gotta tell ya, Douglass...I don't think I've ever felt better, or *worse*, in my life."

"Makes perfect sense." I held her tightly. "A creature just burst out of your body. A beautiful creature, to be sure, but still, that's going to cause a strain."

"You've seen her?"

"I have. They don't come any sweeter. Or redder. Congratulations, Eileen."

"Thank you." Her eyes watered, and she was quiet for a moment. "Hey, did you know someone beat you to the bedside?"

"Really?" I guess I was pretty surprised. "Who? The Corellis?"

"Ugh." She winced. "Thank God, no.... E.M. Asher, the producer.... I guess my agent put him wise. He called the minute I snapped out of whatever stupor I was in. Not that I'm par-tic-u-lar-i-ly"—she had trouble with the word—"alert right now...."

"Now *that's* an employer!"

"Yeah, they're going all in. Makes me feel pretty good."

"You deserve it."

"And you know what else, Douglass?" Her squint contained equal parts grogginess and mischief. "They want to make *Chorines in Arms*! You should be hearing from them soon!"

It was the best news she could possibly have given me.

"I think I'm gonna pass out for a while, Douglass." She sank into her pillow. "See you later?"

I found Tom and Nora asleep on their chairs in the waiting room. Their contorted bodies didn't look very comfortable, but their blissful faces raised a pretty fair argument to the contrary. I left them in peace, grabbing a cab to Eileen's apartment, where Lulu made certain that I relived every agonizing minute of her fifteen-hour stay in solitary. I latched her leash to her collar and walked her back to my place, with an absurd amount of spring in my step.

I was finally going to Hollywood!

As usual, Esther Duncan caught me on the boarding house stairs.

"Douglass!" she called up to me. "You had a phone call!"

As excited as I was, and despite the likelihood that this call would seal the deal with Universal, I knew my tank was nearly tapped.

"Really?" I yawned. "That's great. I guess I'll call them later. They left a message, right? I've had a pretty gruelling night. Eileen had her baby."

"Oh, that's so wondaful!" Esther billowed up the stairs in her layered housecoats and hugged me. "And everything went well?" She stopped herself and shrugged. "What am I talking about? Of course it went well! She's a strong and healthy young girl, ain't she?" Her eyes sparkled. "Not like that fragile Helen Chandleh."

"Esther!" I nearly yelped. "Is that who called?"

"That's what she called husself." She smiled.

"And she left a number?"

"Of course."

Two minutes later, an operator was connecting me

to Los Angeles.

"Hello?" the strange voice fluted.

"Hi."

"Douglass?" she asked.

"It's me."

"I just heard the news."

"About Eileen's baby?"

"About your contract. Universal's going to hire you."

"That's what they tell me."

"So you're coming to California."

"In the fall. Definitely."

"Good." She hung up quickly.

"Was that supposed to be romantic?" Esther handed me a sandwich. I bit into it. Tuna fish on rye. Delicious.

"*Romantic*'s probably not the word."

"Then what is?"

I took another bite and shrugged. "I'll get back to you on that."

I grabbed Lulu's leash and waved goodbye to Esther. I thought the dog seemed a bit tentative as we mounted the stairs, but I chalked that up to my sleep-deprived state of mind.

"Hey, are you all right?" The landlady watched after me.

"I'm absolutely perfect," I called down as I unlocked my door and swung it open.

"That's what *you* think." Dorothea sat cross-legged

on my bed, reading a half-finished script. "You're about to step on time's banana peel."

Book Three

Chapter Twenty-Six

Lulu eyed the intruder with a muttering snarl. Dorothea gave as good as she got.

"Come in and close the door, please." She took gruff command. "We've got a lot to discuss."

I patted the dog's head and followed orders.

"How long has it been?" I sat down next to her.

"Since you told me you'd fallen in love with me?" She inched toward the opposite side of the bed. "About twenty-four hours."

I smoothed my hand along the blanket to her thigh. "It's been a heckuva lot longer for me."

She deflected the move. "Don't start with me, Douglass."

I gave up. "Okay. What's on your mind?"

"I told you." She stood up and paced to the window. "Your plan is about to combust."

"What're you talking about?" I flattened out onto the warm blanket, and Lulu joined me at the foot of the bed. "I haven't made a single wrong move."

"Tell that to the poor saps who are going to have to live in Glenn Beck's America."

The bed suddenly felt much less comfortable.

"I don't understand...."

She pulled a neatly folded piece of paper out of the back pocket of her jeans and flipped it to me. "Maybe that'll help," she said.

Reluctantly, I unfolded the page. It was a Wikipedia entry...on Douglass Infantino.

"Read it," she urged me.

I took a deep breath and dove in.

There was no photo, but the little box in the top right corner contained the following information:

Occupation:	Writer
Born:	February 3, 1894
	Montreal, Quebec, Canada
Died:	Sometime after February 13, 1931
	(disappeared in New York City)

That was ominous as hell.... I moved on to the main body of the piece:

Douglass Infantino was a Canadian pulp fiction author and screenwriter, active for a very short period during the early 1930s. Not much is known about Infantino's life before his work (including the classic story "Cream of the Crop") began appearing in the sci-fi magazine *Corking Tales*, where he also toiled as an editor for several months. The author enjoyed a very close relationship with up-and-coming

Broadway actress Eileen McWade, who claimed (without any corroborating evidence) to be his half-sister.

When McWade signed a contract with Universal Studios, changing her name to Cynthia Ward for the movies, Infantino followed her to Hollywood, writing the screenplay for her debut starring vehicle, *Chorines in Arms* (1931). He also conceived the original story and co-wrote the script (with the multitalented Ward herself) for the star's smash follow-up film, *Boxcar Honeymoon* (1931).

Soon after relocating to California, the screenwriter embarked upon a clandestine affair with married actress Helen Chandler. By all accounts, the relationship was a stormy one, aggravated by Chandler's drinking and depressive tendencies. The pair accompanied Ward to the New York premiere of *Chorines in Arms* at the Roxy Theatre on May 22, 1931. Sometime later that night, Infantino disappeared without a trace from the movie's after-party at the upscale speakeasy "21." The following day, Helen Chandler shot herself in her suite on the fortieth floor of the New Yorker Hotel.

Disheartened by these terrible events, Cynthia Ward announced her retirement immediately, cutting short a potentially brilliant film career at the age of twenty-four. She married prominent Pasadena realtor Carlton Lovering in March, devoting herself to family and charitable activities for the remainder of her long life.

Boxcar Honeymoon premiered to great acclaim during the fall of 1931, and two of Infantino's sci-fi/mystery scripts reached the screen the following year: *The Mutant* and *The Banshee*. Authorities found no evidence of foul play to account for the screenwriter's disappearance. He never resurfaced.

The printout was dated November 1, 2010.

I let it drop to the floor.

"Okay." I tried to smile. "Well, I guess that's not going to work."

Lulu seemed to lose interest in our conversation and hopped over to her food bowl near the window.

"No kidding." Dorothea patted the dog's head.

"So I'll handle things differently."

"I hope so." There was a threatening note in her voice. "Because this clearly *isn't* what I asked you to do."

"Give me a break, Dorothea! It's not easy managing all of these variables."

"Tell me about it. Especially the variable in your pants."

"Can we forget about that for a minute?" I protested.

"Believe me," she said diffidently. "It's forgotten."

The slight struck home—although I did my best not to show it.

"All right then," I said. "Can we talk a little bit about how all of this works?"

"How all of *what* works? Your obsession with unstable actresses?"

"No! Time travel."

Lulu finished her meal and lifted her nose toward the window. Suddenly, she turned toward me and barked.

"What is it, girl? A squirrel?" I asked her.

Dorothea slid the window up as far as it would go and pushed her head out toward the fire escape.

"I don't see anything." Her voice merged with the slow, torturous sounds of garbage collection vehicles in the alley.

"Come 'ere, Lulu." I made clucking noises. "Come on!"

The German shepherd reluctantly obliged me, curling up in a ball on my pillow. Within moments, she appeared to lose consciousness.

"So you want to know what the machine does to the space-time continuum?" Dorothea tried to pick up where we'd left off.

"Of course not. What I want is for you to explain how all of these different timelines relate to each other."

"*All* of these timelines?" She shook her head.

"Douglass, to my knowledge, there are exactly two. The original and the mess you're on the verge of creating. And I think that the relationship between them should be sufficiently obvious."

"Obvious?" I replied. "What could possibly be obvious about it? What happens to one timeline when the other one's in the ascendant? Or is that even the right way to think about it?"

"Oh, that." She shrugged. "How'm I supposed to know? That's more of a philosophical (or even a religious) question than a scientific one, Douglass. Heaven, hell, parallel dimensions. They could exist, I suppose. I kind of hope they do. But, by definition, they can't be apprehended scientifically. We have the tools to measure and analyze phenomena that occur in, at best, a tiny portion of this universe. Our instruments can't tell us anything about what's beyond it."

"So let me get this straight." I stared at her. "You spent forty-some-odd years in World...World X, let's say."

"World X." She nodded. "Fine."

"Then you take a little pleasure cruise back to 1929, tamper with the basic fabric of reality, and return expecting to find yourself in...what? World X plus?"

"No." She shook her head. "Call it World Y. Big or small, change is change. I knew that going in. You can't improve World X with the watch. You have to do that the old-fashioned way. Every time you use my machine, you're booking a one-way passage to World Y."

"And what the hell happens to World X?"

– 220 –

"As I said before"—her tone became especially professorial—"we have no way of knowing, Douglass. Maybe it goes on its merry way without me. Or maybe it just vanishes like last night's airy dream."

"And you're comfortable with that?"

"That's what science is all about. Becoming comfortable with uncertainty."

"That's not how they described it in high school."

"Don't get me started." A bit of warmth crept back into her voice. "But listen. Here's what I do know. Even if that pristine, beautiful World X still exists somewhere, with health care, free education, and a dollop of social justice for all, there's no way for *me*"—she drove her index finger into her breast—"to get back there. None at all. The best I can do is tamper with the fabric of *this* reality and hope that World Z is an improvement."

"All right." I took a deep breath. "That's about all the theory I can handle for now. I don't even want to think about how we all wound up in the same World if we're supposed to be jumping off the cosmic deep end every time."

"Douglass...naturally, everything in World Y will be exactly the same as World X, up until the moment you shift back in time. That includes previous time jumps that you and others have made. But who's this 'we all'?"

"I'm coming to that. I think it's time we started dealing with some facts."

"Facts are good. Let's hear 'em."

"Okay." I paused briefly to consider the best way of massaging the unwanted aspects of the truth out of the equation. "Let's start with the problem of three Dorotheas."

"*Three* Dorotheas?" Curiosity transformed her posture.

"That I know of...yeah.... There's the one who entrusted this mission to me." I extended a finger dramatically. "That wasn't you, was it?"

"You know it wasn't."

"Indeed." I nodded. "Well, I met her on November 2, 2010. The evening of that miserable midterm election, which is still a day away in your present, right?"

"Yes." She settled into Eileen's beloved armchair. "I read some dire predictions about it while ransacking the Internet for you."

"Dire is an understatement. And the world that ambushed Dorothea-1, after she returned from screwing up the timeline, or creating a brand new one, or however you want to describe it, was very similar in nearly every respect to the place you've just come from. Except that in the historical record she ransacked, Eileen McWade never even attempted to make the leap from stage to screen, Helen Chandler died in 1965 after a lifetime of torment, and Douglass Infantino never did anything worthy of a Wikipedia entry."

"Got it. Dorothea-1. Who's Dorothea-2?"

"She's the one who interrupted my mission the

first time. She had witnessed my foolhardy rescue tackle on Bleecker Street and stuck around this era (for seven months!) to study my movements. She finally confronted me in early June 1930. Showed up on my doorstep and forced me to admit that there was probably no way to get Eileen out to Hollywood with Pat Corelli in the picture. We also talked about a host of other things, and ended up having sex, which I enjoyed quite a lot."

Dorothea blushed.

"After we got dressed," I continued, "she headed back to pre-election 2010, while I reset my watch for Thanksgiving 1929 to take another kick at the can. And that's when I met you, Dorothea-3."

"I remember it like it was yesterday."

"So do I." I smiled. "But here's what neither of us knew then. Douglass-1, the guy who went back to save Pat Corelli, must have been lurking in the bushes in Abingdon Square while I talked you into leaving your park bench."

"What do you mean 'must have'? Did you actually see him?"

"Oh, I saw him. He turned up in the morgue about a month later. A couple of cops I'd run afoul of decided that we simply had to meet."

"Charming."

"Oh, they're great humanitarians, those two."

"That must have been horrible, Douglass. I'm so sorry. But then again, something like this was almost bound to happen, given the way you've been using the watch. Didn't Dorothea-1 tell you how to avoid these paradoxes?"

"Ah, now we're getting into it! Something practical for a change. I'm very much afraid she did not."

"God, what could she...what could *I*...have been thinking?"

"I'm afraid neither one of us was thinking very clearly. And I guess what's done is done. But you could explain it to me now. I'd like to avoid any future mishaps."

"Then you'd better follow protocol to the letter when you return to 2010. You don't want to be dop-pelgangered again."

"That would be most objectionable."

She smiled. "Well, you'd all have a tough time get-ting by on one paycheque."

"So what do I do?"

She stood up and slid onto the bed. "Do you know how to set the 'return' toggle?"

I adjusted the setting of the top button on the right. "Like that?" I said.

"Right. That's what you should have been doing all along. You have to make certain to return at precisely the same instant that you left."

"Great." I shrugged. "How'm I going to manage that now? I have no idea what time it was when I left 2010."

"That's not a problem, Douglass," she declared

proudly. "If you press all three buttons on the left at the same time, the watch will replay all of the journeys that it's made."

She performed the operation, and the watch leapt into action, displaying a time jump from 8:00 p.m., October 31, 2010, to 4:30 p.m., November 28, 1929.

"See," she said, "that was my first trip. The one all three of the Dorotheas took."

"Right." I nodded.

After a brief pause, the watch showed a trip back from 6:00 p.m. on Thanksgiving 1929 to 8:00 p.m. on Halloween 2010.

"And that's Dorothea-1's return trip. I did the same thing. Got back in time to hand out the candies. And if I'd died on my errand, those kids at the door (I answered it in my '20s outfit) would have gotten a real trick for a change, to go with the treats that would have fallen to the floor when my hand disappeared from the continuum."

"Don't you mean they did get a trick? On World X. Since nothing can ever get you back there?"

"Hmm." She pondered that for a minute. "Yes. I guess that's true.

"She...I mean you...didn't linger long in '29, did you?"

"Well...no...."

"Did you actually shoot the guys that were going after Pat?"

"No, no." She shook her head. "The gun was

enough of a deterrent. They ran off the other way. But I drew a lot of attention to myself with that stunt.... Oh!" She looked down at the watch. "Damn!"

"What's wrong?"

"We missed the next item in the sequence."

"Oh."

She started the process all over again, gesturing for me to be quiet until we'd accessed the required information.

"What's this one?" She looked at me with puzzled eyes. "1:28 a.m., November 3, 2010, to 3:00 p.m., August 17, 2021?"

"Oh, right." I snapped my fingers. "That. A demonstration trip. To stop me from cracking wise about alternate realities. It definitely worked."

"I imagine so." She bobbed her head at the watch. "Okay, here's the return trip from your little time taste test." She paused expectantly. "And...the winning number is: 4:35 a.m., November 3, 2010. That's when you have to return. Let's set it right now." She wrestled my wrist onto her lap.

"Sounds good." I let her have her way with the watch.

"I hope so," she said sternly. "Don't use this thing to go anywhere but home. Understand?"

"Understood." I tried to sound sincere. "But wait a minute." Something else occurred to me. "What about physical location? Do I have to be standing on the exact same spot too?"

"Ah." She sounded like a proud parent. "That's a very good question, Douglass. Fortunately, the answer is no. I put more than two decades' worth of work into this thing, and it's got some pretty impressive features. The best one, if I do say so myself, is the geochronal stabilizer. Basically, if you're in the same city that you were in when you left, or even the same metropolitan area (although I'm not one hundred percent sure about that), it will find a way to merge the departing and returning bodies into one."

"Great. So that's why there wasn't another Douglass waiting in your kitchen when I got back from 2021."

"That's why. The device also nudges you over whenever there's a chair, a parked car, or a newly built wall in your way."

"You Dorotheas think of everything," I said.

"We do our best. But I don't think any of us could ever have imagined you."

She kissed me lightly on the mouth.

"Stay out of trouble, Douglass-2." She stepped away from the bed, smiling. "She can't be that hard to resist, can she?"

The question took me by surprise.

"I...I don't know...."

"I'll know." Her smile disappeared. "Very shortly. And, Douglass, if you get it wrong this time, I'm gonna have to come back here and take this operation out of your hands before any of the tragic things in that

Wikipedia entry take place. Understand?"

"Why not just go back to Thanksgiving?"

"Because the place'll be crawling with Douglasses and Dorotheas, that's why." She advanced toward me. "It'd become a farce."

"You could go back to the day before," I persisted. "Warn Pat to keep off the street."

"No." She shook her head. "And don't you try it either. We don't need a Douglass-3."

"Well, that'd be symmetrical, wouldn't it?"

She laughed. "It would. In a fearful way."

"Fine." I shrugged, and this time I meant what I said. "No more going back for me."

"Good. That's what I want to hear. Just stick to the plan."

"I will."

"And if it doesn't work"—she moved toward the door—"well, I guess you can take comfort from the fact that it just wasn't ever meant to be."

"Some comfort."

"Either way, Douglass, I'll see you back in 2010." She left.

"Well," a familiar voice wafted in from the fire escape, "we know that's not true."

I had a feeling I was about to meet Douglass-3.

Chapter Twenty-Seven

He wore a slightly longer hairstyle, and he looked a bit emaciated, but the man at the window was unquestionably me.

"Can I come in?" he asked politely.

"You know you're always welcome here." I gestured toward the brown armchair.

"You're a true gentleman." He smiled, a little crookedly. I wondered if I always smiled that way.

He sat down.

"Should I put on a pot of coffee?" I asked him. "You have no idea how tired I am."

"By all means." He nodded. "And believe me, I know exactly how tired you are."

"Right." I fired up the hot plate. "I guess you do.... Do you remember every word I'm going to say?"

He shook his head pityingly. "Douglass...this *isn't* Heinlein's 'By His Bootstraps,' with every jump crammed into one mind-bendingly circular timeline that accounts for everything. I've never been on your side of this conversation. I just went to bed the minute Dorothea left. Is that really so hard to grasp, after everything that's happened? Welcome to World Z."

"I know, I know," I sighed. "So I take it you're the jerk who got us into Wikipedia."

"None other."

While I tended to the coffee, the dog woke up and did a double take.

"Ah, I've missed this splendid creature." My doppelganger rubbed Lulu's chin.

"Don't tell me something happens to Lulu."

"Relax, Douglass," my counterpart soothed. "She'll be fine. I never said that I came straight from '31."

"No, I guess you didn't. So what else have you been screwing with?"

"Pour the coffee first."

I filled a pair of cups and handed one to Douglass-3.

"Thanks." He took a lengthy sip.

"Okay. Go on. The suspense is killing me."

"Don't play innocent with *me*, Douglass. If there's one person you can just be yourself with, it's yourself."

A desperate thought occurred to me, or had been occurring to me, on and off, ever since I'd met Dorothea. "Sabotage?" I whispered.

"Exactly."

"How the hell'd you manage it?"

"Ah," he replied. "That'll take some telling."

"So tell it." I coddled my cup. "There's more where this came from."

He told it.

"All right. You read about the relationship with Chandler.... Or anyway, the final act of it. God, that situation got completely out of hand. I don't know what to tell you. She's exactly as fascinating as she seems. But it still didn't work out. Maybe I criticized her drinking too much. Maybe I didn't criticize it enough. Maybe I thought just having me love her would take care of her problems...and maybe that idea became the biggest problem of all. I don't know....

"Ideally, you'd avoid the whole thing. But I know that ship has sailed. So just remember: If you start something with her, you're gonna have to see it through. There's no walking away in the middle...."

"Why are you even telling me this?" I interrupted. "Why don't you just go back to next year?"

"Because I'd only make things worse now. I'm serious about this. I've internalized a doomed dynamic, and I'll bring it with me, no matter where I go."

"And aren't you infecting me with it right now?"

"No." He shook his head. "Hearing about a thing isn't the same as living it. And you've got a lot of good living to look forward to, so focus on that. Just get her to talk about how much the relationship means to her, and what she expects of you, and things'll probably work out fine. That's all I'm going to say about Chandler."

"You really think that's helpful?"

"I do." His tone made a very strong impression.

"Okay. I'll try."

"All right." He displayed the empty bottom of his cup. "Let's refuel before we push on."

I dumped the old coffee grounds into the bucket

next to my bed and refilled the pot with fresh ones, along with water from the sink.

"That's right," I remembered. "You were going to regale me with the story of your 21st century raid."

"And so I shall." He stood up, stretched, and started examining the few books I'd managed to pile onto the little bookshelf near the window. "Ah, you know, I never did get around to reading our first edition *Maltese Falcon*."

"I'll do it tonight." I smiled. "Flex my history-changing muscles."

"That's the spirit."

I replenished our cups.

"Okay." Douglass-3 returned to his chair. "Here's what happened. My life was exactly the same as yours, up until the moment that *I* popped in here from the fire escape. I played bridge all night, waiting for Mom to be born. I saw Eileen lying there on her gurney, all proud and spent. I came home to the news that Helen had called. And I went through that depressing ordeal with Dorothea-3."

"But wait a minute!" My fingers leapt to my forehead. "Did Dorothea's Wikipedia entry read exactly the *same*?"

"Ah, very good." He nodded. "You're paying attention.... As a matter of fact, it did. So you see, I'm not really Douglass-3, if that's what you've been thinking. I'm Douglass-4, at the very least."

"Right.... So where the hell did number 3 go?"

"Your guess is literally as good as mine." He spread his hands. "Hanging out with the Transcendentalists in 1836? Watching Jackie Robinson's first game as a Dodger in 1947? He could be checking out Buck Rogers' century, for all we know."

"But he didn't come back here to visit you."

"That's the one and only certainty."

"Maybe he just went back to 2010?"

"Anything's possible, but don't forget: The odds aren't too good that anyone like us ever existed there, in this continuum."

"What do you mean?"

"You know exactly what I mean." He grinned macabrely. "You've been worrying about it ever since we went back and allowed Pat to die. What're the chances that the new June Corelli, the one you just saw in her cradle and are planning to help raise as your niece, is going to grow up to marry Dad?"

"Not good, I guess," I groaned.

"And even if she does," Douglass-4 continued, "do you really think that a happy, well-adjusted June will wait until she's forty-five to start a family?"

"God, it all sounds so much worse when you say it out loud."

"Get used to it, Douglass. We've erased ourselves but good."

"But we're still here," I protested.

"Yes, indeed," my duplicate laughed. "Kinda makes you question the wisdom of stealing the watch in the first place, doesn't it?"

I curled up into a fetal ball next to Lulu's soundly sleeping form. "You mean our lives would've continued unchanged if we'd allowed Dorothea to go back and have her way with history?"

"Doesn't that seem likely, given what we know now?"

"*Miseria!*" I exclaimed, in the best Laura Corelli style.

"Come on, man." He patted my head. "It's not as bad as that. So we'll never be ourselves again. So what? We can pretty much be anybody else! And really, let's face it, now that you've got this bond with Grandma, a chance to write your own classic movies, and this thing with Chandler on the way, do you even want to go back to 2010?"

"No." I opened one eye sheepishly. "Not if everything works out."

"So make it work." He sounded like an infomercial life coach. "And don't worry about Dorothea. She's not a factor anymore."

I bolted to my haunches. "You didn't hurt her did you?"

"Don't be an idiot! I'm *you*, remember?"

"Right. So what'd you do?"

"I took her watch out of play."

"What do you mean? She had it tonight."

"Yes." He smiled. "And then she went home to assess our performance. Do you want that hanging over you?"

"No."

"Neither did I. So I did some heavy thinking, just as you would have done in the days and months ahead if I hadn't cleared the problem off your plate. And then I realized: If I travelled forward to any point before the fall of 2010 and pulled some commando stuff, the Dorothea in *this* timeline would never manage to complete her invention."

"I guess." I shrugged. "But then where did the one who threatened us just now go off to?"

"Who cares? To another timeline, I suppose. The one that existed before I destroyed the watch.... She's *fine*."

"Yeah, I guess so.... But what'd you do?"

"Ah." There was a terrifying smugness in his voice. "That's what I've been building up to...."

"So there I was," Douglass-4 continued. "Opening night. *Chorines in Arms*. Things had gone every bit as badly as that crumpled printout had foretold. But that's because no future version of us had ever troubled to come back and nudge me toward the light.... Regardless, I needed to get out of there. Out of her sight. Out of that bar. Out of the city. And then it dawned on me: out of this era entirely....

"I set the watch for January 2008. Close enough, I figured, for all of the elements of the machine to be gathered in one place but early enough that I'd have more than two years' worth of runway in which to implement my scheme, although I was hoping to get the job done far more quickly than that.

"But you know, it's a lot harder to sneak your way into post-9/11 society than it was to establish ourselves here. I had to buy an identity package—and that wasn't cheap. Fortunately, I had loaded up on jewelry when I took my leave of that ritzy after-party. It's amazing what you can work up the nerve to do once you know you can time jump out of trouble....

"I created a new life for myself, under the name of Larry Tremblay, born and raised in Metairie, Louisiana. And I got myself a crusty little pad in the Bronx, not so different from our old one. I had enough money to live on. Quite comfortably, in fact. So I put eight hours a day into creating a blog version of our old *Nitrate Nuggets* column. I poured every ounce of creativity, wit, and insight that I had into that thing. Not just into the blog itself, of course, but into establishing a presence in the online community.... Publicly 'following' sites, sending a few personal emails, leaving tons of comments.... It was pretty slow going at first, but after less than a month, my hit count started climbing. I drew comments of my own and responded to everyone. I got links from message boards. And finally, after another few months of continuous posting, I began receiving frequent mentions on the Turner Classic Movies site.

"At that point, I figured I was in good enough shape to push on to the next phase of my plan, which was to 'meet cute' with Dorothea on the net. That part went remarkably smoothly. Google led me to a message board devoted to 20th Century Fox musicals and a thread which featured a virtually endless discussion of the respective merits of Alice Faye and Betty Grable. And there she was, Dorothea Cullen, insisting that there was no comparison, that Alice Faye had a far weightier presence and an incomparably better singing voice. I agreed with her, but for the sake of my mission, I adopted the opposite position, arguing that Grable's superior dancing and her impregnable sass made her a far more interesting heroine.

"The debate raged across endless scrolled-down screens. Finally, we acknowledged each other's extraordinary competence in this esoteric field and concluded that all Fox musicals are fun. Then we moved on to other, only slightly different, topics. I let it slip that I had a film blog, and discovered that she'd been reading it, without commenting, for quite a while. Soon, we became Facebook friends, sharing YouTube clips on each other's pages, and it was only a matter of time before we met up in person, since we both, miraculously, lived in New York.

"We had our first date just a little before Christmas 2008, and it was no different from any of our other first meetings. There was no hurry this time, though. We were together for months, and I got to know her really well. Did you know her parents are still alive? I met them. They're pretty nice people. It's no wonder Dorothea turned out the way she did, despite the massive social handicap of her genius.

"For a while, I actually considered just staying with her. Why not? We weren't lying about falling in love with her, were we? And what's more, we actually feel comfortable with her...."

"Very comfortable," I interrupted, remembering Dorothea's crushed expression that first night. "Until I let myself think about what a dick I've been to her."

"Sure, that's a problem," he conceded. "But we could have gotten past it. She was always ready to believe the best of us...."

"Maybe that's the biggest problem of all." The thought struck me for the first time. "When you're not at your best (and when have we been, since this craziness started?), you might not want to be called out for your transgressions, but that's probably what you need."

"You think Chandler's going to do that for you?" he laughed.

"No...I guess not.... But I think chasing her might force me to police myself. There's no margin for error there."

"None." My counterpart nodded. "Keep that in mind, and you won't go far wrong.... I had some pretty goddamned sweet times with Dorothea, but it was clear from the start that it would never work.... My Dorothea was just as obsessed with Cynthia Ward as Dorothea-1, even though Grandma's filmography had been drastically curtailed. One night, toward the end of summer

2009, she introduced me to *Chorines in Arms* and *Boxcar Honeymoon*, in their special Criterion DVD editions, and that's when she dropped the bomb about the watch.

"She showed me her lab, behind a secret door in her pantry—and she told me about her plan to go back to 1929 and save Pat Corelli. I tried to talk her out of it, knowing that if she went, she might never reappear in my timeline, and that even if she did, she'd almost certainly have run into *you*, at which point, questions would arise...."

"Ah." My head was spinning. "So you scurried back to the sabotage plan?"

"I did." Douglass-4 nodded. "I contacted the same businessman who'd set up my fake identity, telling him I needed a specialist.... I had gotten to know Dorothea's routines very well, but I took extra special care to make certain that she wouldn't be anywhere near her apartment when the appointed hour arrived. I invited her to spend the weekend at a bed and breakfast in Vermont, during Rutland's annual Halloween parade...."

"You finally went to that?" I'm sure I sounded jealous. "Was it great?"

"It was really great." I noticed a slight glassiness in his eyes. "We went as Frankenstein and the Bride. Took a leisurely hike up to Killington Peak. And spent pretty much all of Sunday in bed. Meanwhile, my operative was working his mischief. I really thought I'd be able to handle the duplicity of it. After all, we've been lying to Dorothea ever since that first night. But the guilt nearly overwhelmed me on the way back to town. Thankfully, she was driving and didn't notice it. I eked out six more hours of her love on cruise control.

"When Dorothea saw the fire trucks and the police cordon, she nearly drove the car into a hydrant. I felt like a monster as I consoled her on the curb. The superintendent was smoking a cigarette in Abingdon Square, along with most of Dorothea's fellow tenants. He toddled over and said, 'Don't worry, honey. Your apartment is fine. Everyone's fine. It's just that little storage space behind your pantry that got roasted.'

"Dorothea's face fell. 'Twenty-two *years*,' she mumbled. Only to me." Douglass-4 grimaced. "And that's all she said."

I couldn't think of anything to say either. I settled for: "Terrible."

"Yeah." He stood up. "Let me tell you something, Douglass. You don't ever want to know what it feels like to finally take things too far with Dorothea." The mischief left his features entirely. "I wish I'd never done it. But since I did, make it count for something, hunh?"

He touched the "go" button and disappeared.

Chapter Twenty-Eight

My last summer in New York evaporated like so much steam from a Lower East Side pothole during a heat wave. Eileen and June received clean bills of health and were released from captivity within two days. I moved in with them a week later. Esther Duncan broke precedent and accompanied me up to the new place.

"Such a baby!" she exulted, pulling June out of the magnificent oaken cradle I'd helped to lug up to Eileen's bedroom. "She's going to be a beauty, just like her mama."

The beauty in question poked her bleary eyes out from the bedclothes and sighed. "Neither one of us is going to look good for long if we don't find a way to get some sleep around here."

"Aw, sweetheart." Esther patted Eileen's head. "You get used to it."

And I suppose we did. I gave my notice at *Corking Tales* (and Tom Katz actually threw me a little party at his house in Long Island). I handled Lulu, the cooking, and just about everything else besides June, and I still think I came out ahead on the deal. Eileen spent nearly every waking minute (which amounted to just about every minute, period) nursing, coddling, or exercising.

"Okay, I think you can ease up on those sit-ups," I suggested one evening in late August. "You look great."

"I know," she said, sweating. "But I don't look *Hollywood* great. I didn't come this far to let a few pounds sink me just before I get to the end of the rainbow."

I shook my head. "Well, just don't let them give you any diet pills."

"Diet *pills?*"

I grinned. "That's the best spot in the world for a question mark."

"You're a strange man, Douglass."

"No question at all about that."

Finally, toward the middle of September, we began packing up. It was a surprisingly painless procedure. I really didn't have much of anything to pack except for a few clothes and books. And even though the studio was paying for everything, Eileen decided not to ship most of the large items.

"The new bungalow's all furnished anyway," she reasoned. "And I guess this stuff would just remind me of Pat."

"Don't you want to be reminded of him?" I was genuinely surprised.

"Yes." She nodded. "But not by a couch. I've got my own ways of remembering."

I thought of the photo album.

She sent the furniture home to the Corellis.

The "bungalow" in question was a modest West

Hollywood "mini-villa" in a development called "Sunset Arcadia." The place was near the corner of Sunset Boulevard (of course) and North Olive Drive, just a few blocks west of the legendary Garden of Allah.

Before Eileen could so much as open a box, I dragged her (along with Lulu and June) out for a peek at that storied locale—an estate built to the quirky specifications of early silent icon Alla Nazimova, just after World War I. The Crimean-born star had even requisitioned a swimming pool in the shape of her beloved Black Sea. In those days, it had been called "The Garden of Alla" (a pun on the title of Robert S. Hitchens' oft-filmed novel)—and it had earned quite a reputation as a site of what Prohibition-era America would not have hesitated to call "debauchery."

Nazimova's Hollywood stock dropped precipitously during the early '20s, when she courageously put her own money into financing a pair of film adaptations of plays that she produced for herself, *A Doll's House* and *Salome* (the latter being a movie rumoured to have an all-gay cast). Neither film did well, and if there's anything the studios disliked even more than "unsavoury" publicity, it was poor box-office returns. They pretty much closed the tinsel door on her. Nearly broke, Nazimova returned to the stage and eventually had to sell her property (although not before she had surrounded the main structure with a whole flock of "villas" intended to generate revenue for her retirement).

By the fall of 1930, Alla's "Garden" (which had acquired an extra, pun-killing *h* somewhere along the way) was well into the second phase of its existence as a combination hotel and trendy apartment complex.

"What's the big deal about this place anyway?" Eileen asked me as we pushed the pram past the compound's stone-paved front court. "It's just a stuccoed nightclub with a weird pool."

She wasn't wrong. And yet, F. Scott Fitzgerald and Robert Benchley, two of my lifelong favourites, were due to wreck their livers here over the next few years.

"Well, I hear they get a lot of interesting guests," was all I could think of to say.

She shook her head indulgently. "You've got to stop thinking like a fan, Douglass. You're part of the club now."

We meandered back through the crisp October air toward the Sunset Arcadia, which, though it wasn't destined to attract a multitude of newsreel-worthy tenants, did offer a beautiful view of Laurel Canyon. The studio had brokered the rental on Eileen's behalf, and the location, just a quick fifteen-minute drive up Cahuenga Boulevard from Universal City, was awfully convenient.

Inside, the bungalow had a nice open-concept feel, with a spacious living room/kitchen coming directly off the foyer and a pair of closed bedrooms in the back (each with its own private bath). The walls were lustrously white and hung with a few placeholder watercolours, all of which depicted various combinations of waves, horizons, and gently descending suns.

"God." Eileen made a face. "Someone must be trying to boost the local art market. I've never been more desperate for a new painting,"

"Not a Maxfield Parrish in the bunch." I grinned.

Then June started crying. That's how the lion's share of our conversations ended.

I didn't meet up with many babies during my 21st century bachelorhood, but I had never cherished any illusions about their generosity of spirit. And yet, after more than three months of relentlessly effervescent egotism, I awoke every morning with the hope that today, or, at the very least, someday soon, we'd see some small show of humanity from our tiny taskmaster.

But that day remained a distant promise when October 13th rolled around. Ready or not, we were contractually obligated to report to the studio, leaving June's fate (at least during working hours) in the hands of Nadine Schatz, a retired nurse whom Eileen's agent had recommended as a nanny.

Just a little over sixty, Nadine had grown up in St. Louis. Her parents had immigrated to Missouri (from Bavaria) a couple of years after the end of the Civil War. Thomas Schatz had opened a leather goods store in town and had apparently done very well for his family. As the first-born daughter, Nadine had been expected to do her part in helping to build the Schatzs' standing within the Midwestern city's sizeable German community. She had earned above-average marks in high school, gone to mass every Sunday (and Confession, whenever it had seemed warranted), learned to play the violin, and developed into an attractive, if perhaps a bit skinny, specimen of late 19th century femininity, with a personably pointed nose, a bowed mouth, and straight blonde hair. She had lived up to every expectation that had ever been set for her. And then, just a few days after accepting an engagement ring from some minor city counsellor's son, she bolted, running off to Chicago to study nursing.

She had pursued that profession in the "Windy City" for more than thirty years, putting in nearly a decade at the Children's Memorial Hospital in Lincoln Park and then partnering up, in more ways than one (from what she implied but never quite stated), with a progressive female pediatrician who worked with children from the South Side ghetto. Tragically, after a good run, the doctor (Margaret) had developed worsening symptoms of tuberculosis, sometime during the early '20s. Eventually, the illness had forced Margaret to abandon her practice. After every other effort failed, she had agreed, reluctantly, to follow the era's prescribed "treatment" for TB, relocating to Flagstaff, Arizona—and Nadine had gone with her.

She had managed to live for fifteen months.

Margaret's death, at the age of sixty-one, had devastated Nadine, who found herself alone and practically penniless in the arid wastes of the southwestern United States. She had driven the rickety remains of her old heap to Los Angeles and applied to work at the city's Children's Hospital Society. But at age fifty-five, Nadine had not exactly conformed to that organization's profile for a new hire. And so she had hung out her shingle as a nanny.

"Because taking care of kids is the only thing I know how to do." She had brought the interview to a close, in her softly matter-of-fact way. "Although I do think it's a shame that I can't help the ones who really need it and still make a living."

"You're hired!" Eileen had practically leaped over the table to shake her hand.

Nadine Schatz was exactly the kind of person you'd want to entrust your infant mother's care to, but that didn't make it any easier to leave June behind on Monday morning. Eileen had to be on the set at 6:30 a.m., so she had ridden out toward Burbank long before I did. Universal didn't require their writers to perform such superhuman feats. We punched the clock at 9:00 a.m. I stayed close to the cradle for as long as I could, but Nadine gently chased me to my car (a two-year-old emerald-green DeSoto Roadster I'd picked up on a used lot for three hundred and fifty dollars) just after 8:30 a.m.

Unlike, say, Warner Bros., Universal wasn't (or, to be more accurate, wouldn't become) particularly noted for its commitment to the screenwriter's art. The studio relied pretty heavily on freelancers for their "A" feature scripts (and they had paid me quite handsomely as an independent contractor for *Chorines in Arms*). The in-house writing staff, to be perfectly frank, was composed almost entirely of people who were either a) related to Carl Laemmle, Sr., or b) related to someone (i.e., Eileen) who was important to Carl Laemmle.

I don't mean to imply that we didn't earn our keep. For one thing, our patchwork corps drew the thankless, but essential, task of supplying transfusions of "additional dialogue" to any current productions that sprang leaks in logic or locomotive fuel. We also enjoyed the dubious honour of coming up with plots, gags, and full scripts for the whole line of "Red Star Comedy" shorts— movies with "stars" even I had never heard of, sporting titles such as *You Said It, Sailor* and *The Laughback*. And of course we churned out an endless string of lobby poster blurbs, trailer title cards, and other obnoxious slogans to slug the public with. Still, it was a fun way to earn a living—and a pretty lucrative one, too. Even starting at the bottom of the ladder, I was earning five times more than I'd been getting from Tom Katz. Plus I had lots of free time to work on other projects, if I wanted to.

To be truthful though, by mid-October, the only "other project" on my mind was seeing Helen. I knew she'd be tantalizingly close throughout the autumn, filming *Dracula* on the lot with Tod Browning. But I couldn't just show up on the set, no matter how much I wanted to. Writers didn't have that kind of pull at Universal. I had no choice but to wait until she wandered my way.

In the meantime, I got to work. I devoted more

than two weeks to the media blitz surrounding the up-coming release of *The Cohens and the Kellys in Africa*. The fifth entry in a rather popular series which de-tailed the exploits of two squabbling Lower East Side families (one Irish, one Jewish) who come into an un-likely joint inheritance that sends them on a global spree, the movie was due out in December. Already built on a foundation of wall-to-wall ethnic stereotyp-ing, the franchise seemed poised to reach new depths now that the cantankerous clans were headed south of the equator. I didn't have to watch the movie, thank-fully, but I was forced to write copy such as: "If you thought these feuding families made a fuss in Paris and Scotland, just wait 'til you see them on safari!"

On October 31st, E.M. Asher hit me with my first important rush job: shoehorning two minutes of new dialogue into a medium-budget comedy called *Free Love*, another film which seemed to have been designed explicitly to remind a 21st century sentimentalist of everything that was wrong with classic Hollywood.

The script began with a fairly interesting premise: upper-middle-class woman divorces her domineering husband at the urging of her psychoanalyst. However, as the story develops, the analyst is exposed as a conniving weasel, and the woman is burlesqued as a gullible fool. Based on a play by Sydney Howard, the movie takes the "long-suffering" husband's side in nearly every way, mocking the wife's expensive search for clarity and play-ing the couple's marital difficulties strictly for laughs. In the end, the society lady (played by brittle comedienne Genevieve Tobin, who'd wind up doing some interesting things at Warner Bros. a little later in the decade) abandons her introspective quest and returns to the calloused arms of her husband.

Somewhere along the way, the director (journeyman Hobart Henley, who was noted for his work with female stars) decided that the movie needed a scene or two which portrayed his heroine as something close to an intelligent adult, rather than a sulky or repentant child. Just to mix things up a bit, I suppose. My task was to whip up a breezy little encounter between Tobin's temporarily assertive character and an obnoxious glove salesman played by Andy Devine. I couldn't do much about the overall tone of the film, but at least I could generate a mild touch of cognitive dissonance by writing the divorcee as a confident woman with a barbed sense of humour, a person who welcomes a challenge in the verbal arena. A person who *disappears* as soon as the script returns to the spirit of Sydney Howard's miserable play....

I finally hammered the scene into satisfactory shape around 8:00 p.m. I handed the new pages to a runner, cleared the day's debris off my desk, and headed out to the parking lot, whistling semi-contentedly. It had been a blisteringly hot day, with the sun bullying the mercury up past 90. But the temperature dropped nicely after dark, and a hearty half-moon brought an approachable air to the aloof Southern California sky. As I strolled toward the DeSoto, a slightly skewed version of the tune I was toting ("Lullaby of Broadway," which wouldn't be written until 1935) echoed from the depths of the convertible.

Heart racing, I leaped onto the running board and peered over the passenger side door.

Helen Chandler was curled up on the soft leather seat, in full post-bite *Dracula* pallor.

"You're working too hard, Douglass," she said. "We're going to miss tricks or treats."

Chapter Twenty-Nine

We didn't go trick-or-treating.

We drove twenty miles due west on Ventura Boulevard and turned down into Topanga Canyon. When we reached a likely pull-off spot in Summit Valley, Helen squeezed my arm.

I parked the car at the base of a sage-covered hill.

"Come on, Douglass." She sank her heels into the close-cropped chaparral.

I clambered up after her.

"No sheep around here." I drank in the arid LA County scenery, with the Santa Monica Mountains looming in the distance.

"You've been listening to some pretty picky sheep." She nestled up against a large rock at the top of the hill. "I'm sure they prefer luscious fields of clover, but they can handle sage just fine."

"Oh, really, Old MacDonald?" I joined her. "When's the last time you had a farm?"

"I grew up on a farm, if you must know," she said with some satisfaction.

As a nostalgia-struck teen, I could have recited every known detail of Helen Chandler's biography by heart. And I'd written several professional articles about her as an adult. But a vast gulf had opened up in my mind between the actress I'd watched and read about all of those years and the woman sitting next to me in 1930. Somehow, I just couldn't line them up. I guess that's not so surprising, considering the direction the legend was headed in and the countervailing drift of my hopes. But a part of me still knew that Helen's father had raised thoroughbreds in South Carolina, before World War I.

"A farm?" I eyed her quizzically.

She grinned. "Well, it was a racehorse stable. But we had some other ungulates around the place, to keep the horses from chomping too much grass."

"Ungulates, eh?"

"Uh-huh. Those sheep were always my favourites. Because we didn't sell them off constantly. They were the ones I missed, when we moved away."

I put my arm around her shoulder. "Sounds like a nice place. What happened to it?"

She shrugged. "Well, South Carolina banned betting, and Dad's business dried up. They've got some poor legislators down there."

"Tell me about it."

"Oh, but they've got some good things, too, beyond the sheep. I got my first nip of mint julep on Christmas, the year before we left."

"Sounds like you've got your next endorsement deal all lined up."

"Oh!" She spun gleefully. "Did you spot my soap huckstering in the magazines?"

I did remember seeing an enigmatic headshot accompanied by inane copy in a winter issue of *Photoplay*.

I put on my best disingenuous society hostess voice: "I'm *devoted* to Lux toilet soap."

She kissed me.

"Imagine getting paid to lie about your bathing habits!" she said after a deep breath.

I kissed her back.

"People want to know what touches you."

"Oh, Douglass! How lyrically lecherous."

❖

I pulled up to the Sunset Arcadia just after 8:00 a.m., ready for a Saturday-long nap. Nadine Schatz was waiting for me, with her third or fourth cup of coffee and a half-read *L.A. Times* spread out on the kitchen table. June was lolling happily in her new playpen, and Lulu's jaw bounced every time the baby nudged a squeak toy.

"Your sister nearly lost her mind this morning." The nanny eyed me with uncharacteristic sternness.

"Oh, no!" I slumped into the chair facing her. "Did you have to come in at six? I'm so sorry!"

"Save the first take for the lady of the house." Her eyes widened indulgently. "You don't want to be dishing out any canned apologies tonight."

"What did she say?" I groaned.

"Just about everything she can't say on camera."

"God." I buried my head in my arms. "I completely lost track of time."

She got up to check on something baking in the oven. "Douglass, that's not exactly news. The question is: Who'd you lose it *with*?"

I lifted my chin off the table. The scent of peach pie wafted across the kitchen.

"I just wrecked your whole morning, Nadine. How can you possibly give a damn about my escapades?"

"I was awake anyway." She spread her oven mitts. "And as for escapades, I'm all for 'em, as you very well know."

"Well...she finally showed."

"Really?" She gave June's wooden animal mobile a spin on her way back to the table. "The actress?"

During the past few weeks, I'd given Nadine a pretty complete account of my adventure in the Big Apple (minus the time travel elements, of course). I'd even filled her in on my near-arrest for resembling an East River stiff. But no part of the saga had piqued her interest more than my premiere night in Central Park with Helen.

"The actress." I nodded. "She ambushed me in the parking lot. A welcome ambush. But an ambush, just the same." I craned my neck to read the wall clock in the living room area. "I guess that was more than twelve hours ago."

"And?" She leaned forward expectantly. "What? You got hitched? Robbed a bank? Woke up in a vat of your own vomit?"

"All very plausible outcomes.... Of course, a marriage would've been bigamous.... But, actually, we just drove down to Summit Valley and convened beside a rock."

"Last time a tree. This time a rock...."

"Our romance respects the local topography."

"Don't you mean affair?" She raised an eyebrow.

"Well, I guess it's that, too."

She sniffed the air. "The pie's just about ready. Would you like a slice?"

"You have no idea how much."

"With whipping cream? I made some earlier. It's in the ice box."

"You must have been one hell of a nurse."

She slid a pair of pieces onto plates, and I ladled out the cream.

"Believe it or not, Douglass." She licked crumbs off her unadorned lips. "I got up to a lot more than nursing, in those days."

"I believe it."

The peaches were fleshy, the crust was buttery crisp, and the whole thing was enlivened by cinnamon.

"So?" She gestured toward me with her fork.

"So...you want to hear about the non-verbal aspects of the evening?"

"Of course I want to hear about the non-verbal aspects of the evening."

"Well, there were a lot of...aspects."

"After five months, I should hope so. And it was good? Despite the lack of trees?"

"It was great," I said, without exaggerating an ounce, "at least from my perspective."

"Did she seem to disagree?"

"No, not at all, but...well, you know, she's enigmatic."

"Of course she is." Nadine went to get June's bottle of Similac. "Would you like her if she wasn't?"

"I hope I'm not quite that predictable."

"I hate to say it, Douglass." She got the baby settled on her lap and pushed the rubber nipple up to her maw. "But I think it's quite possible that you are. If you had any actual sense, you'd have stayed with that girl back in Montreal. What was her name? Dorothea?"

"All right then." I accepted her verdict. "It's possible."

"Ah, we all have our weaknesses, Douglass. God knows I do. Unfortunately, mine is in very short supply."

"You must miss Margaret so much."

"I do." She adjusted the bottle's position slightly. "But, you know, considering I grew up believing that people like her couldn't possibly exist, it seems pretty miraculous that I got to spend twenty-five years with her."

"Was it hard? Having to hide so much of yourself?"

"Oh, I wish things were different, if that's what you

mean. But I was never hard up for friends, once I got to Chicago."

June released the bottle and belched on cue. Nadine toted her back to the playpen. She knelt down with her back to me and stuck her finger through the wooden bars.

"Arizona was hard."

"I'm so sorry, Nadine."

"Me too." She turned toward me. "And not only for the reasons you'd expect. There's a terrible satisfaction in outliving a lover that nobody ever tells you about, Douglass, in realizing they'll never fall out of love with you. It makes you feel ghoulish and smug all at once. And there's no one left to laugh it off with."

"Well...if you were trying to make me feel better about the fact that this thing with Chandler is almost certain to go up in flames before either of us dies, mission accomplished."

"Good." Nadine smiled. "You're calling her Chandler now?"

"It was either that or *The* Chandler."

"So you're going to see her again?"

"Next Friday. She was practically *non-*noncommittal."

"But she's still married?"

"Certainly she is. Chandler's not the kind of girl who leaves her husband on the second date."

"I hope you always find the situation this amusing."

"So do I."

"Get some rest, dear." She patted me on the shoulder.

"You're not done with these questions by a long shot."

Ten minutes later, I was in bed, dreaming of sleeping 'til next Friday.

Chapter Thirty

I got up around 2:00 p.m., sufficiently refreshed to begin feeling really guilty. I convinced Nadine to head home early, which took some doing. Then I brought June to the soft green and walnut sofa and read to her from a colourfully illustrated edition of *Ozma of Oz*.

My mother didn't pay the story much heed, but I think she enjoyed my impersonations of the Hungry Tiger and Billina the yellow hen. At least until she shifted all of her energy toward getting a finger up my nose. After a couple of bottle feedings and one diaper change, I managed to settle the volatile infant into her crib.

Then I found some Waring's Pennsylvanians on the radio and returned to *Oz*.

Eileen got home sometime after 9:00 p.m.

"Let me guess." She sank down into the upholstery beside me. "You got carried off by a twister?"

"I'm so sorry, Eileen." I spread my arms pleadingly. "Please don't be mad."

"I'm not mad." She surrendered to the hug. "Well...not anymore.... I know things can't have been very easy for you this past year. You never wanted a family. Not this kind of a family, anyway. You've got your own life to—"

"Eileen, you wouldn't believe how easy this has been for me, compared to everything that came before it in my life. It's true I never thought much about family before, but maybe that's because I never dreamed one like ours could exist.... I take it back. I screwed up. Please...be mad."

She scrunched her forehead at me. "Good. Because I am. I mean, honestly.... You can't pick up a phone and say, 'Eileen, can we make some other arrangement for tomorrow morning? There's this lunatic I'd like to sleep with....'"

"Oh, I wouldn't call her a lunatic, exactly...."

"No," she chuckled. "*You* wouldn't."

"You were right though, she is a screwball," I said, replaying the night (and the conversation I'd had with Douglass-4 in the spring) in my head. "There's no question about that. She says all kinds of fascinating things, but none of them quite tell you what she's feeling. And yet, I already get the sense that she's counting on me...."

"Counting on you to *what*?"

"Maybe just to keep wondering why she wants me around?"

"That sounds infuriating, Douglass."

"It probably will be. But what can I do?"

◆

There was nothing infuriating about the fall of

1930, apart from the ongoing economic collapse of the West. Hollywood seemed impervious to the downturn, although I knew that wouldn't last forever. For the time being, though, there was more than enough work to go around. Eileen was putting in sixty hours a week on the set of *Chorines in Arms*, and while she was generally too exhausted to offer much of an opinion about the picture (or anything else), the rest of the studio was abuzz with enthusiasm about the rushes. I could hardly wait to write the lobby posters.

I saw a lot of Chandler. They wrapped *Dracula* in mid-November, and part of me wondered if that would mark the end of our tryst. All it changed was our trysting spot. She never said a word about her living situation, or what she was doing with her time when she wasn't with me, but my absurd memory for classic Hollywood factoids told me that *Daybreak* came next in her filmography. An interesting comedy-drama set in Tsarist Russia, the movie gave Chandler a sparkling role as a penniless music teacher who gets involved with a good-hearted but thoughtless member of the Imperial Guard (engagingly played by fading silent-screen heartthrob Ramon Novarro). *Daybreak* was an MGM picture, so I wasn't very surprised when she suggested meeting about halfway between the Universal lot and Culver City, out on Sepulveda Boulevard, where they'd just finished blasting a tunnel through the Santa Monica Mountains in September.

We did our share of aimless hiking around the

area, but once we discovered a ledge with a magnificent view of the canyons running parallel to the coast, we generally made a beeline for that perch. On most nights, the local flora (which included a few live oaks interspersed with the ubiquitous Southern California chaparral) dominated our conversations, but other subjects did creep in occasionally as the weeks flew by.

One chilly evening, two days before Christmas, I felt an odd bulk between our chests as I pulled her toward me in the brush.

"What's this?" I slipped my hand under her blue worsted coat. "A present?"

"It's nothing." Her eyes widened as I pulled a well-worn paperback copy of *Romeo and Juliet* from the lining pocket.

"Looks like a portable literary allusion to me."

"Douglass"—she made the "gimme" gesture—"it's got nothing to do with us."

I surrendered the book without a struggle.

"What's so funny?" She kissed me, a little diffidently.

"I'm just glad you agree there's an *us*."

"There are all kinds of usses."

I ignored that one. "So did you want to read aloud to each other?"

"No...not really."

"Or maybe it's insurance? In case my banter dries up?"

"I just like having it with me. Can we leave it at that?"

I'm pretty sure I wasn't smiling anymore. "We leave *too* many things at that." I pulled away from her.

"It's just a book, Douglass."

"It clearly is not just a book."

We sat there trading hurt looks for at least two minutes.

"I..." she began tentatively, "I got it on the day of my first audition, when I was ten. My father gave it to me. It's a good luck charm, okay?"

"You mean it actually matters to you whether some things happen instead of others?"

"Of course it matters."

"You say 'of course' as if you take it for granted that I know anything about you."

"Why are you being this way?" She touched my face.

Why indeed?

"Because I've seen you, what, twenty times now? And I still don't have a clue what this means to you. Or even if anything can mean anything to you.... And now you tell me you've got a 'good luck charm,' just like any other earnest, anxious, hopeful human being. And I have to wonder: Why haven't I heard about your hopes, your anxieties, the things that are true for you?"

"Probably because my truths change every day. The anxieties, too. Some mornings, my toothbrush scares me. I picture all those little microorganisms thronging in the bristles. When you're not around, I get up at 4:00 a.m., just on the off chance that I'll have to run to the all-night drugstore and buy a new one, before I have to start my day...."

"When I'm not around?" my voice cracked. "What about your husband?"

"He's not a factor. He never has been."

"But I am?" I melted toward her.

"Douglass...."

"What?" I stared into her eyes.

"I gather this is your way of telling me that you're incapable of accepting an implied compliment?"

"I guess so." I pushed my nose into her hair.

"Well," she sighed, "you're a factor."

"Prove it," I whispered.

"I'm sure we'll prove it several times before morning." She shivered a bit. "We always do."

"Not that way." I kissed her earlobe. "Come to my place for Christmas dinner."

"Oh, Douglass." She edged her teeth into my neck. "I don't know...."

❖

I never quite believed she'd show, but I went ahead and set a place for her at the table.

Eileen watched the pendulum. "It's after five...."

"I know, I know." I checked the oven. The turkey was still raring to go. "Can we wait just a few more minutes?"

"All right," she sighed. "But a few doesn't mean twenty, Douglass. I haven't had a decent meal since this movie started shooting…. I need this."

"Ah, poor baby." Nadine squeezed Eileen's shoulders, visibly wringing tension from the actress' eyes.

I started settling the mashed potatoes, corn, chestnut stuffing, turnips, cranberry sauce, and gravy into serving dishes.

"We'll eat in ten minutes," I promised. "No matter what."

"All right," Eileen sighed. "Want me to carve the turkey? You two did everything else…."

"And we're going to finish the job." Nadine darted into the kitchen. "If you want to carve a turkey, cook one yourself."

"You just relax, movie star." I handed her a hot roll. "That's the whole point."

"Is it? We've really scaled things down from 'Peace on Earth'?" She bit into the steaming unbuttered bread. "God, that's delicious…."

The doorbell rang.

In the bedroom, June started crying.

The dog added a half-threatening howl to the chorus.

Outside, on the sunstruck stucco porch, Chandler looked a bit fretful herself.

"Merry Christmas." I put my arms around her.

"If it is, it'll be a first." She nearly crushed my ribs.

"Then it'll be a first."

"Just promise me you've got wine, and mistletoe."

"See for yourself." I led her into the festively decorated bungalow. I had picked up a nine-foot-tall Douglas fir from a well-stocked seasonal tree lot out near the Hollywood Bowl. The thing reached so nearly to the ceiling that there was no room for an angel or a star on the top, but it did provide a wealth of perches for the glass balls and bells I'd splurged on at Robinson's department store. We completed the effect with thick swirls of silver garland and a multicoloured string of bulbs. (I tried holding out for some really "old-fashioned" bubble lights, but the store manager finally convinced me that they hadn't been invented yet).

The mistletoe hung invitingly over the radio alcove. I took one thwarted step toward it.

"Hi, Helen." Eileen rose to greet us. "It's nice to see you again. I'm glad you didn't have any other...commitments...this evening."

Chandler laughed. "Oh, I'm nothing if not unconstrained. Just ask my publicist. But it's nice to see you, too, Cynthia...."

"Are we ready to eat?" Nadine paraded the carved bird toward the table.

"Are we ever." I nodded. "Helen Chandler, this is Nadine Schatz, undoubtedly the finest person I've met in California."

Chandler surprised me by giving Nadine a deep, sincere hug. "I've heard a lot about you. Thanks for taking such good care of these people."

"Why"—Nadine took the compliment in stride—"it's been a great pleasure to do that, my dear.... And I've been looking forward to meeting you, too."

While all of this was going on, I had to yank two different serving plates out of the path of Lulu's wildly wagging tail.

"I think you can guess this creature's name," I added.

"Hi, Lulu." Chandler knelt down and kissed the German shepherd on the snout.

Eileen pulled the chair to her left away from the table. "Helen, sit over here, next to me."

Chandler shot me an uneasy glance before silently complying. The dog trotted briskly after her.

I kissed the back of her neck on the way to my own seat, across the table from Eileen.

Chandler cleared her throat. "Douglass said something about wine?"

"Ah." Eileen patted the guest's nervous fingers. "But did he tell you that we've got five bottles of 1929 Riesling, homemade by our very own bootlegging nanny?"

Nadine brandished a bottle from the icebox and filled our glasses with the pale wine. Together with the steaming honey-glazed turkey; the large bowls full of vibrantly coloured vegetables and sauces; the serving centerpiece laden with walnuts, figs, filberts, and pistachios; and the deep green tablecloth we'd rolled out for the occasion, the gently bubbling liquid completed a Dickensian sketch of gastronomic benevolence.

I reached for the wine.

"Wait a minute, Douglass." Eileen lifted her glass.

"You know, I was getting a little worried about this West Coast expedition.... It seemed like something that we'd worked very hard to build was on the verge of slipping away from us. And for what? A chance to make faces and noises in sterile soundproof rooms?

"Don't get me wrong. I know *Chorines in Arms* is no run-of-the-mill picture.... I know it has a chance to start some conversations that we need to be having in this country right now, and spread a little bit of much-needed happiness in the bargain...but would I be willing to trade my family, the first real family I've ever known, in order to accomplish those things? Maybe I'm just being melodramatic.... I don't know.... But that question's been playing on my mind for some time.

"I'm sure part of it's just being dead tired.... Or maybe it's not being able to spend enough time with my baby.... But the biggest thing I've been conscious of is the fear that my best friend, my brother"—she shot me a heartbreaking glance—"might vanish from my life as suddenly as he appeared in it, on the worst night I ever hope to experience."

"Eileen." I rose halfway out of my chair.

"Douglass." She smiled. "I'm not finished!" She turned to Chandler with the same endearing look. "Listen, for the past few months, I've been convinced that your...your relationship would ruin everything for us.... I never considered, even for a minute, what it might mean to you. I'm guilty of one of the worst crimes a person can commit against another person (and certainly of one of the worst crimes a woman can commit against another woman): I didn't think of you at all, except as some stick figure in a wretched morality play...."

"Making cracks about my *figure?*" Chandler eased against the back of her chair. "What kind of an apology is that?"

Eileen laughed. We all did. Except for June, who resumed wailing in the bedroom.

Eileen moved the glass closer to her lips. "Well, I'd like to say more, but...I don't think my little girl would appreciate it.... So let's just drink to the fact that we're all here together...okay?"

We followed her graceful lead and then dug in, but while Eileen was away from the table, Chandler leaned toward me and whispered, "Better make sure that kid's in the room when they start passing out Academy Awards."

Chapter Thirty-One

Nineteen thirty had ended well, but it's not as if our troubles were over. Chandler was still married—and maddeningly reluctant to discuss that part of her life. Eileen was still working ridiculous hours. (*Chorines in Arms* finally wrapped in mid-January, after a seemingly endless series of retakes, matched close-ups, and last-minute song substitutions; one week later, she reported to the set of *Boxcar Honeymoon*.) And neither of us was spending nearly enough time with the baby. That might not have bothered June (who could complain about palling around with Nadine Schatz all day long?), but I woke up most mornings (often in a hotel room with Chandler) feeling like a poor excuse for a parent.

Plus, of course, the country's economy was in pretty dire shape and worsening daily. No one was calling it "The Great Depression" just yet, but you could see the grim idea taking shape, behind the panicked eyes of people on the street.

Not that I spent a whole lot of time on "the street," you understand. L.A. County isn't New York City. Even before they built the freeways, Southern California was car country. I met up with more faces on newsreels than

I did on my road-bound rambles around Hollywood, Burbank, and the Valley.

As spring dawned, the studio announced a May 22nd premiere date for *Chorines in Arms*, eliciting a jumble of excitement and foreboding in my mind. It was hard not to dwell on that dismal Wikipedia entry, no matter how carefully I'd recalibrated my approach to the relationship with Chandler. Following Douglass-4's advice, I resisted my natural impulse to sit back and soak up her enigmatic charms. I chipped away at her defenses and tried to keep the pressure on; every once in a while, it actually worked.

In April, I even got to see her place. It was one of the last rainy days of the season, and the plan to convene in Griffith Park had lost much of its allure. She called me at the office around lunchtime.

"I'm afraid they're deluging our grandeur, Douglass," was all she said.

"I know." I looked up from the script for a soon-to-be-obscure Lew Ayres melodrama called *Up for Murder*. (E.M. Asher had asked me to create a "coming soon" piece for placement in the fan magazines.) "I guess you're just gonna have to have me over for dinner."

I had made the same half-serious suggestion once a week since New Year's, without drawing anything that even sounded like a response.

"Okay." She mustered her most mischievous deadpan.

"Okay?"

"Seven thirty?"

"Sure."

"You know where it is?"

"How would I know where it is?"

"I'm at 900 South Serrano," she said slowly. "Just below Wilshire."

I coaxed the numbers and letters from my failing pen, making deep grooves in the script's thick bond paper. "I'll be there."

"Good." She hung up.

I spent much of the afternoon daydreaming about 900 South Serrano. I had absorbed enough of the local geography to know that the address was near Culver City, but it might as well have been in Camelot or Xanadu. Or Disneyland, for that matter. Fortunately, the end of this particular rainbow lay a little closer than Anaheim.

I pulled out of my reverie and returned to my ad copy. Given a free hand, I probably would have used the opportunity to play up Genevieve Tobin's worldly-wise performance as a gossip columnist trapped in an unsatisfying and illicit relationship with her publisher. But the studio's wishes were clear: Emphasize Lew Ayres' pedigree as the star of 1930's Oscar-winning *All Quiet on the Western Front*. It was easy enough to do. Like the preceding year's antiwar classic, the new film put the baby-faced actor through a major physical and emotional ordeal (this time on the domestic front). Playing an amiable young reporter who falls in love with the boss' mistress (Tobin), he winds up killing the old capitalist in self-defense when the rival suitors cross paths at the lady's posh Manhattan apartment. Nobly attempting to keep his beloved's name out of the affair, Ayres takes a straight murder rap and almost gets executed for his trouble. Tobin does finally come forward to testify on his behalf, but she takes her sweet time about it. In the meantime, the star does a good job of projecting torment and ennui in his cell. It's almost like he's back in *All Quiet*'s foxhole with the dead French soldier, except this time the corpse is in the scandal sheets. That's the approach I decided to take.

I finished the piece a little before 7:00 p.m.

Twenty-five minutes later, I parked the DeSoto in front of an imposing Norman-style chateau with dripping palm trees on its lawn. Medieval letters on the rich red awning dubbed the building "St-Germaine," and it certainly looked the part. I gave Chandler's name in the lobby, and they directed me to a corner suite on the fourth floor. I relayed the information to the elevator boy.

She greeted me at the door, wearing a loose plaid shirt and a pair of dark blue slacks.

"Nice turrets," I said.

"I didn't choose this place." She rolled her eyes.

Rain slithered down my forehead as I kissed her.

"Oh!" She pulled me across the threshold. "Do you want some hot tea?"

I nodded.

"How about a scone?"

"You've got scones?"

"They're the only thing I make."

I hung my hat and coat in the vestibule closet. "By some miraculous coincidence, they're also the only thing I want."

She galloped down a long hallway, sparsely hung with Old Master prints. I followed her into a cream-walled parlour, equally minimalist in character. A tall bookcase gave berths to immaculate rows of hardcover classics, from Ovid to Shakespeare to Eliot. The fireplace looked unused, and the curtains were a dull off-white. There were no plants and no *objets d'arts*, unless you wanted to count the all-basic earth-toned lamp on the end table, next to a brown sofa that was the opposite of plush. There was nothing, not even an ashtray, on the coffee table.

"Make yourself comfortable." She gestured toward the sofa. "If you can."

She darted off to get the tea and scones. When she returned, she found me curled up on the polished wood floor.

"It's got a little more give than the sofa." I pulled her down to my level, nearly causing her to drop the refreshment tray.

Everything was cold by the time we actually got to it, but the scones tasted fine at any temperature.

"Buttermilk?" I shook a few crumbs out of the clothes piled on the floor and slid my head into her lap.

"Always." Chandler smiled down at me.

Behind her, the austere room glowered.

"I pictured your place a lot of different ways." I scanned our surroundings theatrically. "But never this way."

"Douglass...."

"What? I'm just surprised, that's all. Is this what he's like?"

She shook her head. "You know I don't want to talk about this."

"I'm sure you don't...but how'm I supposed to ignore it?"

"The same way you ignore everything else about me, when it's convenient for you."

"What's that supposed to mean?" I shot back (although it was quite possibly the least cryptic statement she'd ever uttered in my presence).

"It means I don't want to talk about it." Her eyes narrowed to slits.

I crossed my arms and prepared to dig in my heels.

"Look," she continued, "we've got this whole ridiculous place to ourselves for a few days. Is this how you want to make use of it?"

It wasn't.

◆

A month later, Eileen and I were New York premiere bound on the *20th Century* out of Chicago, after a long and, quite frankly, terrifying flight across the

Rockies and plains. She had paid Frank and Laura Corelli's westbound fare and installed them as baby- and dog-sitters in West Hollywood, giving Nadine some much-needed time off, and the grandparents a long-overdue chance to spend a solid week with June without forcing anyone over the age of one to endure their abrasive personalities. The arrangement suited me perfectly. The Corellis still half suspected me of having mob ties, and they treated me accordingly.

Our car was packed with studio dignitaries, includ- ing associate producers E.M. Asher and Albert DeMond, producer/director John Stahl, and staff writ- ers Tom Reed and Richard Schayer. We also had a full complement of *Chorines in Arms* people, including our director, James Whale, and Eileen's co-stars Sidney Fox and Mae Clarke.

Of course, "Cynthia Ward" carried the film with her galvanizing embodiment of revolutionary feminin- ity, seeking a way out of alienation not only from her labour but also from the commodifying gaze of produc- ers, spectators, and social workers alike. Still, Fox brought just the right touch of good-natured naivety to her character, and Clarke delivered a knockout sup- porting performance that anticipated her hard-shelled, volcanic-hearted turn as a self-loathing prostitute in *Waterloo Bridge* (also directed by James Whale and due out in September).

Fortunately, this wasn't one of those reporter- kissing whistle-stop press junkets that Hollywood would perfect a little later in the decade, and we were under no orders to mingle. Eileen and I spent most of the trip playing cards in our adjoining compartments, but I did venture forth a couple of times to discuss melodrama with Stahl, who was on the verge of dashing off an epic run of genre-defining classics.

As the sole screenwriter (on paper, anyway) of an anticipated hit (and the co-screenwriter of *Boxcar Honeymoon*, which had just wrapped its shooting schedule), my stock was rising at Universal, and the director expressed an interest in collaborating with me. I wasn't too keen on the idea. I had no desire to mess with the creative synergy that would soon produce *Back Street* (1932), *Only Yesterday* (1933), *Imitation of Life* (1934), and *Magnificent Obsession* (1935).

"You're an odd one, Douglass," Eileen mused as she counted out a particularly strong cribbage hand. "Always hanging back a little, as if you still can't believe you ever made it across the border.... As if the things that are happening around us didn't have anything to do with you...."

"What can I say?" I did my best to laugh off this eerily on-target diagnosis. "I was born with my eyes open and my hands in my pockets."

"I guess this has something to do with your precognition, or whatever we're calling it.... But don't you ever make an appearance in these visions?"

I could truthfully say: "No."

"That's terrible," she sighed.

"No." I shook a fistful of cards at her. "This hand is terrible."

The train rumbled on toward the uncertain Pennsylvania dawn.

◆

The premiere went off beautifully. *Chorines in Arms* would be the most popular musical of 1931, drowning out fanciful operettas and stale boy-meets-girl fables with its buoyantly sardonic tone. That part was never really in doubt. It was the rest of the night that worried me.

Chandler had come to New York eight days earlier, squeezing in a quick vacation (and a little Broadway schmoozing) in between shooting *Salvation Nell* at Fox and *The Last Flight* at Warner. She had practically begged me, in her oblique way, to go with her, but I had committed to making the journey later with Eileen. Since our parting at Mines Field airport, she'd cabled several times, with an escalating sense of urgency, asking me to meet her at a suite on the fortieth floor of the New Yorker Hotel (the room she would die in—at least in one timeline I hoped never to live through) as soon as I could.

As it happened, our train got in too late for me to see her before the big screening (once again at the Roxy). When she arrived at the theatre, she looked unsteady on her feet. She flashed me a frown and chose a seat on the opposite side of the auditorium. I considered dodging her until we got back to California, but of course that risked bringing on the tragedy I hoped to avert....

As the crowd roared over the studio's distinctive end logo (featuring a rotating globe and the slogan "It's a Universal Picture"), I contemplated my next move. A year ago, I had skipped out on the post-premiere festivities for *King of Jazz* without warning. A repeat of that escapade would hurt Eileen and draw considerable scorn from the brass. On the other hand, if we did go to "21" with the rest of the group, I'd have to keep my distance from Chandler, still very publicly married to a prominent MGM screenwriter.

After more than a week apart, I knew she'd want me to herself. I also knew that even an hour or two of public coldness on my part, mixed with the illicit beverages served up at New York's most exclusive speakeasy, could put Chandler's volatile psyche on the rocks.

I put my arms around Eileen and hooked my chin over her shoulder. "It was amazing," I whispered. "And it's just the beginning."

She seemed pleased until I stepped back and jerked my head toward the exit, where Chandler was waiting impatiently.

"Douglass," she sighed, "you can't be serious...."

"I'm sorry...but this...this really can't wait...."

Her eyes moved from Chandler's face back to

mine. "No." She rubbed my forearm. "I guess it can't."

I ran off before Asher could notice my delinquency.

A block down 7th Avenue, Chandler's heels fell into step with mine. It was a beautiful evening, so we kept walking (the hotel was only twenty minutes away). As soon as we crossed 42nd Street, she took my hand.

"You're doing all right," she said.

Nothing bad happened that night.

Chapter Thirty-Two

Chorines in Arms outgrossed every musical since *The Jazz Singer*. A few months later, *Boxcar Honeymoon* claimed the same distinction. Once again, I'd done little more than kibitz en route to a major screenwriting credit. In fact, having recognized the title from the Wikipedia entry of doom, I'd done my level best to talk Eileen out of writing *Boxcar*. But it was a surefire idea: the story of a young Ohioan couple (played by Eileen and Lew Ayres) who pool their last few dimes to buy a marriage license and then press on with their pre-Depression plan to take a postnuptial trip to San Francisco—by riding the rails, of course.

"They're talkin' Academy Award nominations for this one," E.M. Asher said, pulling a chair up to my desk one day in October. The producer was an unprepossessingly gray man with a touch of middle-aged floridity creeping into his cheeks. His good-naturedly guttural voice added just the right emphasis to lines like: "You're on a roll, kid."

"Thanks." I looked up from the task at hand (trailer text for the upcoming adaptation of Poe's *Murders in the Rue Morgue*). "But I—"

"I know, I know," Asher bustled on. "You wanna work on somethin' different. Like your magazine stories...."

"You read those?"

"I read *everything*, Douglass. That's my job."

"What a coincidence." I winced at my desk. "I write everything."

"Not anymore. This penny-ante stuff is out, kid. I cleared it with Junior. From now on, we want you writing scripts full-time, not monkeying around with ad copy."

"That sounds all right." I smiled. "What kind of scripts?"

Asher jabbed his thumb into my Poe promo material. "Like that, mostly. We're cornerin' the horror market. Gonna make as many good ones as we can. And you've got the right kind of mind for 'em."

"Shouldn't that sentence have concluded with a dollar sign?"

"Four hundred dollars a week. Effective immediately. I'll wanna see some treatments on Friday, so get cracking."

I got cracking.

◆

I told Chandler the news that evening.

"You're really getting comfortable around here, aren't you, Douglass?" she said. Her front teeth bisected a pillow of rosée-sauced ravioli.

"Where? Little Joe's?" I took my eyes for a spin around Chinatown's finest spaghetti joint. We'd met there several times that fall. "Sure, I like coming here. This avocado salad is great."

"Not *here*, Douglass." She aimed her profile at the cars speeding by on College Street, outside our grease-smeared window. "*Here*. Los Angeles."

"Oh." I smiled. "Well, it's not New York. But this is where people like us need to be, right?"

"Is it?" Her eyes widened. "I'm not so sure."

"What are you talking about? You've made five good movies this year. It's all working out."

She dropped her chin into her palm. "Well, I'm going to do a play."

I don't know why this surprised me. In my native timeline, she had spent most of 1932 on the stage, a quixotic move that had killed her momentum in Hollywood. A year from now, she'd return to find nothing but secondary and tertiary film roles waiting for her.

"Why?" I tried not to sound too pained. "Why would you do that now, of all times?"

"They asked me." She shrugged.

"And if I ask you to stay?"

"I might ask you to come."

"You know I can't do that."

"Because of your big promotion?" She never came close to blinking. "Or because of Eileen?"

I had no idea how to answer that question.

"She's going to be bigger than Shearer and Gaynor put together," she answered for me. "She doesn't need you, Douglass."

"And you do?" I shot back.

The waiter refilled our glasses with water, and Chandler signalled for a second bottle of wine. The couple at the next booth exchanged worried glances.

She turned back to me. "I never said that."

"No kidding," I replied peevishly.

"You've said it often enough," she snapped. "But what does it really mean?"

"It means I love you."

"But not enough to stop playing Uncle Douglass...."

I went from sullen to indignant. "Do you have any idea what she's been through?"

"I'd have to have pretty abysmal English comprehension skills not to know that, Douglass. You don't talk about much else!"

I couldn't help smiling, a little. "Then how can you treat this like some trivial thing?" I reached across the table. "It's my family."

"Sure it is." She left her hand within range of mine. "But you know, I'd be willing to bet that, somewhere out there in the world, there are a couple of things going on that are even more important than your sister's struggle to balance her kid and career."

"A few," I conceded. "But not nearly as many as you think."

"There it is again," she said.

"There's what again?"

"That tone you get."

"Really?" I paused anxiously. "When do I get it?"

She watched a stray dog scuffle by with a half-eaten bun in its jaws. "Oh, whenever you don't want to argue about how right you are."

"And what do you think I think I'm right about this time?"

"Douglass"—she shook her head—"I have no idea."

"So what are we talking about then?" I asked her.

"Nothing."

We dropped the matter there.

◆

She left for New York just after Halloween. We didn't meet again until February 1932, when I finally made it out to see her on Broadway, in between horror scripts. The play was *Springtime for Henry*, a four-character farce co-starring Leslie Banks, Edith Atwater, and Nigel Bruce. Chandler turned in a beguilingly brittle performance in the role of a pixyish, reform-minded secretary who straightens out her hedonistic employer (the title character, industrialist Henry Dewlip) but then gradually loses her hold on him as various sordid details of her former life emerge (capped off by the news that she had shot her philandering ex-husband to death).

Half Mary Poppins and half Lizzie Borden, Chandler's "Miss Smith" was a genuinely unique characterization, and I could see why she had been so eager to give life to it. Still, in my opinion, the play itself didn't hold a candle to *The Last Flight*, *Daybreak*, or *Dracula*. I told her so that night, as we crunched across the winter remnants of the Sheep Meadow.

"*Dracula*'s more of a farce than *Henry* ever dreamed of being." She gestured toward the tree we'd spent most of our first date under. It remained magnificent despite its lack of foliage. "But I agree with you about the other two, now that I've seen them on the screen.... You never get any sense of the overall quality of these pictures, playing them out in dribs and drabs the way we do...."

"I guess not." I let her pull me across the frostbitten grass. "You just have to trust the director...."

"Or not give a damn one way or the other."

Her blonde hair had darkened slightly with the months away from the California sun, contrasting even more appealingly with her pale skin and blue eyes. If she was drinking herself to death in New York, it certainly didn't show.

"Or that," I conceded.

"But I'm not going to stay here forever." She squeezed my hand. "The play's closing in May or June."

"Have you got any movies lined up?" I asked her, hoping that, somehow, this timeline would be kinder to Chandler than my own had been.

She leaned against the elm's great trunk and stared up through its branches at the cloud-swaddled stars. "Oh, not yet, but I've reminded my agent that I'm not too particular about scripts."

I knew what dismal results that strategy was likely to yield: a couple of "love interest" parts in "poverty row" productions, followed by a slew of supporting roles (with steadily declining screen time) in 1933 and 1934.

I tried to draw her attention earthward. "Chandler, you've earned the right to be particular. If you don't exercise it, they'll walk all over you. Wait until something really good comes along. Or, at the very least, hold out until you get an offer from a major studio...."

"Doesn't the air smell incredible?" Her eyes leaped right over my careerist patter. "You just know these trees have buds up their branches."

It killed me to think I might miss the bloom.

Chapter Thirty-Three

Nineteen thirty-two and 1933 were the worst years of the Depression, but you'd never have known it by my pay stubs. A quarter of the country was out of work (a situation that wouldn't even begin to improve until well after FDR's inauguration), but Universal kept me pretty busy churning out original horror stories, adaptation treatments, and screenplays.

It wasn't easy out-gruesoming the newspaper headlines during the days leading up to the November 1932 presidential election. With partisans from across the political spectrum polishing their trumps of doom (and not without reason), many commentators seemed ready to say the last words over the American republic. When federal cavalry officers rode down the bedraggled "Bonus Army" of impoverished Great War veterans camped within sight of the Capitol in July, killing four people and injuring more than a thousand in the process, the possibility that some violent upheaval might rock the nation became palpable—even to an observer who knew how tamely this crisis was destined to play itself out.

Or did I know it? There was always a scintilla of a

chance that some inadvertent action of mine (or Dorothea's) might already have knocked this timeline onto a divergent political course, a course that might or might not include the New Deal. The idea took terrifying hold of my imagination during the fall of 1932, compelling me to comb the papers every morning for evidence of some fateful deviation from the historical record that now existed only in my memory.

"You really think Roosevelt can create ten million new government jobs without turning the White House into Tammany Hall?" Nadine asked me one day as she guided June through a bowl of brown-sugared oatmeal.

It had never occurred to me that our nanny might be a Republican. But then again, to many people of Nadine's generation, the Democratic Party still savoured primarily of Unreconstructed Southern racism, urban machine politics, and the spectre of drunken "mob rule." This impression was far from unfounded, given the Ku Klux Klan's prominent role at the 1924 Democratic National Convention and New York City Mayor Jimmy Walker's even more recent graft scandal. But the Depression was transforming the party, pushing the sorely beset blue-collar northerners and rural southerners who made up its strangely mixed base to unite under the banner of pragmatic government intervention in the economy, with a side order of (very mild) wealth redistribution and re-legalized beer to wash it down. Civil rights, on the other hand, would remain off the table for some decades yet.

"He might at that." Eileen peeked in from the bedroom, where she had been furiously girding herself for another twelve-hour day on the set of *Mutiny at the Bijou*. "But political patronage is the least of our worries right now, don't you think?"

"No, I don't, as a matter of fact." Nadine shook her head. "You can't have democratic elections when half the country works for the administration. That's a real worry, believe me. I grew up in a one-party state, part of the 'Solid South' (until they got started getting a little more sensible around the turn of the century), and that was bad enough."

"Okay." Eileen poured the last of the coffee I'd made earlier that morning into a cup and stirred a frightening amount of sugar into it. "Let's say you have a point. Is it a good enough point to justify voting for Hoover? A guy who's already proven that he's ready to let starving people eat their own bootstraps if they can't find a way to pull themselves up by them?"

"You could both go for Norman Thomas," I interjected, with more bravado than I felt, given my recent anxiety over the possible effects of my actions upon Roosevelt's electoral chances. "That's what I would do, if I could vote."

Eileen turned toward me. "Douglass, you can't be serious!"

"Why not? He's the Socialist candidate, isn't he? I'm a socialist."

"Well, so am I, Douglass, but do you think that

gives us the right to throw our votes away?"

"Ah, the question that sank a thousand third parties...." The frustration of nearly a century's worth of sterile politics-to-come seeped into my voice.

"Don't be so fatalistic, Douglass," Nadine soothed. "You're probably too young to remember Teddy's Progressives in 1912, but they put up a terrific fight. Someone will manage that again and make a more permanent success of it, I'm sure. But it won't be Norman Thomas. He's much too radical, and you know it."

Eileen quaffed down her coffee/sugar compound. "Well, I don't agree with that either. The Socialists are no more radical than they ought to be, and I'm sure I'll get in a vote for them someday. Maybe even next time around. But this election is too important to lose over a matter of principle. There are people out there who won't live to 1936 if Roosevelt doesn't win, and who am I to sit here in my West Hollywood bungalow and condemn them to four more years in Hooverville just because the Democrats aren't perfect?"

"It's not that they aren't perfect," Nadine shot back. "They're guilty of the most terrible atrocities.... Both in Northern cities, where they've allowed gangsters to run wild (and are pretty much gangsters themselves), and all across the South, where they've done everything in their power to block anti-lynching legislation, including a bill proposed by my old St. Louis district's representative, Leonidas Dyer. A Republican."

She wasn't wrong about that. Southern white supremacists in the Senate had a long history of stymying these reform efforts (and would persist in doing so well into the '60s), thus helping to empower the terrorists who used the threat of lynching to maintain the Jim Crow system. Moreover, there had been many progressive Republicans during the first few decades of the 20th century. But Roosevelt's victory in 1932, assuming it happened on schedule, would signify a major realignment in American politics.

"That's true, Nadine," I said. "But things are changing."

"Is Roosevelt still counting on the Deep South?" she asked rhetorically.

I nodded.

"Then they aren't changing fast enough." She pulled the toddler out of her high chair and shuttled over to Eileen, whose body language indicated that she was ready to take a studio suspension in order to keep this little discussion rolling. "Say goodbye to Mommy, Junie. Several hundred stylists and technicians are waiting for her."

"Bye-bye, Mom-my." The two-year-old girl hugged her mother. "Ha' a nice day."

"Goodbye, sweetheart." Eileen kissed her nose and forehead. "I guess you'll have to hold up my end of the argument.... Can you say 'FDR'?"

My mother's hazel-green eyes (one of many traits she'd inherited from Eileen) widened. "Efdeeyahr!"

"Very nice." Eileen let go of the effervescent bundle reluctantly. "Don't let them forget it!"

She sped off to Burbank.

Junie ran to the window, waved at the departing convertible, and then sprinted back to the kitchen table, shouting, "Efdeeyahr! Efdeeyahr! Efdeeyahr!"

Nadine fought hard to maintain a scowl during the course of this display.

"And what are you up to today, man of leisure?" She hid her smile behind a glass of freshly squeezed grapefruit juice.

Nadine still couldn't quite wrap her mind around my most recent arrangement with Universal, which allowed me to work from the comfort of the Sunset Arcadia most of the time.

"Well," I yawned, "they don't expect anything from me until Friday, so there's no way I'm doing any work today." (Actually, anxiety-induced insomnia had encouraged me to complete the entire assignment—a treatment for an adaptation of Henry James' *Turn of the Screw* that would most likely never be produced—overnight, leaving me free as a rather exhausted bird for the next two days.) "Whattayasay, Junie? Want to see a movie this afternoon?"

"Movie?!" she exploded. (Suffice it to say, living in Hollywood had done nothing to tarnish her perception of the silver screen.) "Wi' kah-toons?"

We'd been going to matinees once a week since she'd turned two at the start of the summer, and there had never failed to be a cartoon, but she always reacted to my invitations in the same way.

"I'll have them round up the animals just for you," I assured her.

"Oh!" She threw herself onto the sofa in a paroxysm of anticipation. "Animals!"

"What should we see?" I asked her. It was a relief to flip away from the political section of the paper. "How about Laurel and Hardy? You remember them, right?"

Bard's Hollywood, a neighbourhood house on the corner of Sunset and Virgil, was showing the comedy odd couple's latest feature (*Pack Up Your Troubles*) on an afternoon double bill with a goofy Buster Keaton/Jimmy Durante vehicle called *Speak Easily*.

"Aur-el and Lardy?" June pondered the names. "They know animals?"

"I'm pretty sure they do." I nodded.

Bard's Hollywood had a deal with Universal to show Oswald the Rabbit shorts (directed by Walter Lantz, who'd done the animation for *King of Jazz*).

I took Lulu for a nice long morning stroll into Laurel Canyon and then gave Nadine the rest of the day off, perhaps to attend some ill-fated Hoover rally (the incumbent president was destined to lose California, and just about every other state, by a wide margin). Junie and I piled into and out of the DeSoto in time for the 1:00 p.m. show.

At the concession stand, I bought a giant ten-cent bag of popcorn for us to share. Extra buttery, so it'd slide down smoothly. That's just good parenting.

Bard's Hollywood wasn't among the more grandiose cinema palaces of the era, but it was still a pretty impressive place to take in a movie. I doubt any pharaoh or priest of Ammon would have recognized the columns and busts which lined the walls as "Egyptian," but these art deco pieces had an antique (to my eyes) charm of their own. And of course the hieroglyphics made it official.

The house seated well over five hundred auditors, although it was less than half full at matinee time. The people in the seats included haggard-looking men and women (almost all of them alone) who could very well have been skipping lunch in order to finance this afternoon of fun, cavalier teens playing hooky from high school, and quite a few middle-class housewives.

But every single one of them was white.

Even in California, far from the Klan-haunted lynching grounds of the post-Confederate South, *de facto* segregation remained the norm in 1932.

Junie nearly yanked my arm out of its socket when they cranked up the cartoon. *Carnival Capers* opens with Oswald and his lady friend, a rather Betty Boop–ish beagle, bouncing on boardwalk planks that play like a xylophone. A long-eared precursor of Mickey Mouse, the rabbit was considerably less sentimentally endearing than the word-famous replacement whom Walt Disney and his chief animator Ub Iwerks had dreamed up after their split with Universal in 1928.

In previous weeks, we'd seen Oswald kicking a hyperactive puppy, drawing an axe on a mutated gorilla, and blasting holes in his canoe while attempting to kill ducks. This time around, at the carnival, he plunges gleefully into a series of violent altercations with a peg-legged pit bull who seems bent on stealing his date. When this rather ill-tempered adversary (who, it must be admitted, deserves everything he gets) wedges his torso but good between two pickets of a fence, Oswald draws a mouse on his ass and whistles for the carnival's cat.

Junie was beside herself—and, as usual, I found myself wishing I'd known how much she enjoyed cartoons when I was a kid. Then again, this June McWade was already on a very different path from the one trodden by the woman who'd given birth to me. She had almost certainly laughed more in two and a half years than my mother had in eighty....

She settled down and became a rather prim little popcorn-eating machine during the live-action short (a by-the-numbers football comedy called *The Quarterwitted Quarterback*). But the newsreel—*The World at Your Door*, narrated by journalist Graham McNamee—put her back on the edge of her seat. The procession of pieces included high-decibel coverage of the Italian Fascists' decennial celebrations, a story on aviator hero Charles Lindbergh's sister-in-law's recently announced engagement to a Welsh businessman, and footage of Franklin Delano Roosevelt's speech from a campaign rally at New York's Metropolitan Opera House, where the challenger hit back at President Hoover for proclaiming that "grass would grow in the streets" if the Democrats took the White House.

When the camera zeroed in on the candidate, Junie hopped up onto her seat and exulted, "Efdeeyahr! Efdeeyahr! Mommy likes Efdeeyahr!"

I held her butter-encrusted fingers through the cheerfully shrill performance, which drew confused stares from the assembled cinemagoers. They probably assumed it was a political stunt, a variation on the old baby-kissing game. But it boded well for Roosevelt's chances in this timeline (and for the orderly progression of Great Depression history as I'd always known it) that no one pelted us with popcorn.

Chapter Thirty-Four

Roosevelt carried forty-two of forty-eight states and took more than fifty-seven percent of the popular vote (Norman Thomas, the Socialist Workers Party candidate, got just over two percent). Prohibition was repealed, bank holidays were declared (while the Emergency Banking Act sped through Congress), and a raft of new agencies, aid programs, and relief bills appeared to buoy up the country's bottomed-out economy.

Nineteen thirty-three progressed right on schedule, with just a couple of very welcome deviations.

As Cynthia Ward, Eileen became one of Hollywood's most "bankable" properties, placing fifth (right between Fox's Charles Farrell and MGM's Greta Garbo) in Quigley's inaugural "Top Money Making Stars Poll." Averaging three large-scale musicals a year, she brought in more than enough profits to keep Universal out of the red.

My own contributions were more modest. Just as Dorothea's Wikipedia entry had predicted (can you plagiarize from an alternate version of yourself?), I launched my tenure on the studio's horror unit with solo scripts for *The Mutant* and *The Banshee*. These films didn't set the world on fire, but they played perfectly on double bills with heavy hitters such as *Frankenstein*, *The Old Dark House*, and *The Invisible Man*.

The Mutant told the radioactive-to-riches saga of a venal Austrian lab assistant named Arnulf who acquires strange powers of mesmeric insight when he overindulges in his favourite after-hours pastime of bombarding the caged animals with x-rays. Without batting a now second-sighted eye, the young thug embarks upon a spree of blackmail and intimidation that soon wins him a special appointment to the office of burgomaster. Half hypno-tized and half terrorized by Arnulf's uncanny knowledge of their deepest secrets and fears, the citizens of his Tyrolean village fall right in line, and only the last-minute intervention of a few similarly psionically empowered rats and rabbits from the lab prevents him from taking his freak show to the national stage at the end of the picture. It was a pretty standard supervillain yarn, but I threw in enough pointed references to Hitlerism to get people talking about its "prescience" (especially since the movie appeared in theatres just a couple of weeks before the German chancellor took office on January 30, 1933—not that I had any control over release dates). *The Mutant* en-joyed the honour of becoming one of the first Hollywood films to be banned in the Reich.

The Banshee was a more supernatural affair, build-ing upon Irish legends of spectral women who appear to bewail imminent catastrophe. It involved the adven-tures of a pair of intellectually inclined American girls on a fall semester exchange at Queen's College in Galway (of course, it was still filmed in Burbank). On their very first night in residence at a cozy oak-sheltered boarding house near the campus, the two students have a hair-raising encounter with the eponymous phantasm while strolling through the woods. When they tell the proprietor what they saw, the kind-hearted old woman begs them to return home while they still can ("the spirits are pronouncin' doom upon ye!").

My protagonists aren't afraid (or, at least, not afraid enough to actually leave). The more philosophical of the pair remarks: "Would there really be any use in running? I imagine doom will catch up to us anywhere, and any time, it wants to." Her friend is convinced that a xenophobic classmate staged the incident to drive them out of town, and launches a quiet investigation with the help of the landlady's son, a medical student at the college. At the end of the film, everyone is proven a little bit right, love has bloomed, and one of the young ladies has become a banshee herself.

Those were the only two original stories I whipped up for Universal, between working on (very loose) adaptations of pre-sold literary properties such as Poe's *Black Cat* and *The Raven*, Dickens' *Mystery of Edwin Drood*, and James' *Turn of the Screw*. I had seen all of these films except the last during my youth (I was particularly fond of Edgar G. Ulmer's *Black Cat*), and I did my best to recreate the scripts as I remembered them. (I saw no reason to change history gratuitously.) I worked a little harder on Henry James' unorthodox ghost story because I knew that project had never been "green-lit" in my native timeline, but I don't think it did any good (the tale still wouldn't reach the big screen anywhere until *The Innocents* came along in 1961).

It wasn't the most exciting work I could have been doing, but no one ever heard me complaining. For every hour or two they forced me to waste in some aggravating huddle with Asher and his herd of sub-producers, I got to spend six or seven at home, writing at my own very congenial pace. And every time I did have to put in an appearance on the lot, I managed to contrive some fascinating meeting with a soon-to-be-legendary figure such as pop-eyed character actor Dwight Frye, ace horror makeup artist Jack Pierce, or husky-voiced theatre star Margaret Sullavan, who came west in the spring of 1933 to make her screen debut in Universal's *Only Yesterday*.

I also seized every chance I got to discuss storytelling technique with Sullavan's future husband, William Wyler. A lifelong favourite of mine, the director was a cousin of Carl Laemmle, Sr. who both benefited and suffered from the mogul's fabled nepotism. Fresh off the boat from Alsace, Wyler had waltzed into a job at Universal at the age of twenty-one, but now after more than ten years with the studio, the most coveted assignments still eluded him. It would take a jump to the Samuel Goldwyn Company in 1936 to unleash classics such as *Dodsworth*, *These Three*, *Wuthering Heights*, *The Little Foxes*, and *The Best Years of Our Lives*. Meanwhile, the finest of his Universal movies, *Counsellor at Law*, starring John Barrymore, was set for a December 1933 release. I could hardly wait to see it.

The rest of the time, I just stuck to playing the role I'd created for myself long before I ever wrote a line for anyone else to say: Eileen's best friend and all-purpose sounding board. She needed me more than ever as the accolades and magazine cover stories accrued. "Someone's got to keep me from taking myself too seriously," she liked to remind me.

Not that she ever played the diva, but like any artist who tries to combine political commitment with popular success, she often worried that a funny thing had happened to her message on the way to the box office.

"Hey," I remarked more than once, perhaps savouring my time traveller's irony a little too smugly, "who knows? Maybe making big money for Universal is the best thing you can do for the cause of social justice."

"Fantastic," she'd reply. "Next, I'll organize a benefit concert for the House of Morgan...."

She never showed any sign of going into the kind of tailspin that Dorothea had described from her own timeline, and I assumed that danger had now passed. But she was under a great deal of pressure. As I knew better than anyone, the studio was depending upon the profits from Cynthia Ward vehicles to remain solvent, and she rarely got more than a few days' reprieve from the frantic merry-go-round of writing, rehearsing, shooting, and promoting that had become her life.

My job was to help Eileen stay focused, without allowing her to surrender entirely to her schedule. My most formidable ally in that quest was the cribbage board. We squeezed in a couple of gregarious games just about every night, before she collapsed into bed. Every once in a while, she'd let off steam about some on-set disaster, but mostly she lamented her abdication of the prime parental role.

"Sure," I'd say, "Nadine spends more time with her. But Junie knows who her mother is." (Here I'd throw in a reference to the FDR newsreel story, or some comparable incident, of which there were many.)

"What good is that," she'd sigh, "if I don't feel like her mother?"

"So let's go up to see her," I suggested one night in mid-November '33 (we'd moved to a two-story unit on the property—one with an extra room for June—more than a year earlier). "You can pick up where I left off in *The Tin Woodman of Oz*."

Eileen's eyes lit up before receding into a wry squint. "I'd love to...but...we can't get her up in the middle of the night just to play with her! It'll wreak havoc on her schedule."

"Eileen, she's three; her schedule can be anything she wants it to be."

"Spoken just like an indulgent uncle." She smiled.

"Spoken just like a conscientious mother." I rested my case.

Of course, I hadn't actually proven a thing to Eileen,

but I know that no part of the rambunctious miracle of Junie's laughing ascent of the giraffe growth chart we'd hung up in the kitchen was ever lost on her mother.

"What's going on with Helen?" Eileen turned the tables on me during the evening's second game. "You haven't mentioned her in ages."

I was genuinely surprised to hear the question. "Well, that's because I know you don't like her."

"I never said that, and you know it! I just...can't say I care much for the effect she's had on your life...."

"It amounts to the same thing, doesn't it?"

"No." She sounded hurt. "It doesn't. She's a beautiful girl, Douglass.... An intriguing girl.... One who thinks more than she lets on, and she lets on plenty.... Besides that, whenever I've actually had a chance to speak with her, I have to admit I couldn't help wanting to reach out to her.... I'm sure she'd be easy to fall in love with. But is she easy to *love*?"

"You know the answer to that one." I shook my head. "She hasn't been."

"And she's still married?"

I nodded heavily.

"Don't you want something more, Douglass?"

"Of course I do." I was getting more emotional than I had expected to. I had never really discussed this with anyone. Not even myself. "But I want it from her."

"You've wanted it from others. I know you have."

I had talked a bit recklessly about Dorothea over the years.

– 305 –

"Not from anyone I'll ever see again," I said.

She put down her cards and touched my hand. "So what's stopping it from happening? It can't be her husband."

"No." I cleared my throat. "It's...I think it's...you...."

She scowled. "Is that supposed to make me like her, Douglass?"

"No." I dropped my chin onto the table. "That's one of the main reasons I haven't wanted to talk about it. Haven't wanted to think about it...."

"What do you mean 'it's me'?" she pressed me.

"She's jealous of our closeness. Of this family we've created. She doesn't understand it."

"What's to understand?" Eileen shrugged. "Who does understand it? It just is, that's all."

"Yeah, but she doesn't believe you're my sister."

"Jesus Christ, Douglass! She thinks we're sleeping together?"

"I don't know what she thinks. Probably not that. But she's jealous, all the same."

"She's told you all of this for a fact?"

"No," I admitted. "Our arguments are pretty cryptic.... Everything we say to each other is cryptic. I suppose it could be something else entirely...."

"But still, your guess is it's me."

"Yes."

"Great."

I squeezed her fingers gently. "Ah, well, it could be worse. She's not even in California anymore...."

"I thought she came back." Eileen scratched her head.

"She did," I yawned. "Last fall, just after the election. But did you see the movies they cast her in? *Christopher Strong* was all right, even though it was a Katharine Hepburn vehicle...."

"What's wrong with Hepburn?" Eileen seemed perplexed.

"Not a thing!" I said emphatically. "I love Hepburn. But she takes up a lot of screen, especially in a silver lamé moth gown, complete with antennae.... Chandler had gotten used to being in *Chandler* vehicles...."

"Well," Eileen said matter-of-factly, "she shouldn't have taken off when she was hot."

"I guess she knows that. Now. But anyway, this time she took off while she wasn't hot. Maybe she thinks it'll have the reverse effect.... Regardless of her reasoning, she's got a play lined up for January."

"So she's in New York now?"

"As far as I know."

"Want to fly out there with me next week?" she asked.

"You're going?"

"Uh-huh." She grinned. "Remember I told you about wanting to adapt Irving Berlin's new show, *As Thousands Cheer?*"

"Of course." I nodded. I also remembered Dorothea's allusion to the finished film, which contained a crushing dramatization of Ethel Waters' "Supper Time," a black woman's lament for her lynched husband. This landmark of Hollywood progressivism had never reached the screen in my timeline. "Pretty controversial stuff.... I mean, it shouldn't be. But it is."

"Yes." She took a deep breath. "But I met with Carl, Jr. and convinced him that we need to do it! You know what the show is, right? A revue with songs drawn from a year's worth of headlines, most of them lightly satirical and not likely to upset anyone, except maybe a few people who don't really matter, such as Herbert Hoover and the Woolworth heiress.... But then it's got 'Supper Time'.... Have you heard the recording?"

I had. Many times. "Yes."

"It's so powerful." She was practically vibrating. "And if I can use whatever clout I've built up to get Ethel Waters into a few thousand cinemas, I'll consider every hour I've thrown into this career well spent...."

I suppose I could have said the same about my career as a time tamperer.

"It'd be something to be proud of," I said.

"It would." She led me over to the window. Her eyes didn't need any help from the moon, but they got it all the same. "As it happens, Marilyn Miller is definitely through with the movies, so that opens up some parts in the sketches for me, but I want everyone else to repeat their roles, as soon as the show closes.... Waters, Clifton Webb, Helen Broderick, the whole tight ensemble...."

"Some pretty intransigent theatre types on that list."

"I know it." She smiled. "That's why I've got to invite them in person. Next week. Are you coming?"

I thought about seeing Chandler again, for the first time in months.

"I'm coming," I said.

Chapter Thirty-Five

I packed as lightly as I could for the cross-continental journey, leaving plenty of room in my suitcase for two novels (Wilkie Collins' *Woman in White* and Sheridan Le Fanu's *Uncle Silas*) that the studio was considering adapting and the half-finished first draft of my script for *The Black Cat*. This time, the entire trip would be by plane, with a transfer in Chicago.

"Are we going to miss cartoons this week?" Junie asked me as we said our goodbyes on the porch.

I smiled. "Of course not. Nadine'll take you... right?"

The nanny nodded magnanimously, showing no trace of her general dislike for noisy, crowded cinemas.

Junie bit her lip. "O-kay, but...next time...?"

"I'll be back for sure," I promised. "And I want you to remember everything Oswald does in this one. When you tell me about it, it'll be just exactly like we were there together."

"It will?"

"You'll see."

She clamped her arms around my leg, and I pulled her up to proper hug level. She dropped a few silent tears on the way.

"I've gone to New York before, you know," I whispered to her.

"You have?" She seemed astonished.

"Uh-huh." I nodded. "Twice. And see, you don't even remember it happening.... You're all better. This won't be any worse than the last time you stubbed your toe."

She winced. "Ooh, that hurt!"

"I know," I soothed, "but it doesn't hurt now, does it?"

She wriggled her pink toes in mid-air, thoughtfully. "No!" she exulted.

The dog barked and jumped in for some last-minute petting.

"Okay, my darlings." Eileen joined the huddle, kissing the back of Junie's head. "It's time for us to part."

The girl jumped ship into Nadine's waiting arms.

As we drove away, she was waving and laughing hysterically as Lulu leaped up to take gentle nips at her dangling feet.

❖

Eileen was less inclined to spend the entire trip playing cribbage than I had hoped she would be. Even under 21st century travel conditions (which most definitely were not in effect), I wasn't good for much else on a plane ride. But the promise of an associate producer credit on As Thousands Cheer kept her nose glued to the sheaf of contracts she'd been empowered to offer the Broadway cast. I took a handful of sedatives and tried to forget about the inexorable workings of gravity. The sleeping compartment was pretty cozy.

Eileen woke me somewhere over Ohio, probably a couple of hours before sunrise. The plane was quiet and dark. I switched on my reading lamp and looked up groggily at the knot between her eyes.

"Are you about to hand me a parachute?" I asked.

"Of course not." Her smile was all on the surface.

"Then what's wrong?" I propped myself up on an elbow.

"Nothing." She shrugged. "It's just...this trip, I guess."

"What?" I sat all the way up. "You worried about moving into 'management' or something? I thought you were excited about all of this?"

"I am." She laughed. "I just don't know what I thought I was doing, convincing you to come along...."

I whistled. "Jesus, was my snoring that loud?"

"Don't be silly, Douglass." She planted her fingers in my shoulders. "You've been perfect company, as always...."

"But?"

"But I had a talk with John Murray Anderson a couple of days before we left. It didn't start out to be about Helen.... I just wanted to make sure I'd get a chance to see him the first night we're in town.... After that, I'll be spending every second on *As Thousands*

Cheer…. But anyway…he introduced the subject. He says she's gone completely off the rails…."

"Yeah?" I didn't try very hard to sound surprised.

"Yes. He's pretty sure that play…what's it called?"

"*These Two*," I said.

"Right. *These Two*…. Well, he doesn't think it'll open in January. Or at all, from the sound of things."

"She'll be pretty disappointed if it doesn't."

"Douglass, it's her fault!"

"Even so." I shrugged.

She crossed her arms. "I was thinking it might be a good thing for you to see her in that state. With the mischievous charm stripped away…. But…I've changed my mind…. I think you'll just make excuses for her while she drags you down."

"She's drinking too much, right?" I made it more of a statement than a question. "I take it she hasn't shot any of her cast mates?"

"It's not that she's been drinking too much. It's that no one's seen her sober."

"And you think I shouldn't see her, period?"

"I don't see what good can come of it, Douglass."

"She's just an irredeemable drunk, right?"

"Come on." She slumped away from me. "That's not what I'm saying, and you know it."

"I don't know what I know, Eileen."

I hadn't heard her cry in years.

I touched her hand and changed my tone of voice.

"I know how much you love me," I said.

"That's a good thing to know." Her face swivelled back out of the shadows.

"There isn't much else I'm sure of…. I don't know if I can do anything to help Chandler…. It's entirely possible that I can't. But you know, every once in a while, people can actually save each other…. And it can happen in a lot of different ways."

She nodded, and the tears were still on her cheeks. "You think I've forgotten? I haven't. Not for a second. But think about it this way, Douglass. What on Earth are the odds of that kind of lightning striking twice? And what the hell is going to happen if it strikes foul this time?"

❖

"Douglass!" Esther Duncan put down her broom and greeted me on the front stoop of her Greenwich Avenue domain. "I can't believe it's you! You moving back east?"

"Only for a couple of days." I sank into her house-coated embrace, taking care not to scrape my face on her hair curlers. "But I noticed you've got a vacancy."

Her eyes twinkled. "If I didn't, I'd throw one of these squatters out on his ear."

"Sure," I said. "Right after you cut off his supply of chicken soup."

"Well…whaddya gonna do, Douglass? It's the Depression…."

"Exactly what you've been doing, my friend."

She looked mildly embarrassed. "Well, come on in! This ain't California weather out here!"

Indeed, the temperature wasn't much above freezing, and there were dirty remnants of a November snowstorm on the sidewalk.

"Okay." I followed the bustling form through the door. "Any chance I could use your phone?"

"I'd be offended if you didn't." She smiled. "You still tangled up with Helen Chandleh?"

"Well, now"—I picked up the receiver—"that's something we're going to have to figure out, isn't it?"

❖

I finally reached Chandler on the fourth try. By that time, I'd eaten half a dozen homemade mushroom blintzes, drunk a potful of coffee, and absorbed an afternoon's worth of radio programs. We solved the crossword, too, and it was no pushover.

Chandler sounded fine on the phone. Her voice had a whir in it that never let me down. Still, I figured it'd be safest to steer clear of liquor licenses, so I suggested we meet at the Horn & Hardart automat on 6th Avenue near 36th street, the perfect evenly lit venue for the splash of conversational cold water I hoped to throw upon our poorly defined relationship. She said she'd meet me there in a couple of hours.

I made the journey on foot, for old times' sake, and I got the sense that I was followed. It could have been

Douglass-4 (or some other variant) checking up on me, but I decided it was more likely that three years in Southern California had robbed me of the ability to share a sidewalk with a pack of pedestrians without developing some paranoid delusion about it.

The trek took a little longer than I'd remembered, and I reached the restaurant several minutes late. It was a relief to find Chandler waiting for me, tray in hand. I kissed her in the meat pie section and came away with gin on my tongue.

"H'lo, Douglass." She spoke to her reflection in a wall of glass dispensers. There wasn't a trace of the whir in what she said.

"I missed you." I tried to work my eyes around her nose. Her cheeks were reddish and slightly puffy.

"Well, that's a relief." She dropped her nickels in the slot and pulled out a beef pie.

After eating non-stop all day at Esther's, I wasn't up to ingesting much more than an apple—along with plenty of coffee, which I encouraged Chandler to share with me.

"It won't do any good." She hefted a steaming forkful of meat and pastry.

"What do you mean?" I extended my hand toward hers. She didn't retract it, but there was something about the way it just sat there that made it seem utterly beyond my reach.

She raised her voice slightly. "I'm not drunk, Douglass. I'm just...floating...."

"Floating?"

"Happens to me sometimes.... It's better than sinking...."

"Is that next on the menu?" I couldn't help asking.

She pushed the half-eaten mess of pie toward the edge of the table and said, "Could be."

"I don't understand."

"That's nothing new, Douglass."

"Yeah, but I want to."

"You've had three years." She finally looked at me with wallpaper eyes.

"Sure." I nodded. "And so have you."

"Me? I haven't had a thing."

"I'd love to know where you got that idea from." I was feeling more combative than you'd ideally want to be when leading up to a proposal. "You've been calling the tune for this thing since we started it."

"But only on the dance floor."

"I'm sorry. We might need a translator over here."

"What we need"—she stood up—"is an undertaker."

"Why are you being this way? I came here tonight to ask you to marry me, if you ever get divorced."

The ten tables in our section contained a few couples, two families, a small city work crew, and one teenaged girl with a book. Every single one of those people was now staring in our direction. I suddenly realized I'd been shouting.

"I'm not being any way, Douglass." She stood over me. "I just don't like your script."

"You want to sit down and explain to me how yours reads?"

"My script?" she laughed. "I don't need one. I'm not trying to stage-manage everybody's life! Mine.... Your *sister's*...." She practically reeled from the sarcastic payload of the final word.

"You don't believe we're related?" I phrased the question carefully.

"Douglass, I don't care anymore."

"It always comes back to Eileen with you, doesn't it? You think I'm involved with her?"

"You *are* involved with her! I don't care whether you've actually slept with her, or who the father of that kid is.... Honestly, even if you were the father, it wouldn't have bothered me one bit if you had just done something to show me that I was more important to you now."

She picked up her purse and marched toward the revolving door.

I ran after her, yelling, "Doesn't what I said to you before mean anything? I want to marry you, Chandler!"

Mechanical insect sounds clicked behind me.

I reeled through the doors, caught her elbow on the sidewalk.

"I want to marry you!" I screamed.

"I'm sure you do." She shrugged me off. "And you'll get a bigger house. Out there near the canyon. One with an attic. You'll kiss me and touch me and 'help' me all night, and in the morning you'll go back down to your 'family.'"

"Goddammit!" I grabbed her again. "You don't understand! I'm just trying to keep everything from falling apart!"

Her eyes widened in terror. I let go of her immediately. Then I realized she was looking over my shoulder.

Thick fingers dug into my arm.

"Looks like everything's gonna do just that, friend."

I turned head-on into Detective O'Meara's smirk.

A large crowd of onlookers had gathered outside the automat. Some of them strafed us with camera flashes. Reporters.

A prowl car pulled up to the curb.

"Take these two in." The burly detective pushed us toward the two uniformed cops who stepped out of the vehicle. "Disturbin' the peace."

Chapter Thirty-Six

I spent the night pacing a smoke-wreathed municipal holding cell, waiting for our names to come up on the court docket. After a few hours, I settled into the corner that had the least vomit in it and tried to process what had happened.

O'Meara had tailed me—had probably done so every time I'd ventured back to the city during the past few years—and had tipped off the reporters when things started getting juicy. That's the only way it made sense.

But why?

Had Chandler's husband bribed him to make trouble for us? That didn't seem very likely, but it was less delusional than my first idea: that unknown temporal counteragents had enlisted the detective in their scheme to foil my mission.

The man himself appeared at the gate along about dawn.

"They treatin' you all right in there?" He winked.

"It's nicer than the morgue." I leaned back against the concrete.

"Glad to hear it," he said. "Glad you remember that."

I jumped up and walked toward him. "You trying to tell me something?"

He sipped his morning coffee. "I think I just did, friend."

I eyed his smug face through the bars. "You did all of this just to get back at me for *that?*"

His eyes opened up, but his mouth stayed smug. "It don't sit right with me when a guy puts somethin' over on my beat. Especially when I don't even know what he's puttin' over."

"And what about Chandler? What'd she ever do?"

The cop pulled out a cigarette, lit it, and walked away.

He didn't even bother to show up when our case was called, a little after 9:00 a.m. And the patrolman who brought us in just shrugged. Chandler didn't look up (or at me) the whole time she was in the courtroom. Not that we were there for very long. The judge dismissed the case out of hand.

"Congratulations." A guard shoved me down the aisle.

Halfway to the door, I planted my feet long enough to catch sight of Chandler gnashing her tight shoes against the gray floor—and I had never felt farther from the meadow.

◆

"Nice going, Hollywood!" the property clerk sneered as he emptied the envelope containing my surrendered possessions.

I reached for the stuff.

"I've been meaning to ask you." His eyes popped with a kind of disinterested malice. "What's the point of carrying two of these? Neither one of 'em seems to work worth a damn."

I clasped one gold watch onto my wrist and pocketed the spare (I never left it behind when I travelled).

"You'd be surprised," I said.

I raked in my wallet and keys.

"Here's a note for you." He slid a piece of paper across the desk.

I opened it quickly and read: "Meet me at the restaurant as soon as you can."

I recognized Eileen's handwriting.

"Thanks," I said distractedly.

"Don't thank me," he grunted. "I didn't do it for you."

❖

I took a cab straight to Risotto Voce.

The place wasn't actually open yet, but Paolo (one of the cooks/owners) let me in when I knocked at the curtained front door.

Eileen was sitting at a booth, with her elbows on the table and her ears bunched up into her palms. A tired fork lay on its side on a plate more than half full of cold spinach omelet.

"Did you see the papers?" she asked, without quite looking at me.

"What papers?" I took a seat across from her.

She shrugged. "Pretty much all of them, but I guess this one'll do." She tossed me a copy of the *Daily News*.

The tabloid's cover photograph showed me careening through spinning doors after Chandler. And the headline said everything I'd been hoping it wouldn't:

CYNTHIA WARD'S "BROTHER" PICKED UP IN LOVER'S BRAWL WITH MARRIED ACTRESS

"I'm so sorry, Eileen...." The words were deliriously inadequate. "Do you think this'll spook Universal?"

Her jaw dropped like a broken tire jack. "Oh...I don't know, Douglass.... It's just a nationally circulated story that accuses us both of everything from infidelity to incest, with a little idle speculation about Junie's parentage for good measure.... Why would that disturb a multimillion-dollar company in a sensitive public-service industry?"

I had no clue where to take the conversation from there. It seemed to have ended before I arrived.

"I gather you've already heard from the studio?" I asked quietly.

"You aren't gathering moss," she said with a tone of mock encouragement. "From Carl Laemmle, Jr.

himself. At 7:00 a.m. That's *4:00 a.m.* Pacific time, in case you've lost track."

"What'd he say?"

"You're fired, Douglass—effective immediately. All they want from you is that script for *Black Cat....*" Tears bubbled up under her bluster. "Me, on the other hand, they're ready to fight for.... They'll sic the press agents on these stories, and maybe get a few religious organizations to nominate me for sainthood. Meanwhile, 'artistically,' they'd put me on a crash no-controversy diet...."

"Eileen..." I started to say. But there wasn't a damn thing to put after it.

She slid out of the booth. "I told Junior it was *As Thousands Cheer* and Ethel Waters and 'Supper Time,' or bust—and he said it'd have to be bust. So I quit."

I started to get up, but she pushed my shoulder back down. "I know you didn't mean for any of this to happen, Douglass. I know you were just doubling down on salvation. But you shouldn't have bet my share of the farm."

"I know." I fingered the watch neurotically, actually considered using it right then and there—just to keep from hearing the words she'd clicked into her chamber—but I knew I'd need to think long and hard about where and when to set down next.

"Well, we lost." She looked down at me without an ounce of anything but love. "I'm going to do what's best for Junie now.... Maybe I'll go back to the stage in a few years.... Maybe I never will.... But unless I do, Douglass"—she put her lips to my forehead—"please... don't try to see us."

She whispered something to Paolo on the way out.

I watched her dash across Bleecker and walk into Abingdon Square for the first time since 1929.

"Douglass," Paolo said softly, giving my desolate eyes a wide berth, "Eileen ordered you some blueberry buckwheat waffles.... Is that.... Is that what you'd like?"

I told him I would.

Chapter Thirty-Seven

I spent the afternoon saying goodbye to 1933, making the rounds of all my old haunts in Greenwich Village and Chelsea. I even dropped in at *Corking Tales* HQ. Doreen Katz's brown eyes pulsed with pity as she led me into her uncle's office.

"Douglass!" The publisher invited me to sit down. "I'm glad ta see ya, kid! Don't let those jackals getcha down!"

"I won't." I smiled.

"Sure, sure." He seemed surprised, but delighted, by my response. "You don't need that picture bunch, Douglass. You got what it takes to come back here any time you want. I ain't never really replaced you, y'know."

"Thanks, Tom." I'd forgotten how much I enjoyed jawing with the old man. "I'll definitely keep that in mind."

Indeed, I was counting on reclaiming my old desk, years before I'd landed it the first time.

I still hadn't quite decided how far back to go. I knew I'd have to shoot past Thanksgiving '29, just to prune all of those extraneous Dorotheas and Douglasses from the new timeline. And I'd have to tack on another half decade to prevent the same old no-win scenarios from recurring. If Eileen McWade didn't marry Pat Corelli, I'd never have to stand idly by while he died. I could catch up with her right after high school, before she'd ever heard of my grandfather, and find some pleasant, non-lethal way to stir up her movie star ambitions. The operation might be a little tricky, as I'd aged nearly five years during the course of my two separate trips and was now pushing forty (not that any calendar—or mirror—would have suggested it), but I didn't waste any time worrying about that. Eileen and I would always be friends, no matter which way our ages stacked up.

But my gray hairs wouldn't go over so well if I tried reigniting anything with Chandler (who would have been nineteen in, say, 1925—although already a major player on Broadway). I decided that was probably for the best. Like Douglass-4 before me, I'd lost faith in the relationship ever bringing anything but harm to either of us.

Sadly, there'd be no Junie in the new timeline I hoped to sculpt. That was a bitter blow, but I took consolation from knowing that she'd live on happily with Eileen and Nadine in the continuity I was about to vacate—albeit in a world on a collision course with Ronald Reagan, Newt Gingrich, and the Tea Party.

And without Junie, there'd be no possibility of the original me, either—although that idea bothered me a great deal less. I had to laugh when I remembered why I'd stolen the watch in the first place....

"What strikes you so funny, kid?" Tom Katz asked.

"Nothing, Tom." I stood up and shook his hand. "Just the usual vicissitudes of life.... I'll be seeing you."

I thought I'd take in a "talkie" that evening, before I retrogressed beyond the sound barrier. I walked up to Radio City Music Hall, which had opened while I'd been in California, surpassing the Roxy as the world's largest movie theatre. They showed RKO's *Little Women*, the one with Katharine Hepburn. I enjoyed the film, as always. And the brand new auditorium's immortal art deco sunset proscenium lent an unexpected corona of nostalgia to the experience. I still remembered the first time I'd seen it, at the Rockettes' 1978 Christmas Spectacular. My grandmother had taken me, of course.

I suddenly felt very much out of place in this 1933, whose "New Deal" I had failed to help flourish and whose bravest souls I had ultimately discouraged.

I was ready to leave the past four years behind.

I hailed a cab back to Greenwich Avenue.

I tiptoed up the steps, hoping not to wake Esther. There'd be plenty of time to see her in the past. I'd take a bracing little nap in my boarding house bed and then set the watch for '24. Thanksgiving. Just to preserve some kind of symmetry.

"Silent Cal" Coolidge would be newly re-elected, after convincing the voters he could be even more socially regressive and pro-business than conservative Southern Democrat John W. Davis. The Immigration Act of 1924, which imposed draconian quotas on new arrivals from Eastern and Southern Europe, and pretty much forbade non-European immigration entirely, would be fresh on the books, with the xenophobic will of the country behind it. Prohibition would be in full repressive swing. And the speculation-crazed Jazz Age would be well under way. It'd be a lot more like the America I left behind in 2010, with an ossified political culture that would never for a second have entertained FDR's mildest progressive gains. It would be a pleasure to watch those aspects of the culture go down in flames—and do my part to make sure they never re-gained their bearings.

I opened my door and felt for the light switch.

My hand lighted on a gun barrel instead.

"All right," a determined voice said, "don't move a millimetre. Hear me?"

Soft fingers worked at the watch, skillfully undoing its clasp, while the other five pressed the weapon to my flank.

The machine dropped to the floor with a piano key thud, and Dorothea crunched its gold-filigreed face to crystalline paste with her heel. She turned on the light and ordered me to sit on the bed, with my hands in the air. I did exactly as I was told.

"Who are you?" I asked as guilelessly as I knew how to.

"Perfect, Larry," she snorted. "Really. You might as well be a bastard to the end."

The name threw whatever plans I had half-made into disarray. Douglass-4 had called himself "Larry Tremblay" when he'd launched his pre-emptive strike against

Dorothea's interference. That meant that this woman knew me only as a guy who had callously seduced her, insinuated his way into her confidence, and then blown up her lab. I imagined it would be pretty hard to prove the last part, but the fact that he had up and disappeared immediately after her life's work was destroyed would probably have raised pretty strong suspicions in her mind. She was a world-class thinker, after all.

"All right," I admitted, "I know who you are. But I'm not Larry."

"That's not better." She shook her head. "Not even a little bit."

"I know who Larry is, though. He told me what he did...."

"What *you* did," she corrected me.

"Fine. I guess the pronouns are your department, since you're the one with the gun."

One of Dorothea's brown-gold eyes started to smile, but she squinted it down. "Very amiable of you, I'm sure."

"So you really don't believe that I'm not Larry?" I stretched one foot out toward the floor.

She floated the gun gently up to my face.

I pulled the foot back and kept mum.

"Oh, I guess I'm ready to believe that you aren't the particular version of yourself who tried to pull that miserable stunt with my lab...."

"Tried to?" I couldn't help asking.

"Does it look like you, or he, succeeded?" She

waved her own watch at me.

"No.... I guess not...but...how?"

She sat down next to me on the bed and nestled the gun against my gut. "I fell for you, Larry," she said. "There's no denying that. But I never trusted you."

"Standard research paranoia?" I guessed. "Afraid he'd steal a march on your patent?"

"Maybe a little." She smiled. "But...no...you weren't any kind of a scientist, I knew that.... But I'd seen you before."

"How?" I blurted. "I don't even exist in this timeline...."

"Hmmmmmmmmmmmmm?!" Her eyes lit up. "Now that's interesting! Are you saying that my first trip created you? That'd make you a descendent of Patrick Corelli, am I right?"

"No comment," I grumbled.

"Okay," she laughed. "Fine. Sulk. It's not really that important. What I was trying to tell you is that I'd seen you in a *newsreel*. At the *King of Jazz* premiere? As Cynthia Ward's 'mystery brother'? A certain Douglass Infantino?"

"Ugh," I moaned. "Why the hell didn't he think of that?"

"It's never a good idea to underestimate the extent of a person's obsession, Larry. Or should I call you Douglass? Or something else entirely?"

"Douglass."

"Great. Well, Douglass, I saw that snippet from the newsreel in an obscure PBS documentary when I was thirteen years old. And believe me, I never forgot it. Your man Larry didn't have to go through that elaborate ruse of seducing me through the message boards. All he had to do was knock on my door.... The upshot would have been the same. I would have assumed he was a handsome stranger from the past with an agenda that bore watching. And eventually, after I was really starting to fall in love with him, I would have shown him my lab just to see what he'd do. After stashing my actual research materials somewhere else, of course."

"What a moron." I remembered Douglass-4's haunted expression as he told me about the drive home from Rutland.

"Be nice now," Dorothea cooed. "You're talking about a man I loved."

"Whom you must know is not me." I leaned in toward her like she was a vacillating jury.

"Probably not." She touched my nose. "But you must have done something to me, Douglass, to get your hands on that smear of broken circuits over there."

She had me dead to rights.

"One more thing." She stood up and steadied the gun. "I'm going to need the other one."

"What other one?" I looked up at her.

"The one you were planning to use as soon as I left. The one that made it easy for you to sit there calmly and not make a play for the gun while I was practically in your lap."

"I don't—"

Her finger cozied up to the trigger. "I'll *shoot*, Douglass. Remember, you're not even a unique item anymore."

"Like you shot the one back in 1930?" I wavered.

"Maybe," was all she said.

It was that word—more than anything—that did me in. The idea of Dorothea hating me enough to kill me made life close to unbearable.

A tensed tooth loosed a trickle of blood from her lip.

"Fine!" I reached into my pocket and yanked out the watch. I had my fingers on it long enough to press the "go" button and run wherever it was set to, but I spiked it to smithereens at her feet.

As she knelt to the ground to examine the debris, even the freckles seemed to drain from her cheeks.

"You...you could have used it." She looked up at me with chasmic brown eyes that had swallowed every trace of the gold. "I...wasn't going to shoot...."

"What's the difference?" I slumped back on the bed. "You wanted me to think that you might."

She lay down next to me and cried.

"I couldn't let you do it to me again," she whispered. "I couldn't."

I ran my fingers up her arm to her beautiful face and kissed her the way dew leaps at the sun.

"You did the right thing," I said.

She slid out of bed and was gone.

Epilogue

I'd been shuffling realities for so long, I had no idea how to deal with just one.

Fortunately, I didn't have to—at least, not right away.

I'd been lying in bed for at least a dozen hours when Esther knocked.

I didn't respond, but I knew this was tantamount to an invitation. Sure enough, the landlady slipped through the door about five minutes later.

"When you go a whole day without using your type-writeh," she whispered, "I know there's a problem, Douglass."

My eyes adjusted with difficulty to the lights she switched on. "Plus you read today's papers, of course."

"Naturally." She smiled.

"Some mess, hunh?" I couldn't help smiling back.

"It's shameful, is what it is!" She buried crossed arms in the folds of her housecoats. "I just sent off my letteh to the *Post*."

"You're a good friend, Esther."

They actually printed that letter, but it didn't do any good. My career as a screenwriter was over.

I was glad, in a way. I prefer watching movies to making them. And so I slipped back into the audience—with a ticket for one to the premiere of Ernst Lubitsch's *Design for Living* at Paramount's Criterion Theatre, on Broadway at 44th.

A week later, it was Thanksgiving again. Four calendar years and who knows how many dashed hopes after touching down on the afternoon of Pat Corelli's death/rescue/death, I finally made it to Macy's Thanksgiving Day Parade. More than a million people joined me in the streets, making it the most successful one yet, according to the papers. Santa was badly over-dressed for the unseasonably high 60°F temperatures, and it was odd not to see any Disney characters (not even Junie's beloved Oswald) among the balloons, but I did spot Felix the Cat, along with an impressive array of more generic alligators, turkeys, and ragdolls.

Later that night, Esther served up a delicious holiday banquet for a few of her favourite orphaned tenants. The idiosyncratic menu combined a traditional roast bird with thick mushroom gravy, deep-fried cornbread, onion-tinged pumpkin soup, and latkes.

"There's more to Mrs. D. than chicken soup," said the wry-faced, lush-limbed redhead seated opposite me, taking the words out of my mouth.

The woman's name was Deborah Skelton. The landlady had introduced her as "a burlesque girl with a lot on the ball." A grizzled ex-carnie named Jack and a white-haired Village waitress named Fay rounded out the guest list.

I sensed twin matchmaking schemes in progress, and after taking a careful look across the table, I had half a mind, and even more of a body, to play along.

"Esther's the Coeur de Lion of landladies. She almost justifies the whole miserable political system."

"Don't mind Douglass." The obliging noble in question refilled our coffee cups. "He talks like a thug, but he's really a very sweet boy."

"Sweet, hunh?" Deborah eyed me. "I don't think I've got that kind of tongue."

"Fair enough," I returned her volley. "But let's not stop talking about your tongue."

I have no idea where this conversation might have gone if Esther hadn't shushed us with a very special, and especially reprehensible, holiday episode of *Amos 'n' Andy*. All I know is that things took a far more introspective turn after Deborah and I polished off the dishes.

It was a very mild night, perfect for sitting on the fire escape and watching the cars and the leaves ramble by.

"So. You were doing all right in Hollywood?" she stated rather quizzically, before taking an epic drag on a cork-tipped Craven "A."

I nodded. "Yeah, but you don't want any letters of introduction from me. It couldn't do anything but hurt you."

"No kidding, sport." She winked at me. "I know you're a loser, professionally at least. But I also know a good guy when I see one. So what'd those sons of bitches do to you?"

"Do to me?" I pondered the question. "Oh...nothing, Deborah.... Nothing. Whatever was done, I did to myself. And to a lot of other good people, too...."

"Aw, gimme a break, Doug. You had *plenny* of help, whether you realize it or not. It takes at least as many people to screw things up as it takes to screw."

"Well...maybe." I shrugged. "But I had some unique opportunities. Opportunities you wouldn't understand...."

She jumped down my throat. "Aw, 'course not! I wouldn't unnerstand. I'm just a girl in burlesque!"

"That's not what I meant."

"Well, what didja mean, Doug? I'd really like to know."

"And I'd really like to tell you. But there are limits to the communicability of experience."

"If you talked that way during my act, you'd have a pie in your face by now."

"And I'd deserve it." I nodded.

"Okay, fine." She lit another cigarette. "Nobody knows the trouble you've seen—or caused. What're you gonna do *now*?"

That was undoubtedly the question. And the answer, on the surface, was plain.

"I guess I'll go back to writing pulp fiction."

I dropped in on Tom Katz the next morning. He looked like he'd been expecting me for a while.

"I ain't never really replaced ya, Douglass." He put out his cigarette with tender ceremony and clamped yellowed fingers around my shoulder. "How could I?"

And so I resumed my daily orbit between Greenwich Avenue and West 29th Street.

Little by little, I adjusted to my failure. Universal would resume its collision course with bankruptcy. There would probably be a Blacklist—and a terrible rightward media draft. Socialism would retreat to the margins and (even worse) the universities, leaving oligarchic demagogues free to equate all progressive initiatives with ivory-towerism and Stalinism. I would certainly never be born. Pat Corelli was dead, and Helen Chandler would live out the next thirty years in hell.

It's the worst of all possible timelines.

And yet, to paraphrase my grandfather, that's the world I now live in.

I'm not giving in to it.

After all, I'm still in a better position to affect things than I was in my original 2010. At least this way there won't be any surprises, except for the ones I might possibly set in motion with my daringly "prescient" tales; and those would be good surprises, at least in theory. This novel is slated for serialization in *Corking Tales* next year (1934). Of course, I replaced any references to "Cynthia Ward" with material about a fictional rising star at Monogram. (I don't want to cause Eileen any more trouble than I already have.) And I got rid of the passages with Chandler entirely. But the political content is intact. I know it's unlikely to do any good, but I'm through basing decisions on pragmatic grounds. Look where that led me with Dorothea.

I've gone out with Deborah Skelton a few times, but nothing's happened yet. My days of jumping into the arms of every amazing woman that I meet may be behind me. Or perhaps there are more of them ahead of me. I don't know.

Nadine called me on Christmas morning. Apparently, the whole family's doing fine. If I ever get a chance to keep my promise to Junie, we'll have one hell of a cartoon backlog to catch up on. I hope it happens. I hope a lot of things do.

Acknowledgements

This book would never have reached you if any of these people had defected to a more palatable timeline.

I'm very grateful to Lea Kabiljo for insisting, in no uncertain terms, that Douglass' tale must go on.

I would like to thank Peter Delacorte for showing the world how the political/pop-cultural/time-travel novel is done—and for taking the time to compare notes with me on the genre.

There is no way to overstate Janine MacLeod's contribution to my life or to the composition of this book. Her enthusiasm for the material spurred me on, and her critical eye helped me to refine my objectives.

The entire MacLeod family was extraordinarily supportive of my efforts. Stephanie, Barrie, Jesse, and Khione—I will never forget your kindness, and I hope you enjoy the finished product.

I'm very thankful to Teresa Ortega, Liz Flannery, Bill Ritchie, Emile Fiore, and everyone else who volunteered to read drafts of this text. Their ideas and suggestions kept me rolling through the revision process.

What can I say about Marisa Grizenko's role in all of this? Her influence has been the reverse of nefarious. This is a person who took astute note of the ridiculous number of pie crust passages in the novel and championed it anyway. She is the kind of friend, and the kind of editor, whom no dessert- and dialogue-driven writer can do without.

I am deeply grateful to Jon Paul Fiorentino for providing me with this opportunity—and to everyone at Insomniac Press (particularly Dan Varrette and Mike O'Connor) for bringing my words to you in the pulp.

I want to thank Helen Chandler, whom you know.

There's a real Dorothea in my life, too—a tireless, if catnap prone, companion who rarely left my side during the actual composition of *Hypocritic Days*.

Finally, I want to thank Elise Moore, whom I met just when I, and this book, needed her. Whatever it takes to get a person like me thinking (although not necessarily writing) about the future, instead of the past, she's got it.